MOXiE!

Also by Jennifer Mathieu

The Truth About Alice
Devoted
Afterward
The Liars of Mariposa Island

JENNIFER MATHIEU

SQUARE
FISH

ROARING BROOK PRESS
NEW YORK

SQUARE FISH

An imprint of Macmillan Publishing Group, LLC
120 Broadway, New York, NY 10271
fiercereads.com

Our books may be purchased in bulk for promotional, educational, or business use. Please
contact your local bookseller or the Macmillan Corporate and Premium Sales Department at
(800) 221-7945 ext. 5442 or by email at MacmillanSpecialMarkets@macmillan.com.

The Library of Congress has cataloged the hardcover edition as follows:
Names: Mathieu, Jennifer, author.
Title: Moxie: a novel / Jennifer Mathieu.
Description: New York: Roaring Brook Press, 2017. | Summary: In a small Texas
town where high school football reigns supreme, Viv, sixteen, starts a feminist
revolution using anonymously-written zines.
Identifiers: LCCN 2016057288 (print) | LCCN 2017028191 (ebook) |
ISBN 9781250104267 (paperback) | ISBN 9781626726345 (ebook)
Subjects: | CYAC: Feminism—Fiction. | High schools—Fiction. | Schools—Fiction. |
Sexism—Fiction. | Zines—Fiction. | Mothers and daughters—Fiction. |
Texas—Fiction.
Classification: LCC PZ7.M4274 (ebook) | LCC PZ7.M4274 Mox 2017 (print) |
DDC [Fic]—dc23
LC record available at https://lccn.loc.gov/2016057288

"Rebel Girl" lyrics and portions of the Riot Grrrl Manifesto are used with permission of
Kathleen Hanna

Moxie. Originally published in the United States by Roaring Brook Press
Movie tie-in edition, 2021
Book designed by Elizabeth H. Clark
Square Fish logo designed by Filomena Tuosto
Printed in the United States of America.

ISBN 978-1-250-82287-1 (movie tie-in edition)

1 3 5 7 9 10 8 6 4 2

AR: 5.3 / LEXILE: 840L

For all the teenage women fighting the good fight.

And for my twelfth-grade Current Topics teacher for calling me a feminazi in front of the entire class. You insulted me, but you also sparked my interest in feminism, so really, the joke is on you. Revenge is best served cold, you jerk.

CHAPTER ONE

MY ENGLISH TEACHER, MR. DAVIES, RUBS A HAND OVER HIS MILITARY
buzz cut. There's sweat beading at his hairline, and he puffs out
his ruddy cheeks. He looks like a drunk porcupine.

The drunk part may be true. Even if it is before lunch on a
Tuesday.

"Let's discuss the symbolism in line 12 of the poem," he announces, and I pick up my pen so I can copy down exactly what
he says when he tells us what the gold light behind the blue
curtains really means. Mr. Davies says he wants to *discuss* the
symbolism, but that's not true. When we have our unit test,
he'll expect us to write down what he told us in class word for
word.

I blink and try to stay awake. Half the kids are messing with
their phones, grinning faintly into their groins. I can sense my
brain liquefying.

"Vivian, what are your thoughts?" Mr. Davies asks me. Of course.

"Well," I say, folding in on myself and staring at the Xeroxed copy of the poem on my desk. "Uh . . ." My cheeks turn scarlet. Why does Mr. Davies have to call on me? Why not mess with one of the groin grinners? At least I'm pretending to pay attention.

Neither of us says anything for what feels like a third of my life span. I shift in my seat. Mr. Davies stares. I chew my bottom lip uncertainly. Mr. Davies stares. I search my brain for an answer, any answer, but with everyone's eyes on me I can't think straight. Finally, Mr. Davies gives up.

"Lucy?" he says, calling on the new girl, Lucy Hernandez, who's had her hand up since he asked the question. He stares at her blankly and waits.

"Well," Lucy starts, and you can tell she's excited to get going, even sitting up a little straighter in her chair, "if you think about the reference the speaker makes in line 8, what I'm wondering is if the light doesn't indicate, a, um, what would you call it . . . like a *shift* in the speaker's understanding of . . ."

There's a cough that interrupts her from the back of the room. At the tail end of the cough slip out the words, "Make me a sandwich."

And then there's a collection of snickers and laughs, like a smattering of applause.

I don't have to turn around to know it's Mitchell Wilson being an asshole, cheered on by his douche bag football friends.

Lucy takes in a sharp breath. "Wait, what did you just say?" she asks, turning in her seat, her dark eyes wide with surprise.

Mitchell just smirks at her from his desk, his blue eyes peering out from under his auburn hair. He would actually be kind of cute if he never spoke or walked around or breathed or anything.

"I said," Mitchell begins, enjoying himself, "make . . . me . . . a . . . sandwich." His fellow football-player minions laugh like it's the freshest, most original bit of comedy ever, even though all of them have been using this line since last spring.

Lucy turns back in her seat, rolling her eyes. Little red hives are burning up her chest. "That's not funny," she manages softly. She slips her long black hair over her shoulders, like she's trying to hide. Standing at the front of the room, Mr. Davies shakes his head and frowns.

"If we can't have a reasonable discussion in this classroom, then I'm going to have to end this lesson right now," he tells us. "I want all of you to take out your grammar textbooks and start the exercises on pages 25 and 26. They're due tomorrow." I swear he picks those pages blind. Who knows if we've even gone over the material.

As my classmates offer up a collective groan and I fish around in my backpack for my book, Lucy regains some sort of courage and pipes up. "Mr. Davies, that's not fair. We *were* having a reasonable discussion. But they"—she nods her head over her shoulder, unable to look in Mitchell's direction again—"are the ones who ruined it. I don't understand why you're punishing all of us." I cringe. Lucy is new to East Rockport High. She doesn't know what's coming.

"Lucy, did I or did I not just announce to the class that it should begin the grammar exercises on pages 25 and 26 of the grammar textbook?" Mr. Davies spits, more enthusiastic about disciplining Lucy than he ever seemed to be about the gold light behind the blue curtains.

"Yes, but . . . ," Lucy begins.

"No, stop," Mr. Davies interrupts. "Stop talking. You can add page 27 to your assignment."

Mitchell and his friends collapse into laughter, and Lucy sits there, stunned, her eyes widening as she stares at Mr. Davies. Like no teacher has ever talked to her like that in her life.

A beat or two later Mitchell and his friends get bored and settle down and all of us are opening our textbooks, surrendering ourselves to the assignment. My head is turned toward the words *subordinate clauses*, but my gaze makes its way toward Lucy. I wince a little as I watch her staring at her still-closed textbook like somebody smacked her across the face with it and she's still getting her breath back. It's obvious she's trying not to cry.

When the bell finally rings, I grab my stuff and head out as fast as I can. Lucy is still in her seat, her head down as she slides her stuff into her backpack.

I spot Claudia making her way down the hall toward me.

"Hey," I say, pulling my backpack over my shoulders.

"Hey," she answers, shooting me the same grin she's had since we became best friends in kindergarten, bonding over our shared love of stickers and chocolate ice cream. "What's happening?"

I sneak a look to make sure Mitchell or one of his friends isn't near me to overhear. "We just got all this grammar homework. Mitchell was bugging that new girl, Lucy, and instead of dealing with him, Mr. Davies just assigned the entire class all these extra pages of homework."

"Let me guess," Claudia says as we head down the hall, "make me a sandwich?"

"Oh my God, however did you figure that one out?" I answer, my voice thick with mock surprise.

"Just a wild guess," says Claudia with a roll of her eyes. She's tinier than me, the top of her head only reaching my shoulder, and I have to lean in to hear her. At 5′10″ and a junior in high school, I'm afraid I might still be growing, but Claudia's been the size of a coffee-table tchotchke since the sixth grade.

"It's such bullshit," I mutter as we stop at my locker. "And it's not even original humor. Make me a sandwich. I mean, dude, you could at least come up with something that hasn't been all over the Internet since we were in middle school."

"I know," Claudia agrees, waiting as I find my sack lunch in the cavernous recesses of my messy locker. "But cheer up. I'm sure he'll grow up sooner or later."

I give Claudia a look and she smirks back. Way back when, Mitchell was just another kid in our class at East Rockport Middle and his dad was just an annoying seventh-grade Texas history teacher who liked to waste time in class by showing us infamous football injuries on YouTube, complete with bone breaking through skin. Mitchell was like a mosquito bite back then. Irritating, but easy to forget if you just ignored him.

5

Fast forward five years and Mr. Wilson managed to climb the Byzantine ranks of the East Rockport public school hierarchy to become principal of East Rockport High School, and Mitchell gained thirty pounds and the town discovered he could throw a perfect spiral. And now it's totally acceptable that Mitchell Wilson and his friends interrupt girls in class to instruct them to make sandwiches.

Once we get to the cafeteria, Claudia and I navigate our way through the tables to sit with the girls we eat lunch with every day—Kaitlyn Price and Sara Gomez and Meg McCrone. Like us, they're sweet, mostly normal girls, and we've known each other since forever. They're girls who've never lived anywhere but East Rockport, population 6,000. Girls who try not to stand out. Girls who have secret crushes that they'll never act on. Girls who sit quietly in class and earn decent grades and hope they won't be called on to explain the symbolism in line 12 of a poem.

So, like, nice girls.

We sit there talking about classes and random gossip, and as I take a bite of my apple I see Lucy Hernandez at a table with a few other lone wolves who regularly join forces in an effort to appear less lonely. Her table is surrounded by the jock table and the popular table and the stoner table and every-other-variety-of-East-Rockport-kid table. Lucy's table is the most depressing. She's not talking to anyone, just jamming a plastic fork into some supremely sad-looking pasta dish sitting inside of a beat-up Tupperware container.

I think about going over to invite her to sit with us, but then

I think about the fact that Mitchell and his dumb-ass friends are sitting smack in the center of the cafeteria, hooting it up, looking for any chance to pelt one of us with more of their lady-hating garbage. And Lucy Hernandez has to be a prime target given what just happened in class.

So I don't invite her to sit with us.

Maybe I'm not so nice after all.

CHAPTER TWO

OUR ANCIENT TABBY CAT, JOAN JETT, IS WAITING FOR ME WHEN I
open the front door after school. Joan Jett loves to greet us
when we come home—she's more dog than cat that way—
and she lives to meow and howl and get your attention, which
my mother says makes her a good match for her namesake, the
human Joan Jett, this woman who was part of an all-girl band
in the 1970s called The Runaways before she started her own
group. When Claudia and I were younger, we used to make
videos of Joan Jett the cat dancing to songs of Joan Jett the
singer.

I give Joan Jett a quick pet and then find a note on the counter
from my mother. She could just text me, but she likes what she
calls "the tangible quality of paper."

Working late tonight. Meemaw and Grandpa said come over for dinner if you want. Pls fold laundry on my bed and put away. Love you. xoxoxo Mom

I'm old enough now to stay by myself if my mom has a late shift at the urgent care center where she works as a nurse, but when I was little and she had weird hours, Meemaw would pick me up from school, and I'd go to her house and eat a Stouffer's frozen dinner with her and Grandpa, and then we'd all try to guess the answers on *Wheel of Fortune* before they'd tuck me into bed in the room that had been my mother's when she was young. Meemaw had redecorated it by then in soft pinks and greens, not a trace of my mom's old punk rock posters and stickers left, but I used to peek out the window of my mom's old room and imagine her being young, being wild, being set on leaving East Rockport one day and never coming back. Even though she only managed half the plan, my mother's youth still fascinates me.

Back in those days I'd drift off and, depending on how tired my mother was when she got home, I'd either wake up to my grandpa watching the *Today* show, or I'd be shaken awake in the middle of the night to make the ten-second walk back to our house, clutching my mom's hand, catching a whiff of the minty, antiseptic smell that always follows her home from work. Nowadays I only head over to my grandparents' house for dinner even though they still try to get me to spend the night like the old days.

My phone buzzes. Meemaw.

"Hey, sweetie, I'm heating up chicken enchiladas," she tells me. "Want to come over?" Meemaw and Grandpa eat breakfast at 5, lunch at 11, and dinner at 4:45. I used to think it was because they're old, but my mom says that's how they've been all their lives and that when she moved out at eighteen she felt like a rebel for eating after dark.

"Okay," I tell her, "but I have to fold the laundry first."

"Well, come on over when you're done," she says.

I grab a piece of cheese from the fridge for a snack and answer a few texts from Claudia about how irritating her little brother is before I figure I should get the laundry over with. Joan Jett scampers off after me, wailing away as I head to the back bedroom where I find a mountain of laundry in the middle of my mother's unmade bed. I start folding pastel-colored underpants into nice, neat squares and hanging damp bras up to dry in the bathroom. It's strictly lady laundry. My dad passed away when I was just a baby after he crashed his motorcycle while driving the streets of Portland, Oregon—which was where he and my mom and I used to live. His name was Sam, and I know it's kind of strange to say about my dad even if I can't remember him, but from pictures I know he was kind of a total babe, with dirty-blond hair and green eyes and just the right amount of muscles to be attractive but not so many as to be creepy and gross.

My mom still misses him, and one night about a year or so ago when she'd had too much wine, she'd told me it was weird that she kept getting older but Sam would always be the same age. That's how she referred to him, too. Sam. Not "your dad" but Sam, which is really who he was to her more than anything, I guess. Her Sam. Then she went to her room, and I could hear her crying herself to sleep, which is not my no-nonsense mom's usual approach. Sometimes I feel guilty that I don't miss him, but I can't pull up even the tiniest sense memory. I was only eight months old when he died, and after it happened Mom and me moved back to East Rockport so my grandparents could help take care of me while my mom went back to school and finished her nursing degree. And now, sixteen years later, we're still here.

I'm hanging up some of my mom's simple sundresses when my eye catches on a fat, beat-up shoe box she keeps on her closet's top shelf. In black Sharpie it's labeled MY MISSPENT YOUTH. I slide the final dress into place, tease the shoe box out of its resting spot, and take it to my bedroom. I've looked in this box before. Back when Claudia and I went through our Joan Jett dancing cat video phase, I used to love to take down this box and study the contents, but I haven't pawed through it in years.

Now I open it up and carefully spill the cassette tapes and old photographs and neon-colored leaflets and dozens of little photocopied booklets with titles like *Girl Germs* and *Jigsaw* and *Gunk* out onto my bed. I pick up a Polaroid of my mom where it looks like she was just a few years older than I am now, maybe nineteen or twenty. In the photograph, she has a platinum-blond streak in her long dark hair, and she's wearing a tattered green baby doll dress and combat boots. She's sticking her tongue out at the camera, and her arms are around the neck of another girl who has dark eyes and a piercing through her eyebrow. In black marker written down one of my mom's arms are the words RIOTS NOT DIETS.

My mom doesn't talk too much about her younger years before she met my dad in Portland, but when she does, she always grins a little with pride, maybe remembering how she graduated from high school and drove an ancient Toyota she'd bought with her own money to Washington State just because that's where her favorite bands lived and played. Bands with names like Heavens to Betsy and Excuse 17. Bands made up almost entirely of girls who played punk rock and talked about equal rights and made little newsletters they referred to as zines.

They called themselves Riot Grrrls.

My mother was wild back then. Wild like with half her head shaved and black Doc Martens and purple lipstick the color of a serious bruise. Even though my mom is pretty relaxed compared to a lot of moms—like she's always been up front with me about sex stuff and she doesn't mind if I swear in front of her once in a while—it's still hard to reconcile the girl in the Polaroid with the mom I know now. The mom in butterfly-covered, lavender nursing scrubs who sits down at the kitchen table once a month to balance her checkbook.

I shift positions to get more comfortable on my bed and stare at a page in one of the Riot Grrrl zines. It has a cutout of a vintage cartoon Wonder Woman with her hands on her hips, looking fierce. The girl who made the zine drew words coming out of Wonder Woman's mouth, warning men not to mess with her when she's walking down the street unless they want a smack to the face. I grin at the image. As I flip through the pages, I find myself wishing that Wonder Woman went to East Rockport High and that she was in all of the classes I have with Mitchell Wilson. When Joan Jett meows for her dinner, I have to force myself to pack the box up and tuck it back into my mom's closet. I can't explain why, exactly, but something about what's inside the box makes me feel better. Understood somehow. Which is weird because Riot Grrrl was a million years ago, and none of those girls know me. But I can't help but wish I knew them.

Meemaw has a rooster obsession. Roosters on dishtowels, roosters on plates, roosters made of ceramic walking the length of the kitchen windowsill like they're part of a rooster parade. She even has salt and pepper shakers shaped like—guess what—roosters.

I take the salt shaker in my hand and raise an eyebrow at the rooster's perpetual friendly grin.

"Do roosters actually smile?" I ask, sprinkling salt on my side serving of canned veggies.

"Sure," says Meemaw. "They're very sociable."

My grandpa just grunts and digs his fork through his plate of Stouffer's chicken enchiladas. "How many roosters have you known personally, Maureen?" he asks.

"Several," says Meemaw, not skipping a beat, and Grandpa just sighs, but I know he loves that Meemaw never lets him have the last word.

I appreciate how utterly grandparentesque my grandparents are. I like listening to their banter, to their gentle teasing, to the way two people who have been together for over forty years communicate with each other. I like how my grandpa has funny little sayings that he trots out over and over again and delivers in a voice of authority. (*Remember, Vivian, you can pick your friends, you can pick your nose, but you can't pick your friend's nose.*) I like how Meemaw has never once solved a puzzle on *Wheel of Fortune* but still insists on watching it every night and yelling out whatever answers strike her in the moment. (*"Mr. Potato Head! Fried Green Tomatoes! Sour cream and onion potato chips!"*)

They're cozy, basically.

But like most grandparents, they're totally out of it when it comes to knowing what it's like to be, like, a girl and sixteen and a junior in high school.

"Anything exciting happen at school today?" Meemaw asks, wiping the sides of her mouth with her napkin. I push my green beans around with my fork and consider my day and the homework still waiting for me in my backpack.

"Nothing too exciting," I say. "I got stuck with a bunch of extra work in English because Mitchell Wilson and his friends are jerks."

Grandpa frowns and Meemaw asks what I mean, so I find myself telling them about Mitchell's stupid comment.

"I don't even understand what that means," says Meemaw. "Why would he want someone to make him a sandwich?"

I take a deep breath. "He didn't really want a sandwich, Meemaw," I say. "It's just, like, this stupid joke the boys use to try and say girls belong in the kitchen and they shouldn't have opinions." My voice gets louder the more I talk.

"I see. Well, that certainly wasn't very nice of Mitchell," Meemaw offers, passing Grandpa the salt.

I shrug, briefly fantasizing about what it must be like to be retired and able to spend your days puttering around with your ceramic rooster collection, totally oblivious to the realities of East Rockport High School.

"What he said . . ." I pause and picture the bright red hives of embarrassment burning up all over Lucy Hernandez. Remembering makes me burn for a moment, too, from my scalp to the tips of my toes, but it's not embarrassment I'm feeling. "Well, I think it's totally sexist." It feels good to say it out loud.

"I suppose, I'd expect better manners from the principal's son," says Meemaw, sliding past my last remark.

"Can you imagine what Lisa would have done over something like that?" my grandfather says suddenly, looking up from his enchiladas at my grandmother. "I mean, can you even picture it?"

I look over at Grandpa, curious. "What?" I ask. "What would Mom have done?"

"I don't even want to think about it," Meemaw says, holding her hand out like a crossing guard ordering us to stop.

"Your mother wouldn't have done just one thing," Grandpa continues, scraping his plate for one last bite. "It would have been a list of stuff. She would have started a petition. Painted a big sign and marched around the school. Exploded in rage."

Of course my mother would have done all of those things. The tales of her teenage rebellion started long before she moved to the Pacific Northwest and took up with the Riot Grrrls. Like the time she showed up at East Rockport High with her hair dyed Manic Panic Siren's Song blue the day after the principal announced the dress code would no longer allow unnatural hair colors. She got suspended for a week and my grandparents had to spend a fortune getting it covered up without my mom's hair falling out. I briefly imagine what it must have felt like to walk down the main hallway of school with everyone staring at you

15

because your hair is the color of a blue Fla-Vor-Ice. I cringe just thinking about it.

"The problem was your mother was always looking for a fight," Meemaw continues before draining the rest of her sweet tea. "She had more than her necessary share of moxie. It made things so difficult for her. And us, too, as much as we love her."

"Yeah, I know," I say. I've heard this speech before. And maybe it did make things difficult for Meemaw and Grandpa, but the girl in the Polaroid picture from the MY MISSPENT YOUTH shoe box didn't seem to find life so tough. She seemed to be having fun. She seemed to enjoyed starting battles, even if she didn't always win.

"The good news," Meemaw announces definitively, "is that the rebellious gene seems to have been some strange mutation." She smiles at me and starts stacking the dirty dishes.

"Our dutiful Vivian," Grandpa offers. He even reaches over and ruffles my hair with his big, callus-covered grandpa hand, like I'm ten.

I smile back, but I'm prickly all of a sudden. I don't like feeling prickly toward my grandpa. Or Meemaw. But I don't like being called dutiful either. Even though it's probably—no, definitely—true. So I don't say anything. I just smile and try to bury the prickliness.

After dinner I do my homework (of course), and then I join my grandparents in the family room (or what Meemaw and Grandpa call "the TV room") to watch *Wheel of Fortune*. I laugh as Meemaw shouts out ridiculous answers (*"'Luck Be a Lady To-night!' Lady and the Tramp! My Fair Lady!"*). I accept Grandpa's offer of decaf coffee with cream and sugar. But my mind keeps remembering Lucy's hurt face and the snickering coming from Mitchell and his stupid friends. The burning sensation that flashed through my body during dinner twists my stomach. Makes me restless.

After the bonus round on *Wheel*, I tell my grandparents I have to be heading home, and they do their typical protest to try and get me to stay just a little longer, at least through *Dancing with the Stars*. But I beg off and kiss them each on the cheek and thank them—dutifully—for having me over.

"Of course, sweetie," Grandpa says, walking me to the door and hugging me tight, and I feel guilty for getting so irritated with him earlier.

After I get home and watch some dumb television and mess around on my phone, I decide it's time to get ready for bed, so I throw on my pajamas—boxers and an old Runaways T-shirt my mom gave me for Christmas one year, featuring a very young Joan Jett (the human one). While I'm brushing my teeth, I hear the front door open.

"Mom?" I say, stepping out into the hallway that leads to the kitchen.

"Hey, lady," she answers back, tossing her car keys onto the counter where they skid to a stop by the blender. Then she stops in the middle of our postage-stamp-sized kitchen and stares up at the ceiling before letting loose a loud exhale. "Oh man, what a night," she says, unwinding the bun on top of her head. Her thick black hair slides down her back like a curtain after a performance. She walks over to the fridge and peeks inside, and I finish brushing my teeth and join her.

"Where's that leftover Chinese?" she asks me as she shifts around takeout containers and cans of Dr Pepper.

"I finished it the other night," I say, giving her a sorry face as she shoots me a friendly scowl over the refrigerator door.

"Dang," she mutters. "Well, ice cream for dinner at 10 p.m. never killed anyone. At least not that I'm aware of." She pulls a pint of mint chocolate chip out of the freezer and makes her way to our little den next to the kitchen, the room where we spend most of our time together. I follow her and watch as she collapses into her regular spot on the well-worn couch and then pats the space next to her as a sign that I should join her.

"You okay?" I ask as she swallows a spoonful of ice cream and finally relaxes her body a bit.

"Yeah, just tired," she says, frowning and digging around for another big scoop. "We were slammed from the minute I got there until the minute I walked out."

"Anything gross or scary?" I ask. I watch as she swallows her ice cream and tips her head back to rest, closing her eyes briefly. My mom is still beautiful, even in her cheeseball pink nursing scrubs covered in tiny white daisies. Her dark hair stands in such contrast to her pale skin, and she moves her tall body with total grace. Meemaw says we look alike even if we don't act alike, and I hope it's true even though I'm pretty sure it's not.

"No, fortunately nothing too weird. Just urinary tract infections and ear infections all night long." Sometimes my mom comes home with strange stories that make us both laugh, like the time a kid stuck a bunch of Flintstones vitamins up his nose.

We sit in silence for a bit, and I reach out and stroke one of her long, pale arms. She looks at me and smiles.

"How was school?" she asks.

"The usual," I answer. "School."

"Such a detailed report."

"There's really nothing to say," I insist. Which isn't true, of course. On a different night I would talk through Mitchell Wilson's stupid remark and how sorry I felt for Lucy and how annoyed Mr. Davies made me in English class when he punished all of us instead of dealing with the actual problem. I might even be able to admit that Meemaw and Grandpa annoyed me by calling me dutiful. But I can tell from the way my mom wrinkles her forehead to try and keep her eyes open that she's exhausted.

"Well, it's late anyway," she tells me, "and you should get to bed. I smell like an urgent care center, but kiss me good night anyway, would you?"

I lean in for a hug and a peck on the cheek and as I head to my bedroom, I hear my mom turning on the television to unwind. After shutting my door, I slide under the covers and turn off my bedside lamp. The glow-in-the-dark stars I stuck on my ceiling light up like they're saying hello. Sliding my headphones on, I think about my mom's MISSPENT YOUTH shoe box. I scroll through my phone, looking for Riot Grrrl music, and play a song called "Rebel Girl" by a band named Bikini Kill.

It starts with this pounding drumbeat that's so strong and

angry that I think if I listen to it loud enough I might fly off the bed. Then the guitar kicks in.

But the best part is when the lead singer starts singing and her voice shoots out of her gut like a rocket launching.

That girl thinks she's the queen of the neighborhood
She's got the hottest trike in town
That girl she holds her head up so high
I think I wanna be her best friend, yeah
Rebel girl, rebel girl
Rebel girl, you are the queen of my world

The music thuds and snarls and spits, and as I listen, it's hard for me to imagine that the tired, ice-cream-eating, scrubs-wearing mom on the couch is the same mom from the MY MIS-SPENT YOUTH box. The same girl with the platinum-blond streak in her hair and tongue sticking out and dark eyes that aren't afraid to fight back.

And I know that now she's tired and exhausted and worried about paying all the bills. But there was a time when she listened to this music. When she raged and roared and rioted. When she wasn't dutiful. There was a time when she lived out loud. And no one can take that away from her.

When the song ends I lie there for a moment in silence and then hit repeat, waiting once more for the drums to begin their attack.

CHAPTER THREE

THE WEEK CONTINUES LIKE IT ALWAYS DOES. ON WEDNESDAY I GO TO school, and Mr. Davies doesn't even check the stupid extra homework he made us do in the grammar book. Lucy Hernandez doesn't raise her hand once all class. I go home and do my homework and text Claudia and listen to music and go to sleep. Thursday is pretty much the same routine. It's been the same each year since middle school. Every fall starts with me thinking maybe this year something will be different—something will happen that will shake up my merry-go-round life. But I'm so used to the sameness of every year at East Rockport, I can't even identify what I want that Something to be. I only know that by the end of September it's obvious another school year is sitting in front of me like a long stretch of highway.

The only thing that makes today, Friday, feel at all unique is, of course, that the fate of the East Rockport High football team will be decided a few short hours after the final bell rings.

East Rockport is just a 3A town, so it's not like the big cities or anything, but our football team is pretty good. And by that I mean when I was in the fifth grade we made it to the state championships but we lost, and people still talk about that day more than they talk about the fact that the one of the first astronauts to fly around in space was born right here in East Rockport. On Fridays in the fall, class feels like an excuse to legally require us to come to school so we can admire the football players' lockers decorated with orange and white crepe paper streamers and attend the mandatory pep rally before lunch and participate in the call and response cheers and observe Mitchell Wilson and his crew walking down the hallways like the second comings of Tom Landry and Earl Campbell. And the fact that I even know who Tom Landry and Earl Campbell are should tell you I really have been born and bred in this state.

"So we're driving out together tonight, right?" Claudia says as we file into the bleachers for the pep rally. "My mom said we could take her car. She's staying home with Danny because he isn't feeling good."

"Yeah, okay," I say, plunking my rear end down on one of the top bleachers. I can hear the pep band's horn section getting warmed up. I wince. It sounds like a pack of elephants mourning the loss of their leader or something. In the corner of the gym, the cheerleaders are finishing up their final stretches, dressed in uniforms the color of a Creamsicle.

Claudia and I aren't big football fans, really, but we go to all the games, even the away games like the one tonight in Refugio. That's what you do here. You go to the games. Even Meemaw and Grandpa wouldn't miss one. Grandpa likes to use white shoe polish to write GO PIRATES! on the rear window of their car even if Meemaw always worries he won't be able to drive safely because of it. Claudia and I always sit in the student section on game nights, but usually on the edge of it, like we do at the pep rallies. We split a box of super salty popcorn from the Booster Booth, and we clap our greasy hands along half-heartedly while Emma Johnson and the other cheerleaders lead us in cheers, their voices veering up and down like seesaws. "LET'S go PI-rates."—*clap, clap, clapclapclap*—"LET'S go PI-rates."—*clap, clap, clapclapclap*.

"Come on, let's get this show on the road," Claudia mutters, her eyes darting around to make sure none of the teachers patrolling the perimeter of the gym are watching us before she pulls out her phone to mess with it.

That's when I happen to glance over my shoulder and see him. Two bleachers in back of us and maybe like five people over.

A new boy.

In my experience the new boy is always someone's cousin who's just moved here from Port Aransas or wherever, and he's a total goober with an incredible talent for picking his nose in class when he thinks no one is looking. That's the new boy. That's been the new boy since the sixth grade.

Until right now. Because there's nothing about New Boy that reads East Rockport. First of all, he's wearing tight black jeans and a gray T-shirt and his long, dark hair is hanging in front of his eyes like he's trying to hide behind it. He turns his head a little to scratch the back of his neck, and I can tell the hair on the back of his head is cut short, almost shaved. Boys in East Rockport don't cut their hair like this. Boys in East Rockport have their mothers and their girlfriends cut their hair into neutral guy haircuts while they sit on stools in the middle of their kitchens. Boys in East Rockport go down to Randy's Barbershop on Main Street and flip through *Playboys* from 2002 while they wait for Randy to charge fifteen dollars for the same terrible cut he's been giving them since preschool. The one that makes their ears stick out for weeks.

New Boy must never go to Randy's. Ever.

In addition to the super cool haircut, he's got olive skin and full lips and dark eyes like two storm clouds. He's watching the activity on the gym floor below him with confused interest, like the pep rally is part of some documentary on one of those strange tribes in the Amazon that has never had contact with modern civilization.

I nudge Claudia.

"Don't look in, like, a super obvious way, but who is that guy a few rows behind us? He's new, right?"

Claudia turns and glances, then flares her nose a little in disgust, like New Boy is a stain on her favorite shirt, which is so unfair considering how deeply unstainlike New Boy is.

"Him? Yeah, I know who he is."

My mouth pops open and Claudia grins, relishing the moment.

"Oh, come on, don't hold back," I say. Of course at a school

24

as small as East Rockport High it's only a matter of time before I'll learn New Boy's name anyway, but still, it would be nice to know it as soon as possible so I could begin fantasy boyfriending him right away. I'm much more experienced with fantasy boyfriends than actual boyfriends.

Claudia carefully twirls her long hair with one finger, dragging out the suspense. "His name is Seth Acosta, and he's a junior, too," she says. "His parents are these weird artist types from Austin, and they're renting from my parents. Their house and this finished garage that they're using as their gallery space. Down by the bay."

"Near the mansion?" I ask. The Oakhurst Mansion was originally owned by some guy named Colonel Oakhurst who served in the Republic of Texas Army. Once a year each year in elementary school we were all forced to tour a musty house built in the late 1880s that didn't have any toilets. One of the singular experiences of an East Rockport childhood, I guess.

"Yeah, by the mansion," Claudia offers. "Why? Are you thinking of saying hello to a real live boy for once?"

I shoot her a look and feel my cheeks flush. I'm so awkward around boys that I don't talk to them except when absolutely necessary—like when a teacher puts us in groups to do stupid projects. And Claudia knows it.

"I don't get why two Austin artists would move to East Rockport," I say, changing the subject. I have to kind of shout because the pep band is starting its standard pep rally opening number, "All Hail East Rockport." Some of the kids around us are stomping out the beat on the bleachers with their feet.

25

"Maybe Marfa is done," Claudia yells back. "Maybe they're so cool they're anti-cool. I mean, honestly, can you think of a more not-cool town than East Rockport?"

I shrug in agreement. Claudia is right. There's not much to do on weekends if you're a teenager except cruise the Sonic and the Dairy Queen or try to find a stupid party. In terms of culture, the one museum in town is the Nautical and Seafood Museum of the Gulf Coast and the best part of going there is the fried shrimp-on-a-sticks that they sell in the cafeteria.

"So, are you going to talk to him?" Claudia asks, not giving up. "He sort of reminds me of Johnny Cade in *The Outsiders*. Remember how you read that book in middle school and made me watch the movie, like, ten times? He's so your type." Claudia's right. There's something rebellious about Seth. But not too rebellious. Dangerous but approachable at the same time. I glance in his direction again until Claudia starts making loud, slurping kissing noises near my ear.

"Okay, Claudia, enough," I protest, shoving her gently in the ribs with an elbow. Like I said, I'm great at fantasy boyfriending, but the truth is I've never had a real boyfriend. It always stings to think about it, but I'm in eleventh grade and I've never gone out with anyone. Or even kissed a boy. I want a boyfriend because I kind of feel like a dork for never having had one, but I've pretty much given up on the idea that it's going to happen for me in high school.

As the cheerleaders form a pyramid and the pep band forces out a few more pep-filled notes, I manage to sneak one more peek at Seth. He's still sitting there, his expression wandering somewhere on the border of neutral and bored. He lifts up one lanky arm and drags his hand through his hair and his bangs fall in front of his eyes.

I wonder what his middle name is.

I wonder what he smells like.

I wonder what music he listens to, and I wonder what he looks like when he brushes his teeth.

"Let's hear it for the East Rockport Pirates!" comes a booming voice from the center of the gym floor. Principal Wilson is standing behind the microphone, his gut hanging over his belt, his face cherry red before he even starts yelling. Pretty soon he gets even redder as he bellows and shouts about the best football team in the world and how we all have to support the mighty Pirates and on and on and on.

"I'm bored," Claudia announces, her voice flat. She stares out over the heads of the girls in front of us, then yawns as if proving her point.

Principal Wilson introduces Coach Cole and then Coach Cole introduces the football players and Mitchell Wilson and all the other boys trot out in their jeans and football jerseys over their shirts and Emma Johnson and the other Creamsicle girls do backflips and the pep band exhibits pep and Claudia yawns again.

Sometimes I wonder what it would be like to live in a town that doesn't revolve around seventeen-year-old boys who get laid way too often just because they know how to throw a football.

"Folks, I want to remind y'all how important it is to come

out and support your Pirates tonight because we're going to need every one of y'all cheering as loud as you can, am I right!" Coach Cole hollers. The crowd hollers back, like they're at a church service run by one of those preachers you see on TV. The rally continues like this until the bitter end when Jason Garza, the senior captain, whips his football jersey over his head and swings it around like a lasso before throwing it into the crowd, where a bunch of girls scream and lunge for it like a bouquet at a wedding.

"Oh, shit, look at what he has on," Claudia mutters. "Another one of his gross shirts."

Under his football jersey, Jason is wearing a white T-shirt with big black letters. It reads GREAT LEGS—WHEN DO THEY OPEN?

"Gross," I mutter. Jason is wearing the shirt in front of Coach Cole and Principal Wilson, but it won't matter. He can get away with it. He always gets away with shirts like these, and he's not the only boy in the school who likes wearing them. Boys being boys or whatever. The rest of the football players, including Mitchell, are laughing. I catch the expressions of some of the guys in the front bleachers, and they're laughing, too. Jason even does a little attempt at a sexy dance in front of a few of the girls up front, shifting his hips around like he's trying to keep up some invisible Hula-Hoop. The thatch of dark hair on his head makes him look like a rooster strutting around up there. The girls laugh and put their hands up in front of their faces, and I can't tell if they're grossed out or if they're actually liking it.

Then I notice one of the girls is Lucy Hernandez. Even from all these rows back, it's easy to see she's not smiling or giggling or laughing or even pretending to be grossed out. She's just grossed out for real. This isn't the first pep rally of the year, so poor Lucy should know by now that you never sit in the first few rows unless you're a hardcore Pirates fan. Better to hide toward the back, like people who only go to church on Christmas.

Jason must get Lucy's disgust because he makes a point of gyrating his hips right up near her face, and she just looks away, down at the floor. She's blushing. Everyone else is hooting.

Something charges through my body, and I look down and see my hands are balled up into fists. I stare at them for a moment, surprised, and then will them to release.

"All right, all right," Principal Wilson announces on the microphone, "let's get going to lunch, y'all. Why don't we save that energy for the game, Jason."

The band plays its last notes as we stream out of the gym. I look back but Seth has been swallowed up by the crowd. I hope Seth Acosta is not the sort of guy who would wear a shirt that reads GREAT LEGS—WHEN DO THEY OPEN? He could look as hot as a young Ralph Macchio in *The Outsiders*, but I still wouldn't want to hang out with a guy who wears a shirt like that. Even my fantasy boyfriends have to have standards.

As Claudia and I head toward the cafeteria for lunch, we get pushed and bounced through the shuffle of the crowd, and I realize I've ended up near Lucy. She walks toward the edge of the hallway, her shoulder bumping into the row of lockers every so often. Her cheeks are still pink, and she's not really looking at anyone as she makes her way down the packed hallway. I think about asking her to eat with us in the cafeteria, but the idea of breaking out of my regular social routine and talking to someone new seems exhausting somehow.

After she spoke up in Mr. Davies's class, I know Lucy is the kind of girl who isn't afraid to be the center of attention even if it doesn't make her too popular. It's not so much that I want to be popular, because popular people at East Rockport High School are basically assholes, but I like flying under the radar. I wish I didn't give a shit about what people think about me. Like my mom coming to school with blue hair. She was never dutiful or under the radar when she went here. That's why she became a Riot Grrrl.

When Claudia and I get to our regular table in the lunchroom with our friends Meg and Kaitlyn and Sara, I look for Lucy but I don't see her. I don't see Seth Acosta either. But I do see Jason with his dumb shirt on, cutting in line in front of some freshmen.

Great Legs—When Do They Open?

I have the urge to clench my fists again until the slivers of my mostly bitten fingernails dig into my palms.

I wonder what Wonder Woman would do right now. Or my mom. Or the girl who sings that rebel girl song. The one whose voice was a weapon. The one who didn't care if all eyes were on her. In fact, she liked it that way. What would she do to Jason?

Maybe march right up to him and tell him how gross his shirt is? Maybe take a pair of scissors and cut it right off his body?

He'd probably like that, though. He could show off his stupid six-pack.

I take a bite of my ham sandwich and listen as Claudia and Kaitlyn and the others talk about where we should try to sit at the game tonight. I put my sandwich down and pick at the crust. I'm not really hungry.

"So what time do you want me to pick you up?" Claudia says, kicking me under the table.

"I'm not going," I hear myself saying. I'm surprised at my own response. But also relieved.

"What?" Claudia asks, frowning. "We were just talking about how I have my mom's car."

"I'm not really feeling well," I say, coming up with the easiest excuse.

Kaitlyn reaches over and touches my forehead with her hand. She has, like, five younger brothers and sisters so she's always doing mom-stuff like that.

"You don't have a fever, I don't think," she tells me. "Do you feel achy or cold?"

"It's my stomach," I say, pushing away my lunch.

"Eww, stay away," says Meg, sliding her chair toward the other end of the table. "I don't want to get sick."

Claudia is eyeing me carefully. Just a few minutes ago I was fine, checking out the new guy at the pep rally.

"I don't know what it is," I admit. And I don't. But something has shifted. It happened the moment I said I wouldn't go to the game and now I can't go back.

Or did it happen during the pep rally, when I saw Jason's shirt and realized my hands were in fists?

Or did it happen before that?

"Maybe you should go to the nurse," Kaitlyn says. "Do you want one of us to walk you?"

"No, I can get there on my own," I answer. "But thanks."

"Text me later?" Claudia asks. Her voice is small and a little hurt, I think. But maybe she just doesn't know what to make of my weird behavior. Honestly, I don't either.

Nurse Garcia lets me lie down on one of the cots in the back room of the clinic all afternoon. There's no one else back there, and she turns the lights off for me. It's nice and cool and quiet. When I shift positions, I hear the paper sheet crumple underneath me. The bell for sixth period to start comes and goes, and I pass the time staring at a poster that reads COUGH AND SNEEZE? ELBOW, PLEASE! A little stick figure girl and boy cough and sneeze into their stick figure elbows. I lie there through sixth period, indulging in the fact that I'm tucked away inside my little clinic cocoon while everyone else has to be in class. The bell rings again for seventh period and then again for eighth. And then, finally, the last bell of the day.

"Feeling better?" Nurse Garcia asks as I step into the main clinic office, blinking my eyes at the bright lights.

"Yeah," I answer. "Thanks for letting me rest so long."

"You're not one to fake it, Vivian," she says. "And you don't look quite right, to be honest. Just go home and stick to toast, bananas, and rice, okay? And get rest and drink lots of water. I'm sorry you have to miss the game."

"I'll survive," I tell her.

Usually at the end of the day, Claudia and I meet by my locker, and we walk home together or try to catch a ride with someone we know. But today I grab my backpack and make my way out a side door, taking a different route than I normally do. I walk fast, leaving East Rockport High behind me as quickly as possible.

CHAPTER FOUR

MEEMAW AND GRANDPA ARE GOING TO THE GAME, AND MOM HAS TO work late again. I call my grandparents and tell them I'm not feeling well so I won't see them at the stadium, and I call my mother at work and tell her my stomach is acting up and I'm staying at home. She gives me the same instructions as Nurse Garcia and reminds me to call her if I start feeling worse.

But I don't feel worse. I feel better. There's something weirdly freeing about knowing that almost the entire town is driving into Refugio and I'm safely hidden inside my house all by myself.

I let myself wonder for a minute if that new boy, Seth, is going to the game. If his weird artist parents are taking him there as part of their research for some performance piece they're doing on Small Town Texas Life. Maybe he's already begged them to let him move back home to Austin. Maybe he never even existed at all and is just a figment of my imagination.

As dusk falls outside, I heat up a mini frozen pepperoni pizza and take it into my bedroom with me, balancing it on a paper towel. I love eating in bed. It feels so lazy and wrong and also so luxurious and awesome at the same time. After I carefully pick off and eat all the pieces of pepperoni but before I start in on the cheese, I find this documentary I watched once with my mom and start playing it on my laptop. It's about Bikini Kill's lead singer, the girl with the rocket-launching voice who sings that song about the rebel girl. I remember that when my mom and I watched the movie the first time, I glanced over at her during the closing credits. In the semi-darkness of our den, her face lit only by the flashing images on the television screen, I could see she was blinking away tears. But I could tell by the way she was smiling through her tears that she felt good and sad at the same time. Sometimes I wonder how old you have to be to feel really nostalgic. Sometimes I wonder if it's possible to feel nostalgic for something you never actually got to experience yourself. I think that's how I feel about the Riot Grrrls.

I finish the pizza, wipe off my greasy fingers and face, and pat the bed so Joan Jett will jump up and snuggle with me as I keep watching the movie. One of the things Kathleen Hanna—that's the lead singer's name—talks about in the documentary is the idea of the bedroom culture of girls. Every girl has some super secret world going on in her bedroom where she can make and create things, and Kathleen thought it would be cool if girls could share what was happening in their secret spaces with other girls. That's what Riot Grrrl tried to do. They tried to make ways for girls to find each other. Girls who cared about the same things and fought the same fights and liked the same stuff. But since it was before the Internet, they did it with zines and bands and lyric sheets and shows and cassette tapes they sold for five dollars.

Sitting there in the semi-darkness of my own bedroom, watching Kathleen and the other Riot Grrrls on my laptop screen, I can't stop thinking about my mom's MY MISSPENT YOUTH box. About Wonder Woman taking out street harassers. About old Polaroids of girls with black lipstick who look like they are ready to take over the world with their attitudes. About neon-green flyers advertising a Riot Grrrl convention in Washington, D.C., and fund-raisers for rape crisis centers.

Audacious. That's a fancy vocabulary workbook word that would earn me extra points on any of Mr. Davies's stupid unit tests.

The Riot Grrrls didn't care what people thought. They wanted to be seen and heard.

Because they were audacious.

I cuddle with Joan Jett on my bed while the documentary plays, and an idea that's been building in the back of my brain begins to take shape. It's crazy. It's ridiculous, really. But I can't stop thinking about it.

Up until I was in third grade, my mom smoked cigarettes. She tried to be sneaky about it when I was really little, but eventually she knew I got wise to her and would apologize to me every time she headed out to the back porch to smoke.

"Oh, Vivvy, I'm sorry," she would tell me, sighing. "I'm really trying to quit, but it's so hard."

My third-grade brain came up with an idea. Alone in my

room, I cut out a dozen slips of paper the size of my palm and wrote things on them in black Sharpie like SMOKING KILLS and SMOKING CAUSES CANCER and I DON'T WANT TO LOSE MY ONLY PARENT. Looking back, I cringe at that last one, but I was an earnest third grader, and I was going for the jugular. After decorating them with skulls and crossbones and a stick figure that was supposed to be me crying next to a tombstone that read R.I.P MOM, I commenced the final part of my secret mission. I hid the signs all over the house. Behind her deodorant in the medicine cabinet. In her underwear drawer. Folded into squares in the carton of eggs. I even tucked one into her pack of Camel Lights.

My mother found the first one (buried inside her box of Special K) and waved it at me during breakfast that morning.

"Vivian, was this you?" she asked, arching an eyebrow.

"I don't knooooooow," I said, arching an eyebrow back. "It could be some anonymous anti-smoking person." I loved playing some secret avenger. Even if in my heart I knew I wasn't actually so secret.

My mother rolled her eyes at me, but something funny happened after she found all of the cards.

She stopped smoking. For good.

My mission had worked.

When the documentary is over, I give Joan Jett one last pet and go to my mom's desk in the den for a few supplies. My body hums with excitement. I cross my fingers that our wonky printer that only works half the time will work tonight. And then I get the last item I need from my mother's closet.

I spill out all of my mom's old zines for the hundredth time and look at them with fresh eyes. I'm taking notes. Or, to be totally honest, I'm kind of stealing. But I don't think the girls who made *Girl Germs* and *Bikini Kill* and *Sneer* would mind. In fact, they'd probably be happy about it.

I run one finger over the words of something called a Riot Grrrl Manifesto. I can't remember ever reading it before. It's in one of the Bikini Kill zines, and I wonder if Kathleen Hanna wrote it herself. I swallow up the words.

Because we don't want to assimilate to someone else's (boy) standards of what is or isn't.

Because we are angry at a society that tells us Girl = Dumb, Girl = Bad, Girl = Weak

Because I believe with my wholeheartmindbody that girls constitute a revolutionary soul force that can, and will, change the world for real.

I picture Lucy Hernandez's stunned, hurt expression in class when Mitchell Wilson told her to make him a sandwich. I think about Jason Garza's gross T-shirt and his swiveling, stupid hips. I imagine my life in East Rockport stretching out in front of me, a series of pep rallies and vanilla conversations in the cafeteria with dutiful girls I've known since kindergarten. I picture all the expected things that come after all that—go to college, end up with an okay guy and an okay job, and spend my Fridays in the fall at East Rockport High football games until I'm eighty years old.

I take a deep breath and uncap a black Sharpie. I need the right name to get started. My eyes glide over the well-worn covers of my mom's zine collection. I pick up a copy of one called *Snarla* and hold it close to my face and shut my eyes and take a deep inhale, imagining I can smell the musty basements and warehouses where the Riot Grrrls used to play shows for three dollars. Imagining I can hear them singing out the lyrics they've so painstakingly copied onto the pages of their zines.

I won't be your baby doll
I won't be your pageant queen

Girl let's dance in our bare feet
Let's hold hands all night long

Go ahead and try us boy
We love to fight back!

Those last lines are my favorite.

I can visualize the Riot Grrrls—my mother among them—walking the streets at night in their Doc Martens and their bad haircuts and their dark lipstick, ready to stand up for what they believed in. What they knew was right.

Angry. Untouchable. Unstoppable. And, if you were to use my grandmother's words about my mom during last night's dinner, full of moxie.

Suddenly, I've got it.

My tongue between my teeth, my mind focused, my hand steady, I make careful letters, already imagining what the end product will look like. I finish lettering the title and then at the last minute add the perfect motto. When I'm finished, I crack my neck—it's a little sore from hunching over my creation so intently. And then I admire my work. I can feel the adrenaline pumping through me. I smile.

This is the most excited I've been about anything in ages.

With an hour left before my mom gets home from work, I take my finished pages and place them gingerly in my math folder, then slide the folder into my backpack. Before I lose my nerve entirely, I wheel my bicycle out of the garage and hop on, making my way toward downtown East Rockport.

Since it's game night, the whole town is mostly a dead zone, with signs at the Dairy Queen and the Sonic that read CLOSED FOR THE GAME. The yellow glow of the streetlights illuminates the empty streets and parking lots. But U COPY IT is on the outskirts of the business district, and it's one of the few places in East Rockport that's always open until midnight. I coast past the Walgreens and the hair salon where my grandparents had to pay way too much money to fix my mom's blue hair all those years ago.

It's so quiet I feel like one of the last surviving citizens of a ghost town. The sticky autumn air smells like grease traps and gas stations, and if I take a deep breath I won't catch even a sliver of the scent of the briny Gulf waters just a few blocks away. In East Rockport, it's easy to forget you live by the ocean. Not that the Gulf of Mexico actually counts as the ocean. Last summer there was so much fecal matter floating in it, they shut the beaches down for two weeks. East Shitport is more like it.

Braking gently, I park my bike and walk into U COPY IT,

my eyes taking a moment to adjust from nighttime darkness to the bright fluorescent shine of the inside of the copy shop. There are no customers and just one employee, a guy wearing a frayed red vest that I guess is supposed to be some sort of U COPY IT corporate regalia. Perching on a stool behind the register, he's so busy reading a tattered paperback novel that he doesn't even look up when I walk in. Taking my folder carefully out of my backpack, I approach the counter. The guy's name tag reads FRANK.

"Uh, hi?" I say, and Frank looks up and blinks hard a few times, like he's trying to process that I'm here. He has a little stubble under his chin and a mass of unkempt salt-and-pepper hair that sits like a bird's nest on top of his head. He could be thirty or sixty, I'm not sure. But before he decides to speak to me, he carefully adjusts his frameless glasses and blinks three or four more times.

"Can I help you?" he says at last, setting down his copy of *Carrie* by Stephen King.

"Uh, I was wondering . . . if you could make me some copies?" I hate talking to people in stores, even if there's no one else to hear me. I'm always afraid I'm going to sound stupid.

"Well, the store is U COPY IT, so I can help *you* do it," Frank says dryly. But half a smile pops up on his face so I'm not too anxious.

Frank pulls out a small plastic counting device, walks me over to one of the machines, and slides the device into place. He shows me how it works and offers to observe as I do a practice run to make sure I do it right.

My cheeks heat up, but I pull my pages out of my bag and try to program the machine so it will copy double-sided, like Frank showed me.

"A lady boxer, huh?" Frank says, nodding his chin at the front cover.

"Yeah," I say.

"Cool," Frank says, ignoring how flustered I am. He makes sure my test copy turns out okay, even folding it in half so it's all finished. When he hands it to me, it's still warm as toast.

Holding it in my hand, my idea feels so real that all of a sudden I can't decide whether I should scream with excitement or stop now.

"This looks good," I manage.

"I'll leave you to it, then," Frank says.

Once he's back at the counter, I busy myself making copies. I do a mental count of how many girls' bathrooms I think there are at East Rockport High and punch in the number of copies I need. While the machine whirs, I check my phone for the tenth time. I have to make it home before my mom or she'll never buy that I was so sick I decided to skip the game. It's possible Mom would understand what I'm doing, but I can barely grasp the fact that *I'm* doing this, so I don't know how I would even begin to explain it to her.

And anyway, there's something delicious about it being my secret.

At last I pop out the counting device and head back to the counter to pay with some of my birthday money leftover from last month. Frank offers me another half smile before I walk out.

And then, just as I step through the door, he calls out, "See ya, Moxie!"

It takes me a moment to realize he's talking to me, and by the time I turn around to wave, his eyes are already buried deep in his book again.

I beat my mother home and slide the paper sack into my backpack—I'll have to fold the rest of them over the weekend. That is, if I don't lose my nerve.

I should listen to "Rebel Girl" on repeat tomorrow and Sunday so I don't.

I pull my Runaways T-shirt over my head and brush my teeth, and as I turn out the lights and slide into bed, my mom's car pulls into the driveway. Soon there's a sliver of light shining across me, and I squint my eyes like I've been sleeping all this time and have just been taken by surprise.

"Viv?" My mom's silhouette is peeking through the doorway, her voice a whisper. "You feeling better?"

"Yeah," I answer back, hoping the kitchen doesn't smell like pizza. I'm supposed to have a stomach bug, after all.

"Let me know if you need anything, okay?"

"'Kay," I whisper.

After my mom shuts the door, I slide deeper under the covers and feel my body buzz with anticipation when I think about the copies inside my backpack. No one else on the planet knows about them. Well, except Frank at U COPY IT. And anyway, he doesn't know the next step of my plan.

Finally, after a few minutes, I sense myself drifting off and when sleep overtakes me, I dream about marching through U COPY IT with Frank, the two of us dressed in matching Runaways T-shirts, leaving copies of my creation on top of every Xerox machine.

Hey ladies!

are you tired of a certain group of male students telling you to "Make me a sandwich!" when you voice an opinion in class?

Are you tired of the football team getting tons of attention ⅗ getting away with anything they want?

Are you tired of gross comments ⅗ disgusting T-shirts?

THE GIRLS OF MOXIE ARE TIRED TOO!!!

what would East Rockport High look like if MOXIE was in charge???

Attention Grrrls of East Rockport High!

If the words you've read make sense to you — draw some ♥s and ✭s on your hands before school next FRIDAY OCTOBER 5

Find girls who feel like you!

CHAPTER FIVE

A SCHOOL SUPER EARLY IN THE MORNING FEELS HAUNTED. IT DOESN'T look all that different on the outside, but without teenage bodies filling its halls and slamming its lockers, it seems like a cavernous, creepy space on the outskirts of some parallel universe, full of the spirits of teenage dreams that died sad, tragic deaths involving multiple-choice quizzes and prom-night disasters. All I can do as I pull open a side door is shake off the weirdness and hope there isn't anyone inside to catch me.

I pick the language hall as my secret entry point. I know the head custodian, Mr. Casas, gets here crazy early to unlock the doors and turn on the lights and power up the air-conditioning or the heat—both always seem to break on the hottest and coldest days of the year, respectively. It's not technically against the rules to be here at 6:30 on a Monday morning, but if this plan of mine is going to work, no one can see me.

My heart thrumming, I slide into the first girls' bathroom I see. Once inside, I take a breath and reach inside my backpack for my copies of *Moxie*. My hand slips around a stack of about twenty zines, then pauses. If I pull them out and put them down and walk out, I can't take it back. Not with the early bell ringing in thirty minutes.

The *plink plink* of a drippy sink taunts me in the background.

You. Can't. You. Can't. You. Can't.

I'm a girl who studies for tests. I'm a girl who turns in homework on time. I'm a girl who tells her grandparents she'll be over in five minutes and shows up in three. I'm a girl who doesn't cause a fuss. I even shrink into my desk when a teacher calls on me in class. I'm a girl who would prefer to evaporate into the ether rather than draw even positive attention to herself.

Drip. Drip. Drip. You. Can't. You. Can't.

Total truth? Sometimes I catch myself lip-syncing lyrics into the mirror alone in my bedroom, and I get embarrassed for myself even though there's no one there to see me but my own reflection.

DripDrip. DripDrip. DripDrip. YouCan't. YouCan't. YouCan't!

If I get caught distributing *Moxie*, I can only guess what kind of punishment Principal Wilson will dream up. A zine criticizing his precious school would definitely earn me a huge, public punishment. Way worse than anything that would have happened to my mother when she walked down the hallways of this very building with illegal blue hair. I glance at the lady boxer on the cover of *Moxie*, trying to channel her total badass attitude.

But damn it! I'm dutiful Vivian, and I'm going to be dutiful about this, too. After all, these zines exist because I made them. They're real. I can't stop now.

And with my breath held, I slide the stack onto the windowsill, just underneath the filmy first-floor windows that the girls crack open sometimes so they can smoke without getting caught.

There. It's done. I look at the copies for a moment, trying to imagine how they'll appear to someone who has no idea where they came from. Hopefully like a Christmas present. Or a treasure hunt clue.

Walking quickly through the hallways, my mind running excuses as to why I'm here so early. (*I'm supposed to meet a teacher to make up a quiz. I wanted to see my college counselor. I had insomnia so I decided, what the hell, I might as well get here early.*) I stop at each girls' bathroom and drop off stacks of *Moxie* until there's only one copy left. I never see Mr. Casas or any other adult. Finally, I make it to my locker and slide the final remaining issue underneath some old spirals.

The first bell rings, and it's not long until bodies start streaming into the building as the sun rises. As I walk to American history, I scan the faces of my classmates, wondering if every girl I spot has already been inside a bathroom. Wondering if an issue of *Moxie* is tucked inside a notebook or folded inside the back pocket of a well-worn pair of jeans. I feel my heart pulsing, full of something important.

I take my seat in the second to last row as the bell rings, and Claudia runs in a beat later, sliding into the seat next to me. Our teacher, Mrs. Robbins, is fiddling around with papers at her desk. She doesn't even look up to greet us.

Our friend Sara is seated in front of us, and she takes advantage of Mrs. Robbins's lack of preparation to turn around and face Claudia and me. It's then that I see a copy of *Moxie* in her hands. I can feel my cheeks redden and tip my head forward so my hair covers my cheeks.

"Did y'all see this?" Sara asks.

Claudia reaches her hand out. "No, what is it?"

Sara hands the zine over, and I watch as Claudia's eyes skim the words I wrote Friday night while she was half-heartedly cheering the East Rockport Pirates on to a win over Refugio.

"Whoa," Claudia says.

"What is it?" I ask instead, praying I look normal as I peer over Claudia's shoulder.

"See for yourself," Claudia says, and I lean over the zine so I can read my own creation. I try to contort my face into one of surprise and curiosity.

"Huh," I manage. I feel so unnatural I can't believe they're not all staring at me.

But my friends' eyes are on the zine. "It's totally right on," Sara says. "I mean, all of this is totally accurate. But I wonder who made it? Like, who are these Moxie girls it's talking about? Are they some sort of club or something?"

"Did you see the thing on the back?" Claudia asks. "About coming to school on Friday with stars and hearts on your hands?" She shrugs and raises her eyebrows. "Not sure what the hell that's going to accomplish."

Claudia's words sting because it hits me that I never really thought about what the stars and hearts are going to do. Riot

Grrrls used to do similar things to help like-minded girls find each other at punk shows. But I'm not sure what the girls with decorations on their hands will do on Friday. I'm not sure any girls will show up to school with their hands marked up at all.

"I guess it's cool it got made, at least," I say, fishing for some validation.

"Too bad Mitchell Wilson and his asshole friends won't even realize it exists when they're the ones who need to read it," Claudia says. "Here." She tosses *Moxie* over Sara's shoulder and slumps back in her seat as Mrs. Robbins heads over to her podium to begin her millionth lecture on the Teapot Dome Scandal or something else equally mind-paralyzing.

When the bell rings to end class, Sara leaves *Moxie* behind on her desk as if it's a forgotten homework assignment. I resist the urge to pick it up and take it with me like some sort of overprotective mother.

By the time I walk into English class with Mr. Davies, I feel like a firecracker dud. I've seen a handful of girls with copies of *Moxie* in their hands, but since Sara and Claudia in first period, I haven't heard anyone talk about it. A visit to one of the girls' bathrooms reveals half a stack of *Moxie* zines sitting sadly on the counter, one haphazardly knocked to the floor, a faint footprint right on the front cover. People seem more excited to discuss the Pirates' win and the upcoming game against Port Aransas this week.

But as I take my seat in English, I spot Lucy Hernandez in

the front row with a copy of *Moxie* in her hands, her lips locked tight and her brow furrowed as she reads the inside. She flips the zine over to read the back. Then she opens it and reads the whole thing again. I can't help but watch her as she studies it, and I catch the tiniest sliver of a smile break out on her face.

The bell rings, and Mr. Davies walks in. I'm resigning myself to beginning the worst class of the day when I notice that following him is the new boy from the pep rally. The artists' son from Austin. Seth Acosta.

"Uh, hey?" Seth says to Mr. Davies's back. Mr. Davies turns around and stares at Seth.

"Yes?"

"I'm new," he says, handing Mr. Davies a slip of paper. "I just got put in this class." His voice is low and thick.

As Mr. Davies looks over Seth's schedule, I hear snickering coming from the back of the room. Mitchell and his beefy, empty-headed buddies are cracking up, probably because Seth is new and dresses like he's from Austin and not East Rockport, and this must be amusing to them. But Mitchell Wilson could live a thousand lives and never attain the perfection that is Seth Acosta in his sleeveless Sonic Youth T-shirt and perfectly tousled black hair.

"Take a seat, Seth," Mr. Davies instructs, nodding toward the desks. Seth chooses an empty one in a corner nowhere near me. He chews on a thumbnail and stares blankly at the chalkboard while I try not to stare too much. I wonder what he had for breakfast and which Sonic Youth song is his favorite and whether or not he's ever had sex with anyone before.

That last thought turns my breathing shallow.

Mr. Davies begins a lesson that is only slightly less boring than Mrs. Robbins's from first period, and I spend my time gazing from Seth to my notebook where I'm trying to take notes. Seth takes notes, too, which makes me think he's smart or at least cares about doing well in school, which is a turn on, honestly, even if I'm pretty sure that East Rockport High is not a place that makes anyone smarter.

I'm so consumed with watching Seth that I almost don't notice that Lucy has a copy of *Moxie* sitting on the corner of her desk. But about halfway through the tedious fifty minute class I see it perched there, like a good luck charm. She leaves it there through the whole lecture, but she keeps her mouth shut the entire class, even when Mr. Davies asks questions, so I guess she's learned her lesson. I can't help think, however, that there's something deliberate about the way she keeps *Moxie* visible, and it's sort of cool.

Finally, Mr. Davies sits down at his desk to zone out on his computer while we're allegedly "working independently" (actually messing around with our phones as surreptitiously as possible). That's when Mitchell Wilson gets up from the back row where he's almost certainly been sleeping without consequence and waltzes up to the front of the room to throw something away in the garbage can. On his way back, in one smooth motion, Mitchell slides *Moxie* into his hand and takes it back to his desk. Lucy whips her head around, her mouth in an O as if she's about to speak, but then she just shuts her lips tight and turns toward the front of the room. I catch her crushed expression in profile, even though her face is half-hidden behind curls.

"What the hell is this?" Mitchell says over the snap of paper that must be him opening the zine. I don't turn around. It's one thing to criticize Mitchell in the pages of *Moxie*. But being in his sightline as he reads my words makes my *Moxie* secret terrifying instead of thrilling.

"The girls of Moxie are tired?" he asks. "Maybe they should take a nap then." The guys sitting next to him respond with a chorus of heh-hehs.

I glance over at Mr. Davies, who seems to sort of startle awake at his desk. He glances at the clock.

"Okay, hey, y'all . . . you can chat for the last few minutes of class, but keep it down, please."

Great. Now the hounds have really been released.

"Okay, wait a minute, listen to this," Mitchell continues as most of the class shift in their seats, leaning in toward him. Even Seth is looking over his shoulder, his dark eyes taking in the goon in the back row. Maybe not turning around actually makes me look suspicious. I crane my neck and see Mitchell's eyes skimming the pages of *Moxie*. My pages.

"Are you tired of a certain group of male students telling you to 'Make me a sandwich!' when you voice an opinion in class?" he reads, then looks up, his grin spreading wide like he's just been named All-American. "Hey, that's me!" He shrugs his shoulders all guilty-as-charged. *Sorry not sorry!*

"Wait, read that one," says Alex Adams, another football player in the back row. He points a finger at *Moxie* and smacks at it once, then twice, enjoying himself. "Read that last part."

I'm trying to keep my face normal and neutral, but I'm

pushing my feet into the bottom of my shoes so hard one of them squeaks against the tiled floor.

"Okay, let me," Mitchell agrees. "It says, 'Are you tired of the football team getting tons of attention and getting away with anything they want?'" Mitchell laughs out loud like he's just read the Earth is flat or time travel exists. (Actually, Mitchell might be dense enough to think those things are true.) "Is this thing serious? They're pissed we're doing our job and winning football games? I'm sorry, I didn't realize I was supposed to lose so a bunch of girls don't feel all sad and shit."

Cackle cackle, heh-heh, belchy, burpy dumb-boy noises follow, but the truth is some of the other kids in the class are smiling and laughing, too. Even some of the girls.

Mitchell leans forward in his seat, looking toward Lucy, who is packing her stuff inside her backpack. She stares up at the clock like she's willing it to speed up.

"Hey, new girl," he says in the general direction of Lucy's back. "New girl, turn around, I have a question for you."

Lucy's shoulders sink just a bit. But she turns around.

"Yeah?" she says.

"You write this?" Mitchell asks, waving *Moxie* around between his fingers.

Lucy waits a beat longer than she needs to before offering a cold and clipped, "No," and then turns around to continue packing up.

"There were copies in all the girls' bathrooms this morning," someone says. Mitchell shrugs again, his gaze on Lucy. It lingers for too long.

"Whatever, it's a bunch of shit," Mitchell mutters under his breath. He crumples *Moxie* in his quarterback hands and tosses it toward the front of the room where it bounces off the whiteboard.

"Please, let's use the trash can," Mr. Davies says, coming to life briefly.

The bell rings at last, and I catch Seth making a break for the door, not looking back.

In the crowded hallway, I find myself bumping up against Lucy. She has her eyes fixed forward, her mouth a firm line.

"Hey," I say, my voice low. "I have an extra copy of that thing if you want it. My locker's right there."

Lucy turns, surprised, her eyebrows popping up.

"Yeah?" she asks.

"Sure."

She stands off to the side as I fiddle with my combination, and once I find the one copy of *Moxie* I saved, I hand it to her.

"Thanks," she says, grinning. "This thing is so cool."

"Yeah, it is pretty interesting," I answer.

"I didn't make it, you know," she says. "Do you know who did?"

I shake my head no. If I speak she'll know I'm lying.

"That Mitchell guy is a complete asshole," Lucy says, and when she says it I find my eyes darting up and down the hall, double-checking that Mitchell isn't nearby. It pisses me off that my first reaction is to make sure he can't hear us, but I don't want to get caught by him and become the next brunt of his jokes. He scares me too much.

"He can kind of do whatever he wants around here," I offer, my voice quieter than it needs to be.

"I've figured that out," Lucy says, arching one eyebrow. "Anyway, thanks for this." She tucks *Moxie* inside a notebook. "Hey, what's your name again?"

"Vivian," I tell her. "People call me Viv."

"Right, I thought so. You never really talk in class, so I wasn't sure."

I shrug, not sure how to respond at first. "I don't think talking in that class gets you anywhere," I finally manage.

"Seriously," she says. "Anyway, I'm Lucy. And as that asshole pointed out, I'm new this year."

I smile and nod. "Yeah, I know." I'm not sure what else I'm supposed to say. In East Rockport I run into so few new people.

Lucy smiles back, but when I don't say anything else, she offers me a little half wave and starts off down the hall. I raise a hand goodbye, and it's not until she's filtered through the crowd that I realize I could have asked her where she was from or why her family moved here. I could even have asked her if she was planning on coloring stars and hearts on her hands this Friday as *Moxie* instructed.

I stare down at my own bare hands and realize I need to answer that same question for myself.

CHAPTER SIX

I ALWAYS PUSH THE CART WHEN MY MOM AND I GO GROCERY SHOPPING so my mom can focus on the list—written on paper, of course. It's been that way since I was in middle school.

"Black beans or refried?" she asks me, examining the canned goods in front of her.

"Refried."

"Black beans are healthier."

"Refried."

My mother shoots me a look, but she gives in.

We almost always go shopping on Thursday nights if she's not working. My mom can't handle the craziness of the store on the weekends, and it's a ritual we have together. But as I push the cart, trying to overcorrect its sticky rear left wheel, I find myself looking at my hands gripping the cart's handle instead of talking to my mom.

My hands don't have a single birthmark or freckle on them. My fingernails are naked—painting them always feels like a hassle. I try to imagine stars and hearts scrawled on these hands tomorrow. I try to imagine what it might feel like to walk the halls of East Rockport like that. My heart beats quickly, but I'm not sure if it's out of excitement or anxiety. I picture everyone looking at me and all my friends asking me questions. I clench my hands into fists and take a deep breath.

"Okay, let's head to frozen foods," my mom says. She's different from Meemaw and Grandpa in a lot of ways—except for a Stouffer's addiction. I follow her, pushing the cart.

All week I've been trying to figure out what I'm doing. The truth is, since Monday morning everything has been pretty much . . . exactly the same. The biggest development was probably me giving Lucy my extra copy of *Moxie*. Claudia never mentioned it again, and Mitchell didn't even bother making fun of it after that one time in Mr. Davies's class—at least that I know of. I've wanted to mention it at lunch with Sara and Claudia and the other girls, but I'm worried that talking about it too much might make me look suspicious even though me being the creator of *Moxie* is about as likely as me visiting the International Space Station or inventing the cure for cancer in my chem class. At least that's what the people who know me would say.

I'm not sure if I expected anything to come of it. Maybe it's all over now. Maybe making *Moxie* was just a way to vent.

Sure, Vivian, but why did you include that thing about the hearts and stars if you didn't want it to go anywhere?

I grimace, trying to ignore the question, but that's impossible.

Because somewhere inside I do want the *Moxie* zines to go somewhere. I know I do. I'm just not sure I want to commit to being the one to take them there. Wherever *there* is.

I scowl at the can of refried beans as I keep pushing the cart forward. It would be easier to just think about Seth, but I haven't even seen him this week except for in Mr. Davies's class. He walks in at the bell and leaves at the bell, and he never talks. Just takes notes and sits there all mysterious. Yesterday he wore a shirt that said Black Flag on it, and I spent the night listening to their song "Rise Above" on my phone. It made my toes curl and my chest ache, but in a good way.

I shiver through the frozen foods section as my mom tosses in a few boxes of lasagna and Salisbury steak. Finally, we make it through checkout, and I help unload the bags into our Honda. I'm making sure a carton of eggs isn't placed too precariously in the backseat when I hear a male voice behind me.

"Lisa?"

There's a pause, and then I hear my mom, her voice all tinkly and light. "Oh! John, hey. How are you?"

I slide out of the car to see my mom facing a guy around her age. He's wearing green scrubs and a loose-fitting gray hoodie, and his face is covered in a red, scruffy beard. My mother's face looks all lit up, like this guy is handing her a big Lotto check instead of just saying hi.

"Getting your grocery shopping done?" scruffy redhead dude asks.

"Trying to," my mom answers, her voice still a little off somehow.

"You're on tomorrow morning, right?" he asks.

"Yes," my mother answers, rolling her eyes. This whole interaction seems like it could have taken place in the East Rockport High cafeteria, and my hope that the adult world is nothing like high school crumbles a bit as I lean back against my mom's car in the HEB parking lot. Why is my mom behaving like a teenager? Who is this weird guy with a red beard?

"By the way, this is my daughter, Viv," my mother says, nodding her head toward me and smiling. I raise a hand and smile slightly.

"Nice to meet you, Viv," redhead dude says. "I'm John. Your mom and I work together."

"Nice to meet you, too," I answer on autopilot, eyeing him carefully. My mom has never mentioned any guy at work.

"Well, we'd better get going," my mom says, even though she barely makes a move.

John smiles and nods, and finally after way too long my mother and I get in the car and she starts up the engine, but I notice a big blue-and-white DELOBE bumper sticker on the back of John's SUV as he pulls out of the lot.

"Gross, he voted for Delobe," I announce, my voice louder than normal. I know I sound childish, but this John guy weirds me out.

"Oh, Delobe was a moderate, really," my mom answers, an absentminded grin on her face.

"Mom, he ran for mayor as a Republican," I say, irritated. "You said you'd never vote for a Republican even if your life depended on it."

My mom shrugs and pulls our car out of the HEB lot. "It's Texas, Vivvy. Sometimes a moderate Republican is the best we're going to get. At least he's pro marriage equality."

I can't believe her dreamy, distracted mood—she's not even listening to me—so I shut my mouth and lean my head against the cool glass of the passenger window, frowning at my reflection. When I was in middle school, my mom dated this guy named Matt that she met through a friend of hers. It went far enough that Matt would come over to watch movies with my mom and me and go on walks with us around our neighborhood and take my mom out to dinner while I spent the evening at Meemaw and Grandpa's. Matt liked orange Tic Tacs and had a mutt named Grover that smelled like lavender dog shampoo.

He was nice enough, I guess, but when he was around it always felt like I was waiting for him to leave. I didn't understand why we needed him. After all, it had been two people for as long as I could remember. Me and Mom had always been just fine.

Then, out of nowhere a few months later, Matt stopped coming over. Mom told me they moved in different directions, and from the way my mom spent several nights on the phone with a friend or two of hers, her face twisted into a scowl and her voice lowered to a whisper, I guessed I shouldn't ask any questions. After that, Mom never acted like she had any use for any guy in her life except for Grandpa.

And now there's this Republican-loving John dude with hair the color of a navel orange making my mom do a tinkly laugh, and all I can think is how disappointed I am that my mom could like a guy like that.

At home, my mom and I unpack the groceries, making the same light, easy talk we've been making for years.

"Tell me I didn't forget olive oil."

"Where should I put the potatoes again?"

"I'm going to dig into this ice cream tonight, damn it."

After that's done, my mom collapses onto the couch to watch television and I disappear into a hot shower, letting the streams of steaming hot water drum onto my head. Once I put on my old Runaways T-shirt and sweats, I dig through my collection of pens and markers and Sharpies on my desk. I pluck out one black Sharpie and uncap it, pressing the tip against my index finger a few times to make sure it works. The tiny, scattered black dots look like renegade freckles popping up out of nowhere. My heart beats hard under my rib cage. I imagine myself walking into school tomorrow, the only girl with her hands marked. How fast could I wash them clean so I wouldn't stick out?

I swallow hard and place the marker on my nightstand like an alarm clock before I slide into bed. I reach for my headphones and start playing Bikini Kill.

Not one other girl in my first period American history class has anything on her hands. Not Claudia or Sara or anyone. Just me. My marked hands feel like Meemaw's fine china teacups that she keeps in a glass cabinet and never uses. Like fragile things that don't belong in a high school and need to be put away, immediately. The heady, dizzy state I was in when I created *Moxie* disappears, like I'd biked down to U COPY IT in the middle of a dream.

Of course, Claudia notices my hands. She's my best friend. She notices when I get my bangs trimmed.

"Hey, what's up?" She nods toward my lap, where I have my hands twisted together desperately to cover up the markings I made this morning as the sun was coming up. "You did that thing from the newsletter?"

Zine, not newsletter, I think to myself, but I just shrug my shoulders.

"I don't know. I was bored." It's a stupid excuse. For the first time ever, I actually want Mrs. Robbins to walk in and start class on time.

"I guess I just don't get it," Sara says, joining in. "I mean, I thought that thing made some good points, but how is wearing hearts and stars on our hands supposed to change anything?" She eyes my drawings again and my cheeks burn.

"You're right, it was stupid," I say, embarrassed. A lump suddenly fills my throat. If I start crying in front of my friends over this, they'll know something is up.

"No, I didn't mean it like that," Sara says, her voice soft. "I just meant, like, I think this place is crazy, too, but I don't think it's ever going to improve. It was a nice idea or whatever, but . . . you know."

Claudia gives me a reassuring pat on the shoulder. "It only proves you're super idealistic, just like I thought," she says. I try to smile back and swallow away any bad feelings.

Just then, Mrs. Robbins finally walks in, and the first chance

I get to be excused to the bathroom, I take it. I make my way down the halls of East Rockport, imagining a time and a place where I'll be free from the scuffed tiled floors and pep rally banners reading Go Pirates! and mind-numbing classes that make me feel dumber, not smarter. I just have to hang on until I can get out of here, like my mother. If I only knew where I was going. If only I could be sure I would never come back.

I push open the heavy door just as a flush echoes from one of the bathroom stalls. I squirt some soap into my palms and start scrubbing my hands in warm water, rubbing at the Sharpie hearts and stars with my thumbs.

A stall door opens. I look over my shoulder and see Kiera Daniels make her way to one of the sinks. Kiera and I were friends in fourth and fifth grade, back before that weird time in middle school when the black kids and the white kids and the kids who mostly speak Spanish to each other started sitting at separate tables in the cafeteria. She and I used to trade *Diary of a Wimpy Kid* books, and once we even tried to make our own, with me writing the story and Kiera drawing the pictures. Now she sits at a table with other black girls and I sit at a table with my friends, and sometimes we nod at each other in the hallway.

"Hey," she says as she makes her way over to one of the sinks.

"Hey," I say back.

And then I see them. Stars and hearts. Big ones, too. Fat, bubbly Sharpie hearts and stars all the way up her wrists. Her drawings are detailed. I can see she's even created tiny planets in between the stars. Kiera was always a good artist.

Kiera's hearts and stars say *Look at me*. Mine just whisper *I'm here*. But still, she spots them.

"You read that newsletter?" she asks.

Zine, not newsletter. But whatever.

"Yeah, I did," I answer. And I find myself turning the water off and reaching for a paper towel to dry my hands.

"Who did it?" she asks, raising an eyebrow. She's washing her hands carefully, trying not to smudge her hand graffiti.

"No clue," I answer, bending over to scratch an imaginary itch on my knee, hoping it provides me enough cover to shield my face while I'm lying. I can feel my cheeks starting to warm.

"I liked it," Kiera says. "It said a lot of smart stuff. Things here are fucked up. I mean, my boyfriend is a football player, but still. They are fucked up." Kiera drops her voice a few notches. "Did you know they get to eat at Giordano's for free every Saturday? All you can eat?"

Giordano's is the tastiest Italian restaurant in all of East Rockport, and it's my go-to favorite place to order pizza from if Mom says there's any extra money in our food budget at the end of the week.

"The football players?" I ask, my voice matching Kiera's in quietness. "Someone has to pay for that food. The bill must come to hundreds of dollars every week."

"Who knows who pays for it," Kiera answers. "But I'd be willing to bet it's Mitchell's daddy somehow. I do know the girls' soccer team hasn't had new uniforms since my mom went to school here. And I'm not exaggerating."

"Damn."

"Exactly," Kiera tells me. She finishes drying her hands carefully and then the two of us stand there. It's a little awkward. This is probably the most Kiera and I have said to each other since the fifth grade.

"I wonder what the *Moxie* people will do next," I say. I don't know if I'm asking for ideas or just trying to throw Kiera off my trail. Not that Kiera would have any reason to suspect me.

"So you think it's more than one girl?" Kiera asks. "Whoever made *Moxie*, I mean."

"I have no idea, but probably," I say. There's another bread crumb leading her in the wrong direction. Just in case. "I mean, it sounded like more than one girl when I read it."

"Well, whatever they do next, it needs to be something bigger than this," Kiera continues, holding up one hand. "I mean, this is cool and all, but they need a big F U in the face of Wilson. Something that gets more girls involved, too."

Kiera's voice grows louder, more sure of itself, as she talks to me. For one dumb minute I start to think she made *Moxie*, not me. She's probably better suited to lead it, anyway, whatever *it* is. I would rather hide in the back of the classroom than answer a question, and I just tried to wash off my hearts and stars the first chance I got. I bet if I told Kiera the truth she could take *Moxie* over and do a much better job than me.

But the Riot Grrrls tried hard not to have a leader. They wanted the movement to be one where everyone had an equal voice. That's just one more reason for me to keep my identity a secret.

"Anyway," Kiera keeps going, "it was an interesting idea at

least." She makes her way to the door and pushes it open. "Cool talking with you, Viv."

"Yeah, cool talking with you, too," I answer. And it was cool talking with her. It was cool seeing at least one other girl who followed *Moxie*'s instructions. I wish I'd asked Kiera if she knew anyone else who had marked her hands. But just knowing Kiera's out there makes me feel a tiny bit better. Slightly less alone and weird. I take a deep breath and stare at myself in the mirror.

"Just go back to class," I say. I repeat it again and again until finally I do, my hands still covered in hearts and stars.

Maybe running into Kiera was a sign because after American history, I spy a few senior girls who are into all the drama productions and who also sit on the outskirts of pep rallies and football games walking down the hall with their hands marked. And there are two freshman girls whose lockers are near my second period class. And a few more hearts and stars sprinkled here and there on girls I spot in stairwells and corners and in the back courtyard where kids hang out during our ten-minute break during third and fourth. Some of the girls I know by name and some just by sight, but we catch each other's eyes and nod and smile shyly like we're in on some secret. Like we're each other's golden egg on some strange Easter egg hunt.

The same thing happens when I walk into English class and spot Lucy Hernandez seated in the front row with stars and hearts drawn with blue marker in delicate curls and swirls across the backs of her hands and down her fingers and around her wrists.

"Hey," I tell her as I make my way down the aisle, other students filing in, "I like your hands."

Lucy looks up from under her black bangs and a smile spreads over her face. I wonder if I'm the first person to talk to her all day. I kind of think I might be.

"Thanks," Lucy answers. "I like yours, too."

"Yours are really pretty," I say.

Lucy smiles even bigger. "Thanks."

I smile back, and then there's that same awkwardness I sensed in the bathroom with Kiera, and I'm not sure what to say next. Even though I think there's something else I want to say.

Just then Mitchell Wilson and his crew walk in, loud and taking up space and probably warming up their next make-me-a-sandwich joke, and that feeling I got that afternoon in the cafeteria on the day I made the first *Moxie* comes over me again. The feeling that made me want to clench my fists and dig my fingernails into my skin and scream.

I don't, of course. Instead, I take a breath and tuck my hair behind my ears, then pull out my English notebook and a ballpoint pen.

"All right, class," Mr. Davies begins as the bell rings, "let's go back to the notes on the Enlightenment I provided you with yesterday." Just as my brain begins to seize up with boredom, the classroom door opens and Seth Acosta walks in.

He heads to his desk, his binder and books clutched in one hand at the side of his lean boy body.

71

He is dressed in black jeans.

He has on a black T-shirt.

He is wearing black Vans.

And on his hands, drawn with careful precision in black ink, are small hearts and tiny stars.

As he slides into his desk, fireworks explode in my gut and my heart pounds so hard I know I won't be able to hear a thing Mr. Davies is saying, even if I were bothering to listen.

CHAPTER SEVEN

CLAUDIA EARNS A BEST FRIEND MEDAL AND A MILLION FREE chocolate cupcakes for the patience she gives me during the pre-lunch pep rally, when we tuck ourselves up at the top of the bleachers and I start whispering about Seth Acosta's hands.

"Okay, but why are you whispering?" Claudia shouts. "It's loud as hell in here, and anyway, he's nowhere to be found." The school band is warming up again, playing the same five or six rah-rah songs they play over and over at the football games, and Claudia is right—we can't see Seth anywhere in the school gym. "No one is going to hear you freaking out over Mister Magic Hands," Claudia continues. Her eyebrows fly up. "Okay, now I get why you're so into him. Magic hands." She cracks up at her own words.

I blush in spite of myself. "God, Claudia."

"Oh, like it's not like that with you and him?" she asks,

incredulous. "Like it's totally not about sex? You're just into him for his mind, right?"

"Enough," I manage, burying my head between my knees so she'll stop. The truth is, Seth's hearts and stars did make him one hundred times hotter to me. All through class as Mr. Davies had droned on, I'd watched Seth's temporarily tattooed hands taking careful notes, pausing every so often to scratch the back of his neck or quietly tap his fingers on the side of his desk. I'd cringed every time I'd heard Mitchell or one of his friends open his big mouth, worried Seth was going to become the butt of a joke. But nothing like that happened. Seth has done such a good job of sliding himself into the margins of East Rockport by rarely talking or doing anything extremely good or extremely bad that even though he doesn't look like most of the other students, I'm pretty sure I'm the only one noticing his every move.

"Hey, can I sit here?"

I pop up to see Lucy Hernandez standing a few feet away, balancing herself on a bleacher. Something about her standing up in front of us makes me realize Lucy is a big girl. Tall—even taller than me, which is saying something—with big hips, big eyes, big, full red lips. Even her dark hair is big, falling over her shoulders in curly tsunamis. At first I kind of want her to go away because I just want to talk to Claudia about Seth. Then I feel like a shithead for thinking that.

"Sure, you can sit here," I say. There's no need to scoot down to make room. Claudia and I are in the real nosebleed section of the gym, with Sara and Kaitlyn and the other girls we normally hang out with several rows ahead of us.

"Thanks," Lucy says, sitting down next to me so I'm in the middle.

"Hey, I'm Claudia," Claudia says, shouting her name over my lap. "You're Lucy, yeah?"

Lucy nods and smiles and tucks her knees up under her chin.

"So you're into that newsletter thing like Viv, huh?" Claudia asks, pointing at Lucy's hands. On the gym floor, the East Rockport cheerleaders are doing their thing, led by Emma Johnson, as usual. The dance music piped in through the speaker system thuds as Emma and the other girls shimmy and shake in their spotless uniforms. Their moves are so precise, so perfect. The cheerleaders have these legendary three-hours-a-day practices all summer long, and I guess it pays off in the end.

"You mean *Moxie*?" Lucy asks, answering Claudia's question and holding up her hands. "Yeah, I thought it was cool. It reminded me of this club I was in at my old school in Houston."

"Is that where you moved here from?" I ask.

Lucy says yes and, in a voice loud enough to be heard over the noise of the pep rally, tells us how her dad lost his job in June, so she and her parents and her little brother moved in with her grandmother in East Rockport. Her dad recently found a job as head of maintenance at Autumn Leaves, the town's only nursing home, so now they're here to stay.

"At my old school I was vice president of this club called GRIT," Lucy tells us. "It stood for Girls Respecting and Inspiring Themselves. It was, like, a feminist club."

"And people actually went to meetings?" I ask. I try to

imagine a club like that at East Rockport and my brain turns cloudy with confusion.

"Yeah, totally," Lucy says. "We even had a couple of guy members. We did fund-raisers for the local women's shelter and talked about stuff that we were concerned about. I was hoping there would be a club like that here. So I could meet other feminists, you know?" The way she says the word *feminists* so casually, so easily, sort of blows my mind. Claudia nods and smiles politely, but her eyebrows jump a bit.

I've heard my mom use the word *feminist* when she talks to old friends on the phone. (*"I mean, honestly, Jane, as a feminist that movie just pissed me off."*) Riot Grrrls were into feminism, obviously, but up until this moment in the gym I didn't think of them as feminists so much as super cool girls who took no shit.

"I don't think we've ever had a club like GRIT here," Claudia says. "Wait, correction. I *know* we've never had a club like that here."

Lucy nods, her face wistful. Then she turns to me and asks, "Did you see that guy in our English class who had his hands marked?" I feel my cheeks heat up just a bit, but Claudia keeps her lips sealed, her eyes focused on the pep rally. I know she won't ever say anything about my crush on Seth in front of Lucy.

"Yeah," I answer. "I think he's new, too. Like you. I thought it was kind of cool."

"It was," Lucy says. "But I'm surprised he didn't get his ass kicked."

"Maybe none of the guys noticed," I respond. "They were all too busy thinking about this." I float my hand out in front of my

76

face in the general direction of the pep rally. Principal Wilson is giving his usual come-to-Jesus speech about supporting our boys and blah, blah, blah. The football players start walking out in their team jerseys, and the students in the first few rows roar so loud my ears hurt. I glance around at the other students in the back rows. A girl I don't know is slumped in a bleacher alone, totally asleep. A few skinny, pimply boys are grouped in a clump, staring blankly down at the gym floor.

"Do you guys actually go to these games?" Lucy asks, her brow furrowed.

"Usually," shrugs Claudia. "But Viv bailed on me for the last one."

"I wasn't feeling good," I remind her. "But yeah," I continue, answering Lucy's question, "there just isn't much else to do around here. So we go."

Lucy's eyebrows furrow deeper as she thinks, I'm sure, of the one movie theater in town and the one twenty-four-hour Sonic Drive-In and the one main drag. None of those things are things that are any fun by yourself.

"Hey, you want to come and hang out at the game with us tonight?" I blurt out, glancing at Claudia out of the side of my eyes, hoping she's okay with it. But Claudia just smiles and says, "Yeah, you should come. It's a home game. We won't even have to drive far or anything."

Lucy chews on a thumbnail, her eyes still on the activity in front of her. My heart picks up speed a bit until she turns and looks at us and says, "Okay, why not. I'll go." Then she stares back at Mitchell Wilson and Jason Garza practically beating on their chests as they urge the crowd to yell louder and louder for them. Lucy's eyes widen. "God, it's honestly like Roman gladiators or something out there," she says, giving the gym floor her best what-the-fuck face. "Like, they're acting like they're about to go wrestle tigers or lions or whatever."

"I know, right?" I answer, smiling. It really is the perfect description.

On the Friday nights when my mom isn't working and there's a home game, she'll sometimes join Meemaw and Grandpa to watch the East Rockport Pirates play football. I wonder if it's intensely depressing for her to have to sit in the same bleachers that, when she was a teenage girl, she totally shunned in favor of driving to Houston to go to punk rock shows. But she always says it's fun for her now, as an adult, to just sit back and observe the spectacle.

"It's a display of testosterone-fueled hypermasculinity, sure," she told me once, "but a person can only watch so much on Netflix all by herself on a Friday night before it starts to get really sad."

But this Friday afternoon as I stand in my bra and jeans digging through my closet to find something to wear to the game, my mom pops her head into my bedroom. The first thing I notice is her cheeks have a little more blush on them than usual and her lipstick looks fresh.

"Hey, you're going with Claudia tonight, right?" she asks.

"Yeah, she's picking me up."

78

"Okay," she says, nodding. Then she moves into my room, but her steps are uncertain. My mom and I never hesitate to go into each other's rooms.

"Look, Vivian, I'm not going to be driving to the game with Meemaw and Grandpa, okay?" she begins, and I notice her smile is stretched sort of thin, the freshly lipsticked corners of her mouth not really turning all the way upward.

"Are they not going?" I ask.

"No, it's just . . ." She pauses so long I finally pull a T-shirt on over my head. This seems like the type of conversation in which a person should not be standing around in just a bra and jeans.

"Mom, what is it?"

"Do you remember John, from the HEB?" she starts, her smile still fighting to stay a smile, her lighthearted voice sounding forced. I can feel the sides of my mouth sliding downward, but I'm not forcing it at all.

"That guy who voted for the Republican?" I ask. I attempt to arch an eyebrow. I know I'm being a little pain in the ass.

My mother rolls her eyes. At least her expression is finally authentic. "Yes, Vivvy, that guy."

"Yeah, I remember him."

"Well, you know, we work together at the clinic, and it turns out he's one of the doctors for the football team. You know, he's on the sidelines during all the games in case of an emergency. He just started doing it."

Wow, so he votes Republican and he tends to sexist Neanderthals on the side. Sounds like a real winner. To my mom I just say, "Okay?"

79

"Anyway, he asked me to have a drink with him after the game. Maybe down at the Cozy Corner." The Cozy Corner is the one bar in East Rockport that my mom goes to on the super rare occasion that she goes out with some of the other nurses from work. She says she likes that they have the Runaways on the jukebox.

"Okay," I say again because I can't think of what else to say. I wonder if this Republican John dude likes the Runaways. Highly doubtful.

"I just wanted to let you know I might be a little late getting home, but not too late," she says, her fake smile back on her face, her voice a half-assed attempt at cheerful.

"So he's taking you to the game?" I ask.

"Yeah. He's picking me up. You don't have to come out of your room or anything. I told him I'll just come out when I see his car."

"The car with the DELOBE bumper sticker on it?"

"Yes, Vivvy." Deep sigh. Half hopeful eyes.

"Okay," I say. "Well . . . have fun."

My mom lingers a few beats too long, and I know she's debating whether or not she should keep on trying to talk about this. But she just pulls me in for a hug and a kiss on the temple. She smells like the vanilla extract she loves to use as perfume, and all of a sudden I'm sorry for everything.

"Mom," I say as she heads out of my bedroom.

"Yeah?"

"Have a good time."

Her eyes light up for real at last.

*　*　*

The game is actually fun. Claudia picks me up and then we go to Lucy's neighborhood, where she's waiting on the porch of a little green-and-white bungalow. When Claudia's Tercel pulls into the driveway, Lucy bounces up, dressed in jeans and a white T-shirt with red piping on the sleeves and collar. At least a dozen red plastic bracelets dance on one wrist. Her hands are still marked, too, like maybe she's even touched up her hearts and stars a little.

"Hey," she says. "Thanks for coming to get me." She slides into the back and immediately pops her head in between the driver and passenger seats. "This is the first time I've gone out or, like, done anything since I moved here." She sounds a little breathless, like maybe she's kind of nervous.

"It was no big deal to come get you," says Claudia, and the truth is, it's easy to be around Lucy. When we meet up with Sara and Kaitlyn and Meg and the other girls we always hang out with, Lucy keeps up with them no problem, her easy, bubbly chatter acting as super hilarious new-girl commentary on the ways of an East Rockport football game.

"Wait, how much money did they spend on that Jumbotron? Aren't our math textbooks from the '70s?"

"When does Mitchell Wilson get trotted out on his golden chariot, pulled by white horses?"

"If the Pirates don't win, do we all have to drink spiked Kool-Aid, or what?"

The other girls and I take time to catch Lucy up on all the

81

town gossip, pointing out the half dozen former Pirates football players in the stands who were going to be big NFL stars until they suffered injuries or got kicked out of college for too many DUIs. Now they're old men with potbellies that stretch out their orange East Rockport Booster T-shirts, and they watch every move on the field with expressionless faces. During halftime when all of us make our way through the crowd to the Booster Booth to get popcorn, we run into Meemaw and Grandpa, and Lucy smiles and introduces herself and looks them in the eyes and shakes their hands, and I know Meemaw will describe her later as "that lovely Spanish girl who was so darn charming."

I spy my mom way down at the front of the bleachers, behind the team bench, watching the game but not clapping or shouting or anything. She doesn't see me. I purposely ignore looking too carefully at the mass of men and boys on the East Rockport sideline. I don't want to spot John.

The Pirates win, so we don't have to kill ourselves, and even though I've had a lot of fun with Lucy, once Claudia and I drop her off and she waves and thanks us for inviting her, like, five times as she gets out of the car, I'm grateful it's just me and my best friend since forever.

"Wanna spend the night?" I ask Claudia. I'm not crazy about going home to an empty house, the emptiness forcing me to imagine my mom and Republican John at the Cozy Corner.

"Sure, why not," Claudia answers, and the fact that she doesn't have anything with her doesn't matter, because we spend the night at each other's houses so often that we keep toothbrushes and extra sets of pajamas there.

Later, after we've changed and spent some time catching up with stuff on our phones and eating pretzels dipped in peanut butter and talking about how John is all wrong for my mom, we collapse into my double bed. The glow-in-the-dark star stickers light up for a little while before the room slips into darkness.

"I like Lucy," I say, staring at the fading stars.

"Yeah," Claudia agrees, yawning. "She's cool."

"I think that game was, like, culture shock."

Claudia rolls toward me. "Yeah, she hasn't been indoctrinated since birth." We both laugh.

In the dark I can't see if the hearts and stars on my hands have faded. It seems like so long ago that I tried to wash them off in the bathroom sink at school. "You know," I say, "I think it's kind of cool that she calls herself a feminist."

Claudia doesn't answer right away. For a second I think she's already fallen asleep.

"Yeah, I guess," she says, and I can tell she's being really careful about what words she uses.

"You mean you're not sure it's cool?" I ask, choosing my words carefully, too.

"I mean, I just think you don't have to label it," Claudia says. "Like the word *feminist* is a really scary, weird word to people. It makes people think you hate men. I'd rather just say I'm for, you know, equality."

"But isn't that what feminism is?" I say. "Equality? I don't think it means you can't want to go out with guys. I mean, I'm not trying to be difficult or whatever." The truth is, I hate disagreements. Especially with Claudia. Which is why we've literally never had a single fight in all our years of being friends.

"No, no, I get it," Claudia says, and I know she wants this conversation to end. "I mean, I think you can call it humanism or equalism or peopleism or whatever." She yawns again, louder this time. "I just think girls and guys should be treated the same."

"Me, too," I say.

"So we agree," Claudia says.

"Of course," I say, even though I don't actually think we do.

Claudia yawns one last time, and, after we wish each other good night, I hear the gentle, even breathing of my best friend, signaling to me that she's drifted off. All of a sudden, my mind is wide awake even though I thought I was tired. It replays through the day, and I find myself thinking of the hearts and stars on Lucy's hands. On Kiera's hands. On Seth's.

Lying there, staring at the ceiling, listening to Claudia breathe, I realize I'm waiting. Waiting for what, I'm not sure. Maybe for the sound of my mother's keys in the front door. Or maybe for something important to start for real.

CHAPTER EIGHT

AS OCTOBER STRETCHES ON, LUCY HERNANDEZ STARTS EATING LUNCH with Claudia, me, and our other friends. Sometimes when she gets to the lunch table first, she pats the empty chair next to her and says, "Viv, sit here!" Once I catch Claudia rolling her eyes at this, but she does it so slightly I think I'm the only one who notices. With her sincere, bubbly personality, Lucy fits in pretty easily. And I make sure I sit next to Claudia as often as I sit next to Lucy.

Just as Lucy has joined us at lunch, it seems like Republican John is joining my mom's life, whether I like it or not. One evening, a few weeks after my mom goes to the Pirates game with him, they have dinner plans, and my mom gives me a heads up that he's coming over to meet me officially. ("He's nice, Vivvy, and I think you'll really like him!") My mom's in her room getting ready when he rings the doorbell, so I have to let him in. He's dressed in some dumb button-down shirt and khakis. At least his scruffy, red beard is trimmed for the occasion.

"Hey, Viv," he says, smiling way too big.

"Hey," I answer back. I smile, too, to be polite. Then I lead him into the kitchen as my mom hollers, "Just a sec!" from down the hallway. Standing there, John examines the refrigerator and the dishwasher like they're the most interesting appliances he's ever seen. I lean against the kitchen counter, my face neutral. Maybe the polite thing would be to offer him a glass of water. But I've already smiled at him, so I figure I'm okay.

"So how's school treating you, Viv?" John asks, finally cracking the awkward silence.

"Oh," I say, pushing out another smile, "you know. The usual."

"Yeah," he says, crossing his arms and immediately uncrossing them. "I'll bet." What can John know about my school anyway? He grew up in Clayton, not East Rockport, but if he's the kind of doctor who wants to work with the football team, I'm willing to bet his high school experience was nothing like mine. He was probably president of the Young Conservatives and sat at the jock table.

Just then my mom walks out wearing this gorgeous green dress and strappy sandals. This is no casual dinner.

"Hey!" she says, her eyes bright. John grins back at her, and I wish I could disappear.

"Hey!" he says. Then he slips a paperback out of the pocket of his pants. "Before I forget, I have that Faulkner novel I was telling you about. I mean, if you were serious about wanting to

86

borrow it." I guess he's trying to wow her with his intellectual prowess, but my mom just thanks him in that high, tinkly voice and says, "We'll see if this is the one that gets me to change my mind about his work."

"I promise, you'll love it," John says. Gag. Why is he trying to get my mom to like an author she told him she didn't like?

After some goodbyes and a quick kiss on the cheek from my mom, I shut the door after them and head back to the den to curl up on the couch. With the house empty, it almost feels like my mom is at work. Almost. But she's not, and so I feel lonelier than I would if she were busy taking temperatures and checking blood pressures. I watch television but whenever a kissing scene comes on, I change the channel. Finally I give up and go to bed. Later that night when I hear my mom coming back in the house alone, I make sure the lights are off and I'm buried deep under my bedspread even though I'm still awake.

The date with John is still on my mind Monday morning as I make my way into school. The hearts and stars from the first issue of *Moxie* are long gone from the hands of the few girls who drew them. It was cool that the drawings gave me and Lucy a chance to meet and Kiera and me a moment to talk for the first time in years, but nothing has really changed at East Rockport. Mitchell and his buddies are still gross and the football team still rules all (even though their record is only 3–2). Yesterday while my mom was at work I spent the afternoon digging through her MY MISSPENT YOUTH box, but this time, even when I held the zines and flyers in my hands, they felt like something I couldn't touch.

They are artifacts from a different time and I'm a girl today, right now, in East Rockport, Texas, and I'd better just accept it.

As I walk toward the main building shrouded in my sour mood, I hear a "hey" very clearly directed at me. A guy "hey," not a girl "hey." I look up to see where it came from.

He's standing in the doorway of the school like some modern sort of James Dean, a phone in his hand instead of a cigarette.

Hearts-and-Stars New Boy Seth Acosta.

"Oh!" I say, jumping a bit. "Hey." All the other students milling around East Rockport High's front walkway disappear into the ether. I don't hear them or see them.

Seth's eyebrows dart up and hold there for a minute. "Sorry. I didn't mean to scare you."

Oh, you didn't scare me. Just rendered me mute. Give me like five years, and it should wear off.

"I'm fine," I manage.

"That's good."

SILENCE. Awkward silence. Please, God, don't let me be getting those freaky hives on my chest and neck like I sometimes do when I'm nervous. I glance down to check.

My chest looks like a strawberry farm had a bumper crop.

Dang it.

"We're in the same English class, right?" Seth asks. He shifts his weight a little. He doesn't seem to notice the hives. Probably he's just too cool to say anything.

"Yeah, I think we are," I say, faking uncertainty.

"Do you remember what the homework was for last night?"

he asks. He bends over and fumbles through a few binders and notebooks, finally pulling out a slim green assignment book. His actions are so weirdly pedestrian and normal that I find myself relaxing a little bit.

"Uh, he assigned the grammar exercises on page 250 and 251, the stuff on adjective clauses," I say from memory before I have a chance to worry if my ability to memorize homework makes me look like a total weirdo.

"Yeah, that's what I had written down," Seth says, shutting his assignment book and sliding it into his backpack. That's when I notice a Runaways sticker on the corner of one of his binders, sticking out of his backpack like it's waving hi.

"You like the Runaways?" I ask. "They're so cool."

Seth's eyebrows pop up again, then he looks down and notices the sticker.

"Oh, yeah. That. My mom put that on there. They're okay, I guess."

"So your mom likes them?" I try. I can feel the strawberry field in full bloom. It's probably super impressive to Seth that I like the same music as his mom.

"Yeah," Seth says, and he cracks half a smile. "She used to play them for me when I was a kid. Like, constantly."

Standing there listening to Seth, it's almost as if I can visualize myself in the future relating this conversation to Claudia, reviewing point-by-point the brilliant ways I kept conversation going.

For instance: 1) My mom is also into the Runaways, and she would also play them for me as a kid or 2) Why did you move here? or 3) So what do you listen to other than your mom's old music? or 4) Hey, do you want to make out?

Okay, maybe not the last one. But any of the others would have worked.

Instead, this is what I say:

"That's cool. Well, see you later."

That's.

Cool.

Well.

See.

You.

Later.

And I walk away. I just stroll off, like I can't be fucking bothered. I can't decide if I'm the biggest idiot ever or if my anxiety levels are so high they decided to do me a favor and just end the conversation before I turned into one giant pink hive.

Either way, my neck and chest and even my cheeks are still burning as I walk into school. It's been this way for me with guys ever since I was the tall girl in middle school and never got asked to dance by boys at the sock hops, so I'd hide in the bathroom during the slow songs, practicing my excited face in a stall so I wouldn't look jealous or fake when Claudia told me about dancing with Scott Schnabel.

Heading down the main hallway, I spot Claudia by her locker, and she tucks in next to me as we make our way to first period American history.

"Listen, you will never believe the shirt I just saw Jason Garza wearing," she says. I'm grateful she doesn't seem to notice how worked up I am so I don't have to explain my stupid social faux pas with Seth.

"Does he have on the one about what time a girl's legs open?" I offer, still a little jittery.

"No," Claudia says. "This one is worse. There's a big red arrow on it pointing to his junk, and it says Free Breathalyzer Test Blow Here."

I scowl. "God, really?"

"Yes," Claudia says.

"Gross."

"Yup."

We slide into American history and take our seats at the back. As the bell rings Mrs. Robbins announces a pop quiz on our reading from last night, and all of us collectively groan, like we're actors in a bad sitcom about high school.

"If you read the chapters, you have no reason to be worried," Mrs. Robbins says, playing her part perfectly.

As she starts handing out the papers, there's a knock on the door, but the knocker doesn't wait for Mrs. Robbins. The door pops open, revealing Mr. Shelly, one of Mr. Wilson's assistant principals. Whereas Mr. Wilson actually wields legitimate—if ridiculous—power over the high school, Mr. Shelly is just some second-in-command worker ant. But he walks around with a pathetic amount of swagger like he gets off on ruling a bunch of captive adolescents. Probably because he does.

"Doing a dress code check, Mrs. Robbins," Mr. Shelly barks, letting his eyes skate over us. Mrs. Robbins sighs and waits, then jumps a bit just like the rest of us when he says, "Lady in the back.

Is that you, Jana Sykes? Stand up, dear." He's got a piggish little face and beady eyes, and it's hard to imagine him ever looking any different. Like his mother gave birth to a fiftysomething assistant principal with a hair loss problem and rosacea.

Of course we all turn and look, and Jana Sykes stands up uncertainly, shrugging her shoulders. As it turns out, her shoulders are the problem.

"Jana, those straps on your shirt are pretty thin, aren't they?"

It's super likely that Jana is so high right now she doesn't know what she's wearing. She peers down and blinks hard once, then twice, at her black top pulled lazily over her boy jeans hanging low on her thin hips.

"Um, they're . . . straps?" Jana says. There's the tiniest ripple of giggling. I'm wondering when Mr. Shelly is going to clue in that the bong rips Jana did in her pickup before school are a larger concern than her outfit, but he doesn't.

"Jana, come with me. We need to get you changed."

"They're about to take a quiz," Mrs. Robbins says.

"I'll have her back in a jif," Mr. Shelly insists, and soon Jana is making her way out of the classroom and Mrs. Robbins is handing out the quiz, which she clearly printed off the Internet, and probably this morning, too. At least it's easy. But Jana never does come back.

All throughout our morning classes, girls get pulled out by administrators. Sometimes it's Mr. Shelly who does it and sometimes it's other assistant principals and counselors. In my second period math class, Jasmine Stewart and Kelly Chen get pulled out for their pants being too tight even though they don't seem extra tight to me. In fourth period chem, Carly Sanders gets told her shirt is inappropriate. It's just a T-shirt with a scoop neck, but maybe the fact that Carly's boobs aren't the smallest in the school have something to do with it.

I glance down at my boring jeans and plain gray T-shirt. Each time a girl has been called out by an administrator, she's been forced to stand up like some doll on display as the administrator scans her carefully. When Kelly Chen had to stand in math class, her cheeks pinked up so quickly that I felt myself blushing out of sympathy. I'd rather die than have the whole class's eyes on me analyzing my clothes and body.

When I walk into English, I see two girls in the back row practically drowning in oversized East Rockport High School gym gear. The bright-orange-and-white shirts drape almost to their knees, and one of them tugs at the collar like it itches. That must be the clothes that girls who break the rules have to change into.

"What the hell is going on?" Lucy asks as I slide into the seat behind her.

"With what?"

"With the Hester Prynnes over there," she says, nodding her chin toward the back row. "You know, those weird dress code checks."

"Who knows," I answer. "The administration gets all excited about the dress code every once in a while."

"It seems totally arbitrary," Lucy says, but I don't get to answer her because the bell rings, and Seth Acosta walks in. I watch as he makes his way to his seat, wondering if he'll acknowledge our conversation this morning, but he doesn't. Mitchell Wilson and his crew crowd through the door a few minutes late, but of course Mr. Davies doesn't say anything to them.

Then a soft, sweet voice rings out from the doorway.

"Mr. Davies, sorry to interrupt, but I got a schedule change into this class?"

The boys in the back hoot a little as Emma Johnson saunters over to Mr. Davies and hands him a pink slip of paper. She slides into her seat like a bird to its nest, delicate and lovely, each movement perfectly coordinated. She ignores the hoots of Mitchell and his friends until the last possible second, when she flips her honey-colored hair over her shoulder and gives them one of those looks Emma Johnson has been giving to boys since we were in the fifth grade. A look that seems irritated and inviting at the same time. I've always wondered how she pulls it off.

Emma lives what Meemaw would refer to as a charmed life. Beautiful, popular, good student, richer than most, head cheerleader, and actually fairly nice if you talk to her, which I estimate I've done five times in my entire life. Girls like Emma Johnson are supposed to be nasty and snooty, but Emma isn't like that. Not really. She holds herself like a politician running for office, which makes sense considering she's class vice president. She's careful. Mature. Goal-oriented. Once in ninth grade Real Life class—which was this class where we were supposed to learn stuff like how to balance a checkbook, but mostly we just watched public service announcements about the dangers of crystal meth—I spotted Emma working on her résumé. In the ninth grade.

As Emma settles herself in, I glance sideways at Seth Acosta to see if he's noticed her. I can't help myself. After all, she's gorgeous by anyone's standards.

But Seth is glancing at me.

I raise my eyebrows a little out of shock or terror or delight and then Seth glances back down at his desk.

God, I'm an idiot.

He doesn't look at me for the rest of the class.

After the bell rings, Lucy and I head down to the cafeteria to meet up with Claudia and the other girls. Lucy is still on a tear about the dress code checks.

"This whole thing is just so gross and sexist," she says, her angry pace of walking so quick I have to double-time my own steps to keep up despite my long legs. We pause only so we can get our lunches out of our lockers. Then Lucy starts up again. "I mean, it's totally random. These girls have to stand up and allow themselves to be looked at and endure this . . . like . . . public *shaming*." She spits out the last word.

"I know, it's gross," I answer, waving to Claudia, who is waiting for us near the entrance to the cafeteria.

"So this has happened before?" Lucy asks.

"Yeah, a couple of times last year. Whenever the administration decides we're falling out of line in terms of our clothes or whatever."

"But that asshole Jason whatever-his-name-is is allowed to wear insulting T-shirts every day of the week, yeah?"

I don't have to answer because she already knows what I would say.

When Claudia joins us at the door, she leans in close, her expression muted. "Y'all, Sara is really upset."

"Why?" I ask.

"Just now in French class," Claudia explains. "Mr. Klein came in and busted her for her top."

"But she was in first period with us!" I'm confused. "Why didn't she get busted then if they were going to bust her?"

"Why bust her at all?" Lucy says, her voice rising.

We take our seats with Kaitlyn and Meg and a few other girls as Claudia explains how horrible it was when Mr. Klein made Sara get up in front of the entire class. "He told her top was inappropriate and she should have known better," Claudia says. "He really laid into her."

"It's because she has biggish boobs," Meg says under her breath. "Like you can control that."

Just then we spot Sara coming toward us, dressed in an ugly-as-sin East Rockport gym shirt that's way too big. Grass and dirt stains as old as the school are embedded into the orange fabric.

"Hey," Sara says, sitting down. Her voice is soft, almost a whisper. Nobody knows what to say. Sara puts her paper bag lunch on the table, opens it, and pulls out a carton of chocolate milk. Then a shaky exhale slips through her lips and her eyes tear up.

"Sorry," she says. "I had to change. Mr. Klein was so rude about it. He accused me of wearing an outfit that could distract the boys." The tears reach the edges of her eyes and one blink is all it takes to make them spill over. Meg, Kaitlyn, Claudia, and I begin a chorus of "I'm sorry"s and Meg reaches over to squeeze

Sara's shoulders. But Lucy just slams her hands down on the cafeteria table so loudly we jump.

"This is bullshit," she says, and none of us respond. We just stare at Lucy as Sara wipes her eyes with a napkin.

"I mean it," Lucy continues. "It is. Making girls monitor their behavior and their appearance because boys are supposedly unable to control themselves? That is one of the oldest fucking tricks in the book." She falls back against her chair as though she's worn out. The other girls are staring at her, almost a little nervous, but I'm hanging on every word. Lucy's little speech sounded like it could have come out of one of my mom's zines. It's exhilarating.

"At my old school in Houston, the administration never could have gotten away with this shit without a fight," she continues. "The girls in my GRIT club would have found some way to fight back."

"I know, Lucy, but this isn't Houston," Claudia answers, and there's something just under the surface of her voice. Annoyance, maybe? Frustration?

"Trust me, I know this place isn't Houston," Lucy responds. She puffs up her cheeks and then exhales loudly, angrily. I tense up, anxious that my best friend and my new friend are upset with each other and unsure what I should do about it.

"Hey, look, I just want to forget about it and eat my lunch," Sara says, opening up her milk carton. "Can we please change the subject?"

"Of course," Claudia says, and she glances at Lucy with watchful eyes. Lucy doesn't say anything else after that. She just sits there, her chin in her hands, her eyes scanning the cafeteria and all the East Rockport cliques, resting on the girls who are dressed in bright orange gym shirts like Sara. Girls of every color and from every kind of group are scattered around the cafeteria like hazard signs, impossible to miss. Sara and the other girls start chatting about mostly benign stuff like how hard the math quiz was and would the deejay at the Fall Fling be better than the deejay at the Homecoming dance and so on. By the time the bell rings, Lucy hasn't taken a bite from her Tupperware container full of leftovers. I glance down at my lunch. I have't eaten much either.

"You're not hungry?" I ask her.

"No," says Lucy. "I lost my appetite. I'll see y'all later." And with that, she scoots her chair back loudly, gets up from our table, and heads for the exit, her head down. I resist the urge to follow her. To ask her more about what the GRIT girls of Houston would have done to fight these dress code checks. Lucy doesn't seem like she's in the mood to talk much to anyone, not even me.

CHAPTER NINE

THE DRESS CODE CHECKS GO ON ALL WEEK, AND I FIND MYSELF
wearing my biggest, baggiest shirts and sloppiest jeans to avoid
getting called out in front of everyone. Each time a girl has to
stand up in front of the room for inspection, I find myself sinking deeper into my desk. On Wednesday morning, after we re-
cite the Pledge of Allegiance and the Texas Pledge, Principal
Wilson's pinched twang cuts into second period announcements.

"You may have noticed we've put an emphasis on dress code
this week, and we hope y'all will adhere to the rules and regula-
tions detailed in the student handbook about modesty and proper
dress." As he speaks, I notice a few girls near me roll their eyes
at each other. I glance at my shoes and grin. Principal Wilson
keeps talking.

"Please remember that when you get dressed in the morning,
you're coming to a learning environment, and we expect you to

be dressed as a student, not a distraction. Ladies, I'm especially asking you to keep tabs on your outfits and remember that modesty is a virtue that never goes out of style. Now here's Assistant Principal Kessler with the rest of this morning's announcements."

Modesty is a virtue that never goes out of style! What a bastard! I can't help myself. Glancing up to make sure the teacher isn't paying attention, I lean over to the rolling-eye girls—Marisela Perez and Julia Rivera—and whisper, "Have you ever noticed he never goes after the guys wearing those gross shirts about sex?"

Marisela nods furiously. "I know, right?" She doesn't whisper. Her voice is loud enough for everyone to hear.

"Ladies," the teacher drones from his desk, "please listen to the announcements."

Marisela waits a beat until the teacher checks out again. "And have you noticed," she says in a softer voice, "that the dress code doesn't even have anything specific in it about how you should dress? It's, like, super vague."

"That's why they can enforce it however they want," Julia chimes in.

I never thought of that. I scowl and Marisela scowls and Julia scowls, and even though I'm still mad, this tiny little moment between the three of us buoys me. It keeps me afloat until Mr. Shelly appears at our classroom door and Marisela is hauled out for the length of her shorts.

As Marisela makes it to the door, she pauses, turns, and looks at the rest of us.

"If I never make it back, tell my mother I love her." Then she holds her wrists in front of her face like she's expecting Mr. Shelly to slap handcuffs on her.

We all crack up except for Mr. Shelly.

"That's enough, Miss Perez," he tells her, ushering her down the hallway.

Marisela's act of insurrection—however tiny—sets something off inside of me. That little fire that was lit when I made the first issue of *Moxie* feels like it's getting stoked again. When I get to English class, it burns even more strongly because Lucy's hands are covered in fresh stars and hearts, intricately drawn with green ink.

"Hey," I say, nodding at her drawings. "What gives?"

Lucy lets one fingertip glide over her graffiti. "I don't know," she says. "I guess I was feeling pissed about everything with the dress code checks and Sara and this place in general. I thought maybe this would be some sign to whoever created that issue of *Moxie* that there are some of us that really believe in what they're saying. I mean, I don't know if we'll ever hear from them again, but doing this at least makes me feel better." She looks at me, her face open and vulnerable. "Do you think that's dumb?"

I stare at Lucy's hands. "I don't think it's dumb at all," I tell her. "I totally get it." The fire inside me is growing by the moment. I feel warm from the inside out.

"Thanks, Viv," Lucy says, a smile breaking across her face.

"And I think it's really cool," I add.

Lucy smiles again. Then her eyes grow big with excitement. "Hey, I was just thinking. Do you want to come over to my house for dinner tonight? We could hang out after. I mean, if you're up for it."

It's the first time Lucy has asked me to hang out just the two of us. My initial thought is Claudia and what she might say. But then I remember that my mom and I are supposed to have dinner at Meemaw and Grandpa's.

"I wish I could, but we're going to my grandparents' for dinner," I say, halfway grateful for the out, halfway disappointed.

Lucy's shoulders sink. "Okay, I understand."

"But I'd love to come over sometime," I add. Maybe Claudia wouldn't even have to know.

"Cool," Lucy says, brightening.

"Cool," I offer in agreement.

During class I find myself glancing at Lucy's hands. By the time the bell rings, I've filled my notebook with hearts and stars, and my mind is churning with ideas.

That evening, just before we're supposed to head over to Meemaw and Grandpa's, my mom finds me in my bedroom, spread out on my bed doing homework.

"Hey, Vivvy," she says, her voice soft, "I wanted to let you know that I'm planning on meeting John for a drink at the Cozy Corner later tonight. Is that okay?"

"On a weeknight?" I ask, shoving my math book aside.

My mom tucks some of her long, dark hair behind her ear and offers me a shy grin. "Well, our shifts are really different this weekend, and we won't be able to hang out. I mean, you know, to go out. So we thought it might be nice to get together this evening."

"You must really like him, huh?" I ask. "I mean, if you're seeing him on a weeknight." My mom's face falls a little bit. Maybe my words sound more accusatory than I intend them to be.

Or did I mean it?

My mother stands there for a moment, looking at me like she's trying to figure out a math problem. I know I should say something, reassure her that I'm cool with everything, but I can't. Even though I know I should be, I'm not cool with everything. I just don't know what she sees in him.

At last she shrugs and says, "I like him, Viv. He's a really good person. And a hard worker. He's one of ten kids, and his parents didn't help him at all. He put himself through college and med school." Her tone is blunt—irritated even.

"I never said he wasn't a good person or a hard worker," I answer, rolling over onto my back and talking to the ceiling. "I'm glad he's nice." A little rock forms in my stomach.

Silence.

Finally my mom says, "We can talk about it more when I get home tonight, if you want to."

"Okay, but there's nothing really to talk about," I say, wishing this conversation wasn't happening. "It's really totally fine."

I hear my mom take a breath. I stare at the glow-in-the-dark stars above me, dull and plastic under my bright bedroom lights. I can tell without looking that my mother is trying to figure out what to say next. Finally, she tells me, "We should make a move."

"Yeah, we should," I say, and I slide off the bed and walk toward the front door of our house like everything's normal and fine even though everything feels strange and off-kilter between me and my mom, and it's probably my fault but I have no idea how to fix it.

As we sit down for dinner at Meemaw and Grandpa's, Meemaw asks Mom how late we can stay, and Mom answers not for too long because she's going out with John. My grandparents don't seem too surprised, so I guess my mom has filled them in on John's existence.

"I hope we can meet this young man at some point," Meemaw says, carefully setting down a Stouffer's meat loaf in the middle of the dining room table. She slips off her rooster-decorated oven mitts and we pause for a minute while Grandpa says the blessing.

"Oh, you'll meet him at some point," my mother says, passing her plate toward Meemaw. "And Mom, we're both in our forties. I wouldn't exactly refer to him or me as young."

"As long as your knees don't sound like popping popcorn when you stand up, you're still young," Grandpa dictates, and Mom gives me a knowing look and grins. I smile back. Some things between my mom and me—like getting a kick out of Grandpa—are so habitual that it's impossible to fight. The weirdness between us fades a bit.

"So how's school, Vivvy?" Meemaw asks, dishing out my serving.

I frown. "They're going crazy cracking down on the dress code. But only the girls."

My mom takes a bite of meat loaf and looks confused. "What do you mean 'only the girls'?"

"Like pulling girls out of class because their pants are too tight or they're showing too much skin. Then the girls have to wear ugly gym shirts over their clothes for the rest of the day as, like, a punishment." I hear Lucy's words from Monday's lunch in my ears. "It's ridiculous. Why should girls be responsible for what boys think and do? Like the boys aren't able to control themselves?"

Grandpa and Meemaw are silent, looking at me with careful eyes. I guess they're not used to their dutiful Viv getting so upset.

My mother's brow is furrowed, and she pauses before saying, "I think you're exactly right, Vivvy. It sounds ridiculous to me. It also sounds like classic East Rockport High."

I tingle with validation. "It really is," I mutter. The conversation about John slips further out of my mind.

"Well," Grandpa says, wiping the corners of his mouth with a napkin, "as the only person sitting here who was once a teenage boy, I can tell you, they only have one thing on their minds."

Meemaw slaps Grandpa on the shoulder with her napkin in this good-natured way, but my mom sighs loudly and throws down her own napkin in protest.

"Dad, that's ridiculous," she starts. "It's just contributing to the narrative that girls have to monitor their bodies and behaviors, and boys have the license and freedom to act like animals. Don't you think that's unfair to girls? Don't you think that's

105

shortchanging boys? The whole thing is just toxic." She finishes her little speech with a huff, and I feel like I've caught a glimpse of her looking like the girl in the Polaroid in her MY MISSPENT YOUTH shoe box. The one with the dyed hair and the friend with the piercing and the RIOTS NOT DIETS slogan scribbled down one arm. That girl still exists, I know it. Even if I can't quite figure out how that girl is the same woman who is hanging out on a weeknight with Republican John.

"Oh, Lisa, let's not start," Meemaw says, her hands hovering over the dinner table. "Your dad was just trying to be funny."

My mom takes a deep breath. I haven't seen her this frustrated with Meemaw and Grandpa in a long time. It's quiet for a moment. I wait, wondering how much she'll push back. Kind of wanting her to do it, too, even if Grandpa doesn't mean any harm.

"Let's just drop it and eat," my mother says, picking up her napkin and putting it back in her lap. She gives me a soft, sympathetic look. "Just keep getting those good grades and staying out of trouble and give me time to save a little more for your college fund, and we'll get you out of here, Vivvy. I promise."

"You talk about East Rockport like it's some terrible place," Meemaw says, fretting. "Her family is here, after all."

"You'll see how much you'll miss her when she's gone," my grandfather tells her. "When you took off for the West Coast, our hearts broke." This is Grandpa's version of a peace offering.

"We don't have the money for her to go that far," my mother

says. "Besides, Viv won't be running off to follow bands or go too wild. She's just going to college."

"Hey," I say, setting down my fork with a frown. "Who says I can't go wild?"

At this the entire table starts laughing, including my mother.

"You, Vivvy?" she asks, like I've just suggested I swim the English Channel. "Oh, sweetie, you going wild. Unlikely. And for that, I'm grateful."

I roll my eyes at them and dig in for more meat loaf, dropping out of the conversation. When Meemaw asks me how Claudia is doing, I smile and answer, but inside, in a place no one knows about, in a place I think even I am just getting to know, the fire that reignited when I saw Lucy's hearts and stars begins to roar. I think about Marisela's retort this morning when Mr. Shelly came to remove her from class. I think about Sara's crushed expression when she came to the cafeteria, humiliated. And I think about all the girls of East Rockport, living under the creepy gaze of administrators looking way too hard for something that's not there.

Later that night, after my mother has dabbed vanilla extract behind her ears, kissed me goodbye, and headed off to the Cozy Corner to meet John, I put Bikini Kill on and turn the volume up so loud that Joan Jett goes and hides in the hallway closet. My heart racing, my cheeks burning, my fingers working against the clock, I collect my supplies: rubber cement, black Sharpies, fresh sheets of white paper.

And the anger that won't fade away.

Camping out in the middle of my bed, I start working, re-minding myself to stop and breathe every once in a while.

Maybe my mother is right. Maybe I'll leave East Rockport one day.

But first I need to set it on fire.

MOXIE

Moxie Girls Fight Back! Issue #2 FREE!!

These ladies say......
"Screw you, dress code checks!"

Dress code checks are sexist because... ★

* they focus overwhelmingly on girls over boys ★

* they're arbitrary — some girls get in trouble and some girls don't — and the dress code checks are totally vague/random!

* they operate on the idea that <u>girls</u> are responsible for boys' behavior ★ ★

* they operate on the idea that boys are helpless creatures with no self control

* they <u>shame</u> girls! ★

Next MOXie action!

On Tuesday come to school in your BATHROBE! Let's protest the sexist dress code checks at ERHS! If a teacher asks why tell them you're playing it safe so you don't distract our poor male students!

TUESDAY. BATHROBES. MOXIE.

Moxie girls fight back!

CHAPTER TEN

FRANK AT U COPY IT LOOKS OVER MY WORK AS I SLIDE MY COPIES across the counter. I glance outside to where I've parked my ten speed. In East Rockport, you never know who might run into you and when.

"Hey, Moxie girl," he says, flipping through my finished pages. "Weren't you in here about a month ago?"

"Maybe," I say, and I'm surprised at my own sassiness. Frank arches an eyebrow and grins.

"Okay, I saw nothing, then," he answers, handing me my change before putting *Moxie* #2 in a paper bag. "But if you see whoever made the first one, tell her these are even better."

"Really?" I ask, unable to catch myself. Blushing, I take my bag, pocket my money, and try to recover. "Okay, I'll tell her if I see her."

On the ride home, my *Moxie* copies inside my backpack, I

come up with a bunch of excuses for why I'm out so late in case my mom is already back from her date with John. Just my luck, I pull up to my house and see John's car with his stupid DELOBE bumper sticker parked in the driveway, the engine running. The streetlights are bright enough for me to see my mom and John in the front seat. Kissing.

Oh, God. Oh gross.

I head around the house and dump my bike, then scoot in through the back door, praying my mother didn't notice me. A few moments later, I hear her coming in through the front door.

"Viv, was that you on your bike?"

Damn.

We meet in the kitchen, my backpack still strapped to my shoulders. Her cheeks are all pinked up and, God help me, her chocolate-colored lipstick is smudged. She frowns.

"What were you doing out so late?"

I stand there, mute. Then I remember our dinner conversation from a few hours earlier. How my mom told me she would never have to worry about me going wild.

"I was at Claudia's studying for a history test and it just, like, went late, I guess."

My mother eyes me carefully, then puts her purse on the kitchen counter. I can tell she 95 percent believes me. Being a good, not-wild girl has its advantages.

"Okay," she says. "But it is kind of late, you know."

"I know, I'm sorry," I say, walking toward my bedroom with my backpack. I need to busy myself both to hide my terrible lying face and to avoid talking about the John situation. I *don't* want to talk about John.

I change into my pajamas and head to our shared bathroom to brush my teeth. My mom wanders into her own bedroom, her eyes on her phone. Still pushing my toothbrush around in my mouth, I step out into the hallway and glimpse her flopping onto her unmade bed, tapping something into her phone with her thumb. Then she smiles faintly.

Maybe she doesn't want to talk to me either. Even though she said she did before dinner. My tooth brushing slows down, then stops entirely. I watch as my mom's smile grows bigger and bigger while she stares into her phone. It's probably a text from John. Maybe he's replaying their kiss in the GOP Love Bug.

I turn back into the bathroom and spit loudly into the sink, then linger there wondering if the noise will wake my mom out of her post-date stupor. Doesn't she want to ask me more about my day at school or if I'm still upset about the dress-code thing? Doesn't she want to bring up John with me like she said she did?

But when I finally leave the bathroom and pause in her doorway to tell her I'm heading to bed, she only looks up and smiles.

"Good night, honey," she says, turning her gaze back down to her phone.

"Good night, Mom," I say. I pass on our usual good-night hug, go into my room, and close the door.

I follow the same plan as I did the first time. Wake up super early and race to school before the sun starts to rise on this finally-cool Texas-in-late-October morning. I slide into the first girls' bathroom with copies of *Moxie* in hand. This time feels less dreamlike and more purposeful. I keep seeing Sara's hurt face at our cafeteria table. I keep imagining the next gross T-shirt Jason Garza will get away with wearing.

And I keep picturing getting caught and probably getting suspended by Principal Wilson. I visualize the entire school knowing *Moxie* existed because of me. I would go from being an under-the-radar girl to a school weirdo. No, that's not totally true. I would become a *town* weirdo, too. Meemaw and Grandpa would be shocked. Claudia would think Lucy has too much influence over me. And my mom would . . . well, before John my mom would have thought *Moxie* is cool, but lately I'm not 100 percent sure she would back me. After all, getting into massive trouble at school doesn't really lead to me getting out of this town and into a good college.

I know Lucy would be cool with it. Which is something. But in the world of East Rockport High, it wouldn't be much.

I take a deep breath. I grit my teeth. I keep going.

The first floor goes smoothly. Not another soul to be found. But as I venture out of the foreign language wing, my heart thrumming, I make a quick right turn and run right into someone. It's a hard hit, enough that I shout and drop the rest of the *Moxie* copies. Honestly, it's like something out of a bad rom com.

My yelp of surprise still ringing in my ears, I step back and find my eyes resting on Seth Acosta.

"Hey," he says. And I can't really decide what should be declared my cause of death—being caught delivering *Moxie* or running into Seth Acosta in the hallway before the sun is even up. Combine the two, and it's possible I'm already dead and this is my weird version of the afterlife.

"Let me help you," Seth says, and he crouches down, his tight black jeans straining around his knobby guy knees, as I stand there, stunned. I watch as he picks up all the copies of my secret teen lady revolution zine.

I can't move.

Seth's coal-black eyes scan the front of *Moxie*, and then he stands up and stares.

"Are you, like, passing these out?"

I swallow. My cheeks are warm. I peer to my left and my right.

"Yes," I say. What else is there to say?

He flips through a copy, then stares back at me, his face serious. His voice drops down a notch or two.

"Did you . . . make these?"

I take a breath. The pause has given me away already, I know it. So I stand there, quiet.

"You did, yeah?" he asks very quietly. The way he delivers that *yeah*—all soft and yummy and reassuring at the same time. I find myself nodding, transfixed.

"Yeah, I did," I say, my voice a whisper. "But don't tell anyone, okay?"

Seth stares at me for a moment, then nods slowly, and I stand there, still in shock. It's not Claudia or Meg or Sara or even a teacher or administrator who finds me out, but this strange boy. I can't really believe it.

"Hey, maybe you can give me some? I'll put them in the boys' bathrooms."

I guess I'm not so out of it, because I laugh out loud.

"Seriously, the boys here don't care about this. I promise." I stare at my shoes. "I mean, except maybe for you."

Seth hands the stack of *Moxies* to me. "Yeah, I definitely don't want to mess with your plans or anything. I mean, maybe you just want this for the girls."

I hold the zines close to my chest in case someone appears. Then I force myself to speak.

"I guess I do want it for the girls." I pause. "But even though you're a guy, you obviously saw the first issue, right?"

Seth pops up one eyebrow. "Yeah, how'd you know?"

"I saw your hands that day," I answer, aware that I'm actually stringing words and sentences together and not passing out. "You marked them with hearts and stars."

"I did," Seth acknowledges. "I found a copy in the hallway. I guess someone dropped it. To be honest, I thought it was pretty kick-ass."

Pretty kick-ass. Does that mean he thinks *I'm* pretty kick-ass? My chest feels like exploding. I decide that Seth Acosta deciding I'm kick-ass is even better than him thinking I'm pretty. Definitely better.

"I mean, I can see why you'd want this to be a lady thing," Seth says, dragging his hand through his hair. "You're preaching Bibles full of truth." He glances around, his eyes wide and his voice a whisper, then pronounces, "This school is fucked up."

I grin, glad to hear the words out loud. "It pretty much is," I say. "It must be so different from Austin."

Seth nods, then frowns just a little. "How'd you know I was from Austin?"

"Oh," I stammer, "my friend Claudia? I think your family rents your place from her parents? She may have mentioned something about it?" Maybe if I make everything sound like a question, I won't appear to be a total stalker.

Seth just nods again. "My parents moved down here to work on their art or whatever. Like, a change of perspective." He shrugs and rolls his eyes a little.

"Like, they wanted the perspective of a suffocating small town?" I manage. Seth laughs, and my chest explodes again, only this time I'm not sure I'll ever manage to rebuild it.

"I guess," Seth says. "Anyway, we live here now." He says this definitively. With resignation. But then he grins again, and it's quiet and awkward for a moment, and I hug *Moxie* to myself even harder. The last thing I said was witty, and if I say anything else, I might mess this all up. Whatever this is.

"Hey, you should probably get going if you want to pass the rest of these out," Seth says. "I have to go find my Spanish teacher. It's why I'm here so early. I need to make up a test."

I nod, then feel the need to reassure myself.

"Just . . . I mean . . . you won't tell anyone about this, right?"

"I really won't," Seth says, nodding hard. "But can I at least have an issue?"

I slide a copy out of my pile and hand it to him. Our thumbs touch as I pass *Moxie* off. My heart slides out of place for a second.

"Okay, I gotta go," Seth says.

"Yeah, and I have to hurry," I answer, and before I know it he's off down the hallway, and I'm slipping in and out of girls' bathrooms, dropping off stacks of *Moxie*, my chest thumping and my mind racing, a Riot Grrrl soundtrack pounding through me as I move.

My phone buzzes next to me. I roll over onto my stomach, push aside my history homework until it falls off my bed, then glance at the screen.

So you think you're going to do it? The moxie thing next Tuesday?

It's Lucy. We only recently started texting. Not as often as me and Claudia text each other, of course, but often enough. Lucy's texts never start with a *hey* or a *what's up*. She always dives right in, like she doesn't care about small talk. Sometimes after what feels like a few minutes of texting I glance at the time and find an entire hour has passed as we trade thoughts on everything from messed-up stuff at East Rockport to our families and even to me admitting I think Seth Acosta is cute. It's easy to spill stuff to Lucy in my texts. Like I've known her for a lot longer than just a couple months.

But talking about *Moxie* makes me anxious because it's such a big secret. I feel the weight of it with every text I send.

Are you gonna do it? I answer back. I need her to say yes.

Hellz yes, Lucy writes back. *I think it's so brilliant*

In the safety of my own bedroom, I allow myself a big grin.

If you will then I will . . . I just need to find my bathrobe

They have cheap ones at the Walmart in case you can't

I chew on my thumbnail and count up the number of girls who were taken out of my classes today for dress code violations. Five. Principal Wilson and his friends aren't letting up. Today I saw a freshman girl in an enormous, shame-on-you dirty jersey crying in one of the second-floor bathrooms, and when I tried to console her, she just shook her head and ran past me out the door.

I'll find my bathrobe or get one, I text back. I watch Lucy's text bubble, wondering what her response will be.

I wish I knew who was doing this because I so want to be BFFs

Me too, I text back. I grin to myself before telling Lucy I have to go and finish my homework.

I set out the zines on a Thursday morning, but the bathrobe stunt is set for the following Tuesday so as not to be overshadowed by the buildup to the Friday night football game. The season is winding down, and I'm glad it looks like we're not going to make it to playoffs so it will end even sooner. But even without the weekly pep rallies and the pre-game frenzy, I know Mitchell and his friends will reign over East Rockport High well into winter and spring. And senior year, too. Senior year will probably be the worst ever.

I've seen Seth in class and a few times in the hallway since he discovered my secret, and we've nodded and smiled at each other. Today, Monday, he catches up with me as we're walking out of English class.

"You ready for tomorrow?" he asks.

"I think so," I answer.

His breath smells like spearmint gum. I notice the slightest bit of stubble on his chin and wonder if he has to shave his face every day or just once in a while. I picture him shaving in his bathroom with a towel wrapped around his waist and his chest bare like an actual man would do, and my legs go all trembly.

"Well, good luck," he says, and he walks off suddenly, loping down the hallway.

That night my mom is working late, and I skip dinner at Meemaw and Grandpa's, insisting that I have a lot of homework I want to finish. But what I do instead is spend the evening on my bed, texting with Claudia and Sara and Meg and Kaitlyn trying to figure out if they're going to do the bathrobe thing tomorrow, too, or if it will just be me and Lucy.

I don't want to get in trouble, texts Claudia.

Me either, agrees Meg.

But there's no rule saying we can't wear bathrobes, Sara chimes in. I remember how upset she was the day she got called out for dress code.

I'm not sure what it will even do, Kaitlyn offers. *But at the same time it feels like it might be kind of cool to see what happens*

So it's two against and two in favor. Well, kind of in favor. My vision of every girl at East Rockport High showing up in a bathrobe and full of indignation fades from my mind. I should count myself lucky if a quarter of the girls at school go along with it. My stomach knots up, and I wonder, what would the lead singer for Bikini Kill do? Or a younger version of my mom?

Look, I text, *you can always bring your bathrobe and hide it in your locker if you're scared and then if other girls are doing it you can take it out right? I mean I guess what I'm saying is I'm just tired of this dress code BS so why not try?*

There's a pause and a few text bubbles pop up and then go away. Finally, someone responds but only to me. Claudia.

You do know the girls in their bathrobes are gonna have everyone staring at them tomorrow right? You don't care about that???

I frown. I'm glad Claudia can't see me.

Maybe . . . but if a lot of girls do it then there will be too many girls to stare AT right? Also Lucy is definitely doing it so we won't be the only ones.

Another pause. This time it's longer. Then Claudia texts again.

Of course Lucy is doing it . . . she's into this stuff.
What stuff?
You know . . . this kind of making a big deal about stuff stuff . . .
Yeah I guess . . . but maybe that's just because she's used to doing this sort of thing at her old school in Houston? You know?

My texts with Claudia dissolve into back and forth statements that sound like questions? So we end on a nice note? And don't

123

rock the boat? At last we sign off and I'm 99 percent sure that Claudia won't be wearing her bathrobe to school tomorrow.

But then there's me. After I toss my phone aside, I take out my turquoise terrycloth bathrobe that goes down to my knees and slide it into my backpack. I brush my teeth, wash my face, put on my old Runaways T-shirt, and cue up "Rebel Girl" on repeat. As I'm listening to the song through my headphones for the fifth time, I can make out the sound of my mom coming in the front door over Kathleen Hanna's throaty yell. I reach up to slide the headphones off my head, but then I stop. Normally if I'm still awake when my mom comes home, I go out to the den to catch up, at least for a little bit.

But tonight I don't feel like it. I slide my headphones back on and turn up the music, drowning out every last thought.

CHAPTER ELEVEN

IT'S EARLY NOVEMBER AND CHILLY ENOUGH THAT MY BATHROBE OVER
my jeans and T-shirt feels good and not too hot. But my cheeks
are still burning from nervousness as I walk toward the front
doors of East Rockport High. On my morning walk to school, I
stopped half a block away to slip the bathrobe on over my clothes
before immediately taking it off, then walking a few more steps,
and finally stopping to put it back on again. Now that I'm getting
closer to actually walking into school dressed like this, I have to
fight the urge to rip the bathrobe off one more time.

As I approach the campus, my eyes scan the clumps of students in front of East Rockport, checking if I'm the only one who
looks like she forgot to get dressed before coming to school. My
heart skips up to my throat. I scan left to right and spot jeans,
skirts, jeans, skirts, and then, thankfully, a tight circle of what
looks to be some sophomore girls all dressed in bathrobes over

their outfits. They keep peering over their shoulders like they're checking to see if anyone around them matches.

My heart slips back down to my chest where it belongs. I exhale. I want to walk by them so they'll see me and know they're not alone, but just then I feel someone collide into my left shoulder.

"You did it!"

It's Lucy, and she's wearing not only a puffy pink bathrobe that makes her look like a Hostess Sno Ball, but also fuzzy pink slippers that match.

"Oh my God, you look awesome," I say, and Lucy grins and shrugs like she knows.

"I saw a few other girls by the gym entrance who had them on, too," she tells me. "I think there are already more girls doing this than the hearts and stars thing." She eyes the campus carefully. "I wish I knew which girls were the Moxie girls. I mean, they're here somewhere."

The irony is too much for me to handle with a neutral face, so I just urge Lucy along so I don't have to make eye contact. Along the way into school, we wave to a few other girls who have bathrobes on. I spot Kiera Daniels, and she has on fuzzy slippers just like Lucy, only her getup is lavender. Kiera and I wave at each other. More than half of the girls she's with have bathrobes on.

Inside all the buzz is about the bathrobes. I overhear a few guys asking each other what's going on and some people talking about "that newsletter." *It's a zine, but whatever*, I think as I start toward history. Lucy says she'll see me in English and we split off.

126

Heading into class, I see Claudia in the back row. No bathrobe, just a pale pink top and jeans. She waves at me as I walk in.

"Hey," I say, sliding into my desk next to her.

"Hey," she answers, and it's very obvious we are both Not Talking About It. I'm disappointed she didn't do it, and she's probably disappointed in me for the opposite reason.

"I'm so tired," she says, pushing out a little yawn. It's forced and weird between us, like it almost never is.

"Yeah, I'm tired, too," I say. "I didn't really sleep well last night." That's the truth, actually. I spent most of the night in a half-awake, half-asleep state, hearing Bikini Kill songs in my head and imagining an army of girls in bathrobes, complete with curlers in their hair and wielding blow dryers as weapons.

Just then Sara files into class, and my heart leaps when I see she's wearing this dark blue bathrobe with daisies on it that she's had since we were in middle school.

"You did it!" I say, grinning. I don't look at Claudia because I don't have to. The disconnect between us is almost tangible.

"I decided at the last minute," Sara says. "Kaitlyn did it, too. But not Meg."

Claudia coughs a little and the bell rings. Mrs. Robbins walks in carrying a stack of papers—no doubt some brain-melting "graphic organizer" for us to fill out using our textbook while she stares at her computer screen. As she sets the papers down on her desk, she looks up at us for the first time and her eyes pop open like she's finally awake.

"What's going on here?" At least five other girls in the class are wearing bathrobes in addition to Sara and me. There's tittering at Mrs. Robbins's question, but nobody says anything. I stare down at my notebook, glad I'm in the back row.

When no one answers Mrs. Robbins's question, she takes a step closer to us and peers carefully. "Are those . . . bathrobes? Did y'all not get dressed this morning?"

More giggles. Kate McGowan in the first row cracks a wide grin. She's wearing an obnoxious plaid number that must belong to her father or older brother or something.

"Do you think this is funny, Miss McGowan?" Mrs. Robbins says. "Take that ridiculous bathrobe off right now."

"Sure, no problem," Kate says.

Kate has always been sort of a badass, talking back to teachers when they won't let her go to the bathroom or get a drink of water. I'm not sure if she wore a bathrobe just to stir up trouble or if she honestly thinks the dress code is bullshit. But then she drops the bathrobe down to her waist.

Kate is wearing a bright red bikini top underneath.

"Miss McGowan!" Mrs. Robbins shouts, barely heard over the hoots and gasps coming from my classmates.

"See, Mrs. Robbins," Kate says, like butter wouldn't melt in her mouth, "I wasn't sure if I was following the East Rockport dress code because it's so weird and unclear, you know? So I decided to be safe and cover myself with this bathrobe so as not to distract any of our precious male students."

The class erupts into more hoots and laughter, and of course Mrs. Robbins has no choice but to make Kate put her bathrobe back on. By the time we all calm down Mrs. Robbins's face is as red as Kate's bikini top. She pinches her mouth up tight and passes out the graphic organizers, slamming Kate's on her desk, and then demands that we work quietly and independently.

The entire time I fill in the meaningless and pointless exercise, I think about the Riot Grrrl Manifesto in my mom's zine. It said girls are a revolutionary soul force that can change the world for real. My chest feels heavy with something that feels scary and good at the same time. I picture myself running up to Kate McGowan after class and telling her how cool she is. The urge is so strong that maybe I'll actually do it.

But right now, there is one thing I can do for sure. In pencil, in the bottom right-hand corner of my desk, I carefully print the words MOXIE GIRLS FIGHT BACK. The letters are only half an inch or so high, but I trace them over and over until the tip of my pencil is dull. I smile approvingly at my artwork as the bell rings.

I hope a girl is sitting in this desk second period.

All day long girls walk around East Rockport in their bathrobes. Through the grapevine I hear of a few girls being forced to take them off in class, but they put them back on once they file out into the hallways. As we take our seats in English class, Lucy tells me that when her chem teacher asked her about it, she followed the script in *Moxie*.

"I just said I wanted to make sure I wasn't in violation of the dress code, and I didn't want to tempt any boys," Lucy says, her eyes triumphant. "Mr. Carlson got so confused. It was hilarious." She leans over the back of her desk as she turns to talk to me. "And do you know what? I'm pretty sure some girls brought their bathrobes to school and hid them in their lockers until they realized they wouldn't be alone. I think we've doubled in number since this morning."

I think Lucy's right about some girls joining in late, but I don't know if we've doubled in number. The bathrobe-wearing girls are still in the minority. But it's not a tiny minority. It might be as high as 30 or 40 percent of all the girls in the school. And it's not just one type of girl but all kinds. Jocks and loud girls and girls on the yearbook and quiet girls and black girls and white girls and brown girls.

Except for Emma Johnson. Not that girl. She walks in a minute or so before the bell and takes her seat, flipping her hair over her shoulder in her signature move, lining her pens and notebooks up on her desk. She's wearing a blindingly white hoodie with the words EAST ROCKPORT CHEER stamped across the back in bright orange. When Mitchell walks in he pauses by her desk, leaning on it with his big hand that reminds me of a hunk of ham.

"You didn't join the bathrobe brigade?" Mitchell asks.

Wow, Mitchell Wilson knows how to use the word brigade *correctly. Shocking.*

"No, I didn't," Emma says, peering up at Mitchell through her perfectly made-up eyes. "I'm not sure I understand it, to be honest."

Of course you don't. You would never get caught for dress-code violations because Principal Wilson knows his son has the hots for you so you're, like, protected.

Instantly, I feel bad for thinking this. Emma is gorgeous and demure and all these other things I'm not, but she's never been anything but nice to people. If anything, it just feels like she's not one of us. Like she's actually an actress on a television show about high school, and she's twenty-five playing sixteen.

"Well, I'm glad you're not wearing a bathrobe," Mitchell says, raising one eyebrow, "because it would be a shame to cover you up."

Oh gag me.

Emma pinks up a little but smiles carefully, then flips her hair over her shoulder again. The bell rings and Seth runs in after Mr. Davies, who starts in about being on time to class.

"Sorry," Seth says, taking his seat, and my eardrums melt a little at the sound of his voice.

Mr. Davies ends up putting us into groups to go over comprehension questions for the short story we were supposed to have read last night. By some miracle, I get put in the same group as Seth, and when we begin the awkward process of dragging our desks into a circle, he catches my eye.

"Cool bathrobe," he says to me.

"Thanks," I answer, willing myself not to blush.

As we go over the questions Mr. Davies has written on the whiteboard, it strikes me that Seth is pretty smart. The story is Shirley Jackson's "The Lottery," which I've read once before because my mom told me it was her favorite short story. Everyone in the group is saying how screwed up it is, but Seth says that's the point.

"It's about, like, realizing that just because something is a tradition, that doesn't make it good," he says.

I bite my bottom lip. I never talk in these things. But I want Seth to know I'm smart, too.

"Some people might say tradition is a good thing, though," I offer, doodling a tiny circle over and over in the corner of my paper, not looking up. "Some people would argue that tradition is part of what holds us together as, you know, a community."

The group is silent for a split second and then this boy, Peter Pratt, slides down into his desk and sighs.

"Who the fuck cares?" he says. "I just want the bell to ring so we can go to lunch."

My cheeks flare up. I stare down at my turquoise bathrobe. "I guess I care," I say. "It's a story that makes you think is all." I feel like I'm going to spontaneously combust out of embarrassment at that admission, but somehow I don't die.

When I look back up, Peter Pratt shrugs and yawns. But Seth looks over at me and smiles. I smile back. My cheeks are still warm, but for a different reason now.

During lunch in the cafeteria, my friends and I talk about how many girls have bathrobes on but Claudia doesn't say much. She just sips her Diet Coke and listens, her face still as Lucy prattles on about all the girls she knows who came to school wearing one.

At the end of the day, I find Claudia at her locker, shuffling through her binders, picking out the ones she needs to take home with her.

"Want to walk home with me?" I ask.

"Sure," Claudia says, shutting her locker door carefully.

I want to make things feel nice between us. As a peace offering, I pull my bathrobe off and stuff it into my backpack. After all, the school day's over. Claudia and I walk out the side entrance and head toward home.

"It's so nice out," she says.

"Yeah," I answer. And it is. It's a gorgeous early November afternoon, the Texas summer heat finally gone for good. The autumn sun—as much as we get autumn in this state—feels good on the back of my neck and my arms as Claudia and I trudge down the sidewalk.

"You know what?" Claudia says.

"What?"

"I didn't have a single girl called out of my classes today for dress code. Did you?"

It hits me Claudia's right. I can't believe I've only just realized it. But it's true.

"No," I say, smiling. "I didn't."

"So maybe it worked," Claudia says. "Maybe you were right to do it, and I was a chicken not to."

"No," I answer, shaking my head. "No, that's not true." But I think maybe it is. A little.

"I don't know," Claudia says. "Maybe it's just that I was scared to get in trouble."

"Maybe some things are worth getting in trouble over," I offer.

"Maybe," Claudia answers. I can tell she wants to say something else, but she's picking her words. Finally they come out in a rush. "I don't know if you would have done this bathrobe thing before Lucy got here."

Her words sting enough that for a split second I want to tell her I'm the one who made *Moxie*. Instead I just shrug.

"I think I still would have, honestly," I say. "But you can think what you want." Once they're out, my words sound harsh. I'm not used to talking like that to my best friend.

"Forget it," Claudia says. "Forget I said anything."

"Okay, let's not worry about it, it's over anyway," I answer. Claudia's house is coming up on the left. *Make nice, make nice, make nice.* I dig up some light chatter about stupid homework assignments to warm up the mood before we have to say good-bye. When we get to her driveway, she leans her head against my shoulder. I lean my head toward hers, catching a whiff of her strawberry-scented shampoo.

"Talk to you later?" she asks.

"Of course," I answer. But as I walk off, leaving Claudia's house behind, I find myself pulling out my phone to text Lucy.

Did any girls get pulled out of your classes for dress code? I type.

A few moments later she writes back.

No!!!!!!! Not a single one!

I can't believe it worked

I know right? So awesome

Stopping under a big pecan tree, I grin at my phone and type out one more text.

MOXIE GIRLS FIGHT BACK!!!!!! I add a few heart emojis for good measure.

Lucy texts back right away.

MOXIE GIRLS KICK ASS AND TAKE NAMES!!!!!

I read the text and laugh out loud, standing there in the middle of the sidewalk.

CHAPTER TWELVE

IT'S BEEN THREE DAYS SINCE THE BATHROBE STUNT, AND NOT A single girl has been called out for dress-code violations since it happened. It's gone down like this before—these weird, cavalier explosions of dress code "checks" on girls by the administration that evaporate into nothing after a few days—but I'd like to think *Moxie* had something to do with it this time. And that means that *I* had something to do with it because I started *Moxie*. Last night after I brushed my teeth and washed my face, I caught myself standing in front of the mirror for a full two minutes looking into my own dark eyes. I grasped my hair and pulled it up into a high ponytail. Squinting, I thought maybe I looked a little like Kathleen Hanna of Bikini Kill.

But by today's Friday football pep rally, I'm beginning to feel like the whole thing was some sort of fantastical dream. The band plays the same songs. The cheerleaders do the same flips.

The only thing that's different this time is that if the Pirates lose the game tonight, they're out of the playoffs.

"Wait, is that a freaking fog machine?" Sara asks as we sit down in our usual spot, high up and away from the action. All of us peer down at the billowing clouds of smoke enveloping the entrance where the football team is about to make their appearance.

"Oh my God, it is," Claudia says, rolling her eyes. The pirate mascot is in a fancy new uniform, too, and there's even someone dressed as a bobcat, representing the opposing team's mascot. The pirate is pretending to slice the bobcat's neck with a sword as the bobcat writhes around in mock terror. These aren't Halloween costumes either, but full-on, college-level mascot gear.

"How much does all this shit cost?" Lucy asks out loud. "Have you ever considered that?" She scowls. "Last I checked, the Bunsen burner in the chem lab runs on coal or something, it's so ancient."

"What the football team wants, the football team gets," Claudia says. "It's so dumb."

"Totally," agrees Lucy, and I relish this moment where my best friend and my new friend are in harmony with each other. Since bathrobe day I've been trying to pay extra attention to Claudia—sitting next to her at lunch, waiting for her by her locker in the morning before history—even while I've been sucked into long periods of texting with Lucy after school where we talk about everything from what *Moxie* might do next to music we want to share with each other. (Unbelievably, she's never heard of Bikini Kill or any of the Riot Grrrl bands, and after I make her a playlist, she's hooked.)

After the rally is lunch, but I eat quickly so I can leave a few minutes early and go to the main office to drop off my permission slip for Driver's Ed next semester. As I walk down the nearly empty hall, I catch Principal Wilson approaching the office from the opposite direction, barking into his cell phone. I'm the only other person in the hallway, but he doesn't smile or even nod. I'm a student at his school, and I was in his mind-numbing Texas history class way back before he became Mr. Muckety-Muck at East Rockport High. But I'm not his son or on his son's team or a cheerleader like Emma Johnson or even a member of the pep band. I'm a nothing on his radar. His jowls quiver a little as he speaks in his thick Texas twang, and he brushes right past me as he enters the office, zooming by like I'm a mosquito or fly.

I scowl at his back and revel in the tiny rush it gives me. He continues through the labyrinth of secretaries and assistant principals as he heads back to wherever his lair must be.

After I turn in my permission slip to one of the secretaries, I head back toward my locker to get my books for my next class. At the end of the hall, I spot Seth Acosta, leaning up against a wall, fooling around on his phone. My heart skips.

"Hey," I manage as I walk by, wanting to stop but not sure I can or should. So I just slow down a little.

He looks up. There are a handful of other students at their lockers way down at the other end of the hall. The bell to end the lunch period is a few minutes away.

"Hey back," he says, sliding his phone into his back pocket and standing up straighter. All signs that make me think it's cool if I stop. That he really does want to talk to me.

"So . . . ," I start—because I'm the one who should be speaking next, I realize—". . . thanks for not saying anything. About . . . *you know.*" I raise my eyebrows like we're in some movie about the Mafia or a government conspiracy, and I immediately feel like an idiot. But Seth just nods and grins. I love that he's taller than me if only by a little. Ever since those sweaty, awkward middle school dances where I loomed head and shoulders over all the guys and no one ever asked me to partner up, I've always been self-conscious of my height.

"I wouldn't say anything," Seth says. "Not even if you covered me in fire ants or forced me to listen to, like, I don't know . . . smooth jazz."

I grin. "What's smooth jazz?"

"Garbage," Seth says, not missing a beat.

We stand there for an awkward moment, and when Seth speaks again, he looks down at my feet.

"Hey, do you feel like . . . I don't know . . . hanging out tonight or something?"

My heart is beating inside my throat. I hope Seth keeps looking at my feet because if he looks up, he'll see it just below my chin, all four chambers pulsating at an astonishing rate of speed.

"You're . . . not going to the game?" I finally manage. Great. Now I sound like Suzy School Spirit.

Seth frowns a little. "No, I'm not. But . . . you're going, I guess?"

"No!" I answer, louder than I'd intended. Of course, I had

been planning on going to the game. What else is there to do? Even Lucy was going to come. But that was before Seth Acosta turned my life into an episode of a television show I would totally binge watch.

"So you're *not* going, then?" he asks, confused. He brushes his hair out of his eyes with one hand.

"I wasn't really, like, sure what I was doing tonight. But if you want to hang out, that would be cool."

I've never hung out with a boy or gone on a date with a boy or been asked to a dance by a boy or kissed a boy. Nothing with boys. Ever. And now this. It's too astonishing to be real.

But it must be real because Seth is saying something about coming by my house around 7 p.m. and maybe going to get something to eat, and then he is typing my phone number into his phone and saying he'll text me later.

"Cool," I say, like this has happened to me every day of my life since sixth grade.

Just then the bell rings. I mumble out a goodbye and Seth says goodbye, and as I make my way to my locker, I am totally positive I'm not walking but floating.

Claudia has to be the first person I'm going to tell about my . . . is it a date? A hangout? A . . . what? When I find her at her locker at the end of the day, she squeals at my news, gripping my hand and literally jumping up and down with excitement.

"I hope you don't mind this means I won't be going to the game with you," I say.

"Screw the game!" Claudia answers, tugging me along after her. The entire walk home she helps me plan what to wear, what to do with my hair, whether I should wear lipstick. (I normally *don't*, but it might be fun to this time, maybe.) Claudia has more experience with boys than I do. She kissed a few in middle school—I think her pocket-sized self and her adorable ski jump nose made her nonthreatening to boys in early puberty—and she dated this guy Colin O'Malley for a few months last year before he moved to San Antonio because of his dad's job. In late night phone calls and texting marathons, she'd told me how she let him touch her under her bra and that it hadn't felt particularly great—only like he'd been trying to squeeze the air out of a deflating birthday party balloon.

The difference is Colin O'Malley was just ho hum. Even to Claudia.

Seth Acosta is not ho hum or meh or vanilla or blah.

He's a stone fox.

"What about your mom?" Claudia asks as we approach my house. "Hey, isn't that her car in the driveway?"

I frown. "I thought she'd be at work." My mom is not something I've considered until Claudia mentions it. Since I've never had any interest from any guy, this isn't a topic my mom and I have ever had to navigate.

"I'm sure she'll be cool with it," Claudia says, and I hope she's right. I mean, isn't that who my mom is? The cool mom?

After Claudia hugs me and practically makes me take a blood oath promising to tell her everything that happens immediately

140

after it happens, I walk in and find my mom in the kitchen, making a sandwich.

"You're home early," I say, setting down my backpack on the kitchen table. I thought I'd have at least an hour or two of getting-ready time in which to practice expressions and witty repartee in the bathroom mirror with my music blaring in the background.

"Hey, sweetie," my mom says, coming over to give me a kiss on the cheek. "Power went out at work. Something about a screwed-up electrical box. So I get a free afternoon off." She walks back to the kitchen counter and spreads mustard on a piece of whole wheat.

"So," I start, my heart thumping. I'm actually kind of embarrassed to talk about Seth with my mom. I mean, don't get me wrong. My mom has always been 100 percent straight-up amazingly honest about sex and puberty and all that hormone shit, but it's a lot easier to have those conversations when it's all just theory, not practice. I mean, not that I'm going to be doing it with Seth tonight or anything. I'm not even sure he likes me Like That. Even though I totally pray that he does.

"So . . . what?" my mom asks. She stops making her sandwich as she listens to my plans for the night. When I finish talking she gives me a small smile, but her eyes are wide with surprise.

"So, I can go, right?" I can't believe she'll say no, but I realize I'm holding my breath.

My mom presses her lips together, thinking for a second.

"Oh . . . sure. Yes, of course you can go. I mean, I'd like to meet this guy first, of course." She pauses, then laughs and shakes her head a bit. "Listen to me. I sound like a mom in a John Hughes movie."

I exhale. "Well, he's picking me up around 7."

"So you're not going to the game?"

"No . . . we're just going to get something to eat, I think. You're going to the game, right?"

"I was going to go with John, but I can meet him there later." She glances down at her half-made sandwich, like she's just re-membering it's there. I stand in the middle of the kitchen. We're in uncharted territory, and everything feels a little off-kilter.

"You don't have to wait or anything," I say.

"No, I want to," she insists. "And as far as what time you should be home . . . have I ever even given you a curfew, my obedient, well-behaved daughter?" She laughs again, but it's al-most a nervous laugh.

I shake my head no and bristle a bit at her description of me. It's true the only places I go are my girlfriends' houses for sleepovers. Or sometimes to cruise the Sonic or the DQ on Saturday nights. My mother has never had to give her duitiful Viv a curfew. It makes me feel like a dork.

"Let's say 10-ish, okay? I'll be home from the game by then."

I nod. Anyway, I'm not sure I'll even be able to find enough to talk about with Seth for three hours without passing out from anxiety.

"Well, I hope you have a great time," my mom says, and this time her cheer seems more sincere. I head to my room to

142

contemplate outfits, trying to shake off the awkwardness between us.

Butterflies is too small a word to describe what's going on in
my stomach when Seth pulls up to my house at five minutes after
seven. I peer through my bedroom window, my heart hammering. I see him get out of the car, slam the door to the red Honda
he's driving, and head up the front steps. I blink and swallow.
How can he be showing up to my house? To see me?

"Viv!" my mom calls out from the kitchen. "Your friend is
here!"

Your friend? You're making this sound like a playdate, Mom.

I walk out, hoping my black jeans and my mom's old Houston
Oilers T-shirt are cool but not trying too hard.

"Hey," I say.

"Hey," Seth says back, nodding.

"Mom, this is Seth from school." *What kind of a ridiculous
introduction is that? Where else would he be from? The bus station
downtown? The meth house?*

"Hi," Seth says to my mom, who's stretching out a hand. She
and Seth shake and she's pretty normal, actually, only asking how
long it's been since his family moved to town. He gives sentence-
long responses, but not kiss-ass answers, which is good because
my mom could see through that in a heartbeat.

"Well," my mom says as Seth and I start to scoot toward the
door, "have fun then, and I'll see you by 10." As she walks us out,
she presses something into my hand. Once we head outside I peek
down and see it's a twenty. I slide it into my jeans pocket and
catch my mother's eye. She gives me a smile, and I smile back.

"So, I get the sense the town's going to be dead, huh?" Seth says, pulling out onto the street. "Because of the game? I didn't think about that before."

"Yeah," I say. "All the fast-food places are closed. Most of the restaurants, too." Seth is driving out of my neighborhood, heading up Broadway toward town. He can't have had his license for too long, but he drives cool somehow, his head back and his hands casually resting at the bottom of the steering wheel. After we get going, he adjusts the volume. The tinny sound of some band I don't recognize but that sounds pretty catchy starts to spill out of the speakers.

"Are you hungry?" he asks.

"Not really," I say. The truth is I'm too nervous to eat, but I forced myself to down a granola bar before he came so my stomach wouldn't start grumbling. "Maybe later after it opens we can cruise the Sonic."

"Wait," Seth says, pulling up to a stop light and turning to look at me. "What's 'cruise the Sonic'?"

I grin, and my eyebrows pop up.

"Cruising the Sonic and the DQ is, like, what we do here on weekends. It just means driving aimlessly around those places to see who's hanging out there and who you can talk to or whatever."

"Really?"

"Yeah," I answer. "You didn't cruise the Sonic in Austin I'm guessing."

Seth laughs. "No. Definitely not." His eyes glance out the

driver's side window at the empty strip malls and storefront churches and resale shops. "I'm still getting used to this place."

It feels easier, somehow, to talk when we're in a moving car. I don't have to look Seth in the eyes. I can glance out my own window instead.

"You must miss it, I guess?" I ask. "Austin, I mean."

"That's an understatement," Seth says. He twists his mouth a bit like he's considering what to say next. "The thing is, my parents are artists. I mean, honestly, they can call themselves that because my mom comes from a shitload of money, if I can speak frankly. My grandparents are loaded and she lives off this trust. So she and my dad spend all their time prepping their art for different gallery shows. They do stuff with, like, textiles. My mom said she wanted to get away from Austin since it's growing so fast and it's not like it used to be in the '80s or whatever. Like she needed some authentic small-town experience to be a real artist."

"So they picked here?" I ask, incredulous. "Of all the small towns in America?"

"Yeah," Seth says, his voice heavy. "I don't think it occurred to them that it wouldn't have killed them to wait two more years until I was done with high school. But whatever." A tiny frown crosses his face.

"Do you at least like their art?" I ask, glancing at him.

"I guess," he says. "I mean, it gets shown and stuff. I think they're big names in the world of abstract textile art, which is, unbelievably, a world. People pay a lot of money for it. But to be honest, to me it just looks like a bunch of bedsheets folded weird."

I laugh out loud and Seth laughs with me. Just then we pass the U COPY IT with its OPEN sign flashing. I think of Frank in his red vest inside, flipping through a paperback.

"Hey," I say, pointing out the passenger window. "That's where I make the copies of *Moxie*."

Seth peers out the window and nods approvingly. "Cool. That bathrobe thing seems to have worked."

"Yeah," I say. It feels so strange to be able to talk about making the zine out loud with someone. But really good, too. "I'm not sure if I'm going to make another issue. But I kind of want to."

"You totally should," Seth says.

As we drive through town without a destination, the sun setting around us, I find myself telling Seth about my mom's Riot Grrrl past and how it inspired *Moxie*. Then we start talking about bands. He's heard of Bikini Kill but never heard them, heard them, so at Seth's prompting I pull up "Rebel Girl" on my phone. From the opening beats, he likes it. I can tell.

"That lead singer sounds like she could kill you with her voice," he says, his fingers drumming on the steering wheel. "But, like, kill you in a good way."

"Totally," I tell him, and my heart swells.

We go back and forth on bands for a while, and Seth describes a couple of live all-ages shows he got to go to in Austin. I've never seen a band play live except for the East Rockport High School pep band, and I'm super intrigued as he describes how his ears rang for days afterward and how cool it was to get to talk to the band members while they were selling their own merchandise (only Seth calls it "merch") at the shows. After I've stored up a list of bands in my head to check out later, Seth drives by Eternal Rest Funeral Home on Front Street. A small sign displayed in the front lawn under a floodlight reads DON'T TEXT AND DRIVE! WE CAN WAIT!

"Wait, is that for real?" Seth says, nodding toward the sign.

"Yeah," I answer. "It's this thing they do. They change it out every once in a while. Once they had one that said 'It's a beautiful day—look alive!'"

"Are you shitting me?" he asks. "And people still give them business?"

I shrug. "They're the only game in town, so yeah."

At this, Seth makes a sudden right turn and pulls into the funeral home parking lot. He turns up the music a little bit and starts bobbing his head back and forth to the beat as he spins circles over and over.

"Um," I begin, turning to face him, totally perplexed, "what are you doing?"

Seth grows serious. "I'm cruising the funeral home."

I explode with a loud laugh. "Cruising the funeral home? Seriously?"

"Yeah," Seth insists. He mimes waving at imaginary cars, chin-nodding at invisible people nearby. "This is so dope," he says. "I feel like I've finally figured out what East Rockport is all about. This is such a scene, man."

The nervousness from earlier has drained from me, replaced with aching cheeks from smiling so much.

After we cruise the funeral home for a while, Seth says he's getting hungry, and we find an open Jack in the Box on the outskirts of town. As we pull through the drive-thru, I offer Seth money, but he says he's got it "this time." (Does that mean there'll be a "next time"?) I order a milk shake and some fries.

"Y'all left the game early?" the scrawny, redheaded cashier asks as she hands us our food. She looks like she graduated from East Rockport twenty years ago and has been working at the Jack ever since. Her name tag reads SHAWNA.

"We never went," Seth answers.

"Well, you're missing something terrible," Shawna replies. "I've been listening on the radio and they're down 35–7 at the half."

"Damn," I reply, my small-town instincts kicking in, ready to express dismay anytime the home team loses. "That's a serious beating."

"I have faith they'll come back," Shawna says with a disapproving frown. "Go, Pirates."

"Go, Pirates," Seth answers, holding his Coke up in a salute.

Seth parks the car in the Jack in the Box parking lot and between slurps of his drink and bites of food, he asks, "Is football this big every year or just, like, this year?"

I snort into my milk shake. "You are new," I say. "The answer is every year. Every fucking year."

"You know, I played back home," he tells me.

I whip around, my eyes wide. "Now you're shitting me," I say. He might as well have told me he was studying to join the priesthood.

"No," he says. "I'm not shitting you. I mean, I was the kicker. I'm too skinny for any other position. But I was the kicker on the junior varsity team, and I was going to go out for varsity this year until we had to move."

I slap the dashboard to emphasize my shock. "You were a football player? And you listen to Black Flag?"

Seth's smile cracks his face wide. "Yes! I'm not making this up. I can show you pictures when I'm done eating."

I try to visualize Seth in those weird short pants and huge shoulder pads football players wear and my mind goes blank. I never thought I'd have a crush on a football player. For a split second I feel a little like my mom on a date with Republican John. *If this is even a date*, I remind myself.

"I'm sorry, I guess it's just that . . . I don't know if you've noticed, but here . . . here the football players are . . . like . . ."

"Total assholes?" Seth offers, raising an eyebrow. "Oh, I've noticed. But just because a guy plays football doesn't make him an asshole. Unless, you know, you think I'm an asshole, and you're just hanging out with me because you feel sorry for the sad new kid at school."

I glance down at my milk shake. "You're not an asshole," I murmur, then take a loud slurp. *You're just a hilarious and totally good-looking guy who listens to cool bands and likes my zine, and that basically makes you the boy of my dreams, but you know, whatever.*

"That's good," Seth says, grinning. "That I'm not an asshole. Back home football was a sport people were into and everything, but it wasn't the only thing people cared about, so players were more chill, I guess."

"Well, people aren't chill about football here," I answer. "Those players are the *reason* this town and this school exist. I mean, they're what people get excited about around here. They're what makes East Rockport worth living in for some people. The chance that this year we'll make it to the playoffs, you know? The *hope*. You watch. Starting next week the talk will already be about the next season and how *that* will be the year we take state."

"Damn," Seth says, taking a long drink from his soda.

We talk for a while in the parking lot—I tell him how my dad died when I was a baby and how it's just me and my mom with my grandparents next door. He tells me that his parents are nice enough, just occupied with their art, and that in addition to playing football he wrote a music column for his old high school newspaper. It's an easy conversation, each of us stepping on the ends of the other's sentences, wanting to chime in or add something or agree with something. My body hums with the sure sense that I'm the coolest girl in the world. Sitting there in the front seat, the fluorescent lights of the Jack in the Box parking lot shining on us like the moon on steroids, it's weird to remember that this afternoon in the hallway when Seth asked me to hang out I could barely make eye contact with him because I was so anxious.

After a while, Seth takes my wrappers and empty cup and gets out of the car to throw them away. I lick the salty tips of my fingers as he walks back toward the car, and I realize that the night is coming to a close. It's 9:30.

Seth suggests we head back, and as he drives toward my

neighborhood, the Jack in the Box parking lot disasppearing behind us, my breathing starts to tighten up and my heart begins to hammer.

Seth Acosta is going to kiss me. I know it.

As he pulls onto my street, I glance into the rearview mirror, pretending I'm checking for something in my eye. My lipstick is still holding steady. Is that a good thing or a bad thing when you kiss someone?

Seth slides into the driveway. Here, in the inky darkness of his car, he's going to kiss me. *Remember this, Vivian. Remember everything about this.*

I wait for him to shift the car into park. How can you kiss with the car in drive?

But he doesn't shift the car into park. He only turns to me and says, "I had a lot of fun hanging out with you tonight, Vivian."

It's definitive, the way he says it. There's no question that this is The End of the night.

"I had fun, too," I say, forcing a smile while dying inside. "Thanks for asking me to hang out."

"Honestly," he continues, "I haven't really, you know, made a lot of friends since I got here, so, you know . . . this was really cool. I'm going to check out some of those bands you told me about. Especially more of that Bikini Kill one." He sort of looks over my shoulder when he says it. Like maybe he can't wait for me to leave.

"Cool," I say, my hand on the door handle and my hammering heart twisting hard.

I haven't really made a lot of friends since I got here.

Friends.

FRIENDS.

"See you Monday?" he asks.

"Yeah, see you then," I answer, itching to get out of the Honda and into the safety of my bedroom.

"And I promise I won't say a word about *Moxie*. I mean it."

"Thanks," I answer, "I really appreciate it." I get out, slam the car door, and race up the front steps, grateful my mom is still at the game and the house is empty. Seth waits until I've let myself in and then drives away, and as I step into the living room and shut the front door behind me, I can't help it. I start crying. Not heaving sobs or anything like that. Just a few warm tears peek out of my eyes and slip down my cheeks.

"Don't be stupid, Viv," I say out loud. "You still had a great time tonight, right?" Joan Jett saunters in at the sound of my voice, purring as she loops herself around my legs. I pick her up and bury my face into her fur. Then I put her down and get ready for bed, eagerly sliding under my covers, wrapping self-pity around myself with the blankets.

The truth is I did have a great time with Seth. And maybe we will hang out again. But I don't want to just hang out with Seth. I want to know what it feels like to have a boy's lips on mine. I want to press my entire body up against his and kiss him. I want a hot, cool, smart boyfriend, not a hot, cool, smart boy *friend.*

As I climb into bed, my phone buzzes from my nightstand. I reach for it, hoping for the tiniest second that it's Seth.

It's Claudia.

We got our ASSES KICKED tonight—lost 42–7 . . . but who cares HOW WAS YOUR DATE?!?!?!?

I know Claudia will hate me for not responding, but I toss my phone onto the carpet and slide deeper under the covers, hoping I'm asleep before my mom gets home. I don't think I could stand one more person asking me how the night went.

CHAPTER THIRTEEN

CLAUDIA AND I ARE IN CLAUDIA'S BED STARING UP AT THE CEILING.
It's the morning after one of our Saturday night sleepovers, and she's listening to me talk over my "date" with Seth for the ten millionth time. It's been a few weeks since I was left kissless in his car, but that hasn't stopped me from analyzing the night over and over. At least Claudia humors me. A little.

"Maybe he was just intimidated by you," she says, stretching her arms out and yawning.

"I feel like that's what you're supposed to say so I don't feel bad for being rejected."

"Vivian, come on."

"Well, I'm serious. I was sending him signals. I was alerting him to my lips. So what the hell happened?"

Claudia rolls her eyes and yawns again. A buzz interrupts us.

"Hey," she says, nudging me. "Your phone."

I reach toward Claudia's nightstand. It's my mom.

"Hey, Mom."

"Hey, sweetie," she says. Something in her voice sounds weird. Off.

"Is everything okay?"

"Oh yeah, everything's okay."

"Good," I say. I peer over at Claudia, who is picking at her cuticles.

"The reason I'm calling . . . well, this is awkward, but I know I can be up front with you, Viv," my mom begins, sort of clearing her throat.

"Yeah?" I ask.

"Well, John is here."

Nothing else really needs to be said. My mother knows I'm old enough to understand that John didn't just show up at our house at nine in the morning to catch up on old times. And I know she knows I know. I squeeze my eyes shut as the idea of my mother and John having Sexual Intercourse invades my brain.

"Uh, okay?" I say, my voice flat. What else is there to say?

"Anyway, we're getting ready to go out to get a bite to eat, but I wasn't sure when you were coming home and I didn't want you to be . . . surprised. I'm sorry, Vivvy, I didn't know if you would still be sleeping or walking home when I called or what."

"No, it's fine," I say. "We're not sleeping, we're awake. I'll see you when I get home."

And then I do something I've never done in my life. I hang up on my mom without waiting for a response.

As I fill Claudia in, she squirms appropriately at the idea of

155

my mother and John Doing It. "It's just so gross," I say. "And I think she could do a lot better."

"Is this guy that bad?" Claudia asks.

I don't want to have to make my case to Claudia. She should be on my side automatically. So I just sigh dramatically and say, "I don't want to talk about it."

"Okay," she says, her voice quiet. "Sorry."

"No, it's fine," I say, offering up an exaggerated sad face so she gets how fine it is—even if it isn't. "I'm sorry, I didn't mean to snap."

"No, it's no big deal," she says, throwing back her bedspread and jumping out of bed, signaling the end of the conversation. "But I'm hungry. Let's go make pancakes, okay?"

"Do you have chocolate chips?" I ask, quickly falling into our familiar script.

"Duh," says Claudia.

I eat breakfast at Claudia's house, dawdle a little, and then head home, walking at the pace of a snail. By the time I get there, there's no sign of John. Just my mom reading in the den.

"Hey," she says, when I walk in. A little too eager.

"Hey," I say, wandering over to the refrigerator even though I just ate.

"Viv, can we talk?" she says.

Her simple question seems strange to me. My mother and I have always talked without having to say "Can we talk?" first. We just talk. There's never any prologue.

"What's up?" I say, shutting the fridge and leaning up against it.

"Well, come over here. You're too far away." She pats the couch next to her.

I give in and slide in next to her, trying to ignore the mental picture of her and John that keeps threatening my mind.

"Viv, I'm sorry about this morning," she says, quietly. "I shouldn't have sprung that on you like that. It just . . . the situation was . . . unexpected." She reaches out to touch my arm, but I shrink back a bit.

"It's okay, Mom," I say. "It's fine."

"But is it really fine?" she asks, her voice soft, her mouth a small frown.

"I mean . . . it's . . ." I hesitate. *What is there to say? How disgusting? What do you see in him? How could you do it in our house?* But she's looking at me with such sincere concern—I can't be the brat who makes my mom miserable. "It's weird, a little. But if he makes you happy . . ."

"He's a really nice guy, Viv," my mom says. "I wish you'd give him more of a chance."

I can be nice, but I can't be her BFF who acts all giddy over John. "I am giving him a chance," I say.

"Yeah?" she asks. Her voice is hopeful but her eyes seem skeptical.

"Yes," I say. "Now I'm super tired because Claudia and I stayed up too late, so I'm going to lie down, okay?"

My mom nods, but she doesn't smile. Just shifts a bit in her seat as I get up off the couch and walk toward my room.

"Hey," she says when I reach my bedroom door, "we never

even talked about that Seth guy. He came around a few weeks ago and I never saw him again."

Oh God, now? Really?

"We're just friends, Mom," I say, my hand on my doorknob. "It's nothing."

My mom's eyes go wide. I know my voice sounds harsher than necessary, but I don't care. She doesn't say anything else. I try to block out her hurt expression as I fling myself on my bed and pull out my phone.

Without really deciding to, I find myself texting Lucy.

I'm in a crap mood

She writes back immediately.

Why?

My mom had her boyfriend spend the night last night—I wasn't here or anything . . . but she told me about it and it's just gross.

Is this that super conservative dude you told us about at lunch? Who basically like told your mom what book to read that one time?

Yeah

Groooooooosssssss

I knoooooow

I smile and keep going.

Then she asked me about seth . . . like two weeks after our "date" or whatever . . .

Damn . . . knife in the heart

Seriously

I'm sorry that didn't work out . . .

I kick my shoes off and settle in for a nice long back and forth with Lucy.

I mean . . . he hasn't been an ass to me or anything . . . since we hung out that one time he says hi to me in the hallway and we talk about music sometimes in English . . .

Ugh. Cold comfort.

Seriously. I didn't want a study buddy . . . I wanted more.

The heart wants what it fucking wants

I almost think it would have been better if he'd ignored me from the start . . .

After more back and forth about Seth, Lucy texts me, *I can cheer you up . . . I have a secret*

My eyebrows pop up.

What??? Is it about a boy?

Blerg no. No dude at East Rockport has caught my eye . . . but it's something pretty kick ass

I'm finally genuinely smiling for the first time all morning.

WHAT IS IT?

WAIT UNTIL TOMORROW AND YOU'LL FIND OUT

I try wheedling it out of her for a few more minutes, but Lucy resists and finally says she has to go. After our last text, I toss my phone aside and grin at the ceiling. For the first time in ages, I find myself wishing for Monday to come.

When Monday does arrive, it arrives cold and wet. I'm simultaneously thinking about Lucy's secret and counting the days until winter break when I spot it. Taped to one of the side door entrances.

I read it once. Then read it again. First I'm confused—for a

split second I wonder if I've had some sort of short-term memory loss and I actually made and taped *Moxie* flyers up while I was in a trance or something—but as I peer at it, reading the words over and over, a sense of glee settles over me.

Because I'm pretty sure I know what's really going on.

Inside, I spot more flyers on lockers and by water fountains, pinned up on message boards with brightly colored pushpins. When I get to my locker, I find one taped to the door.

Just then my phone buzzes.

I look down. It's a text from Lucy.

Okay I was going to wait till English to tell you but what do you think of the flyers?!

My hands jump, ready to text right back, but then I have the foresight to use the situation to provide myself with some cover.

WAIT—YOU started Moxie?!?!?

I grin as I hit send.

No! I still don't know who did the newsletters . . . but I figured whoever it was wouldn't care if I added to the ranks . . . like adopted the brand, right?

Students push past me, heading to first period. Shoes squeak on wet, tiled floors and voices holler from one end of the hallway to the next, demanding answers to last night's homework or securing a promise to meet somewhere after class. Standing there, staring at Lucy's message, I realize Moxie doesn't belong to me anymore. It belongs to every girl at East Rockport High who wants to be part of it. I text Lucy back.

I totally love it and I know whoever started Moxie is going to love it too

But if Lucy is aiming for anonymity with this soccer team fund-raising bake sale, she's going about it all wrong. In English class she tells me about making the flyer last night at home and then coming to school early to copy it in the library, but she whispers so loudly she might as well be talking at normal volume, and I'm pretty sure people around her hear. Then at lunch in the cafeteria, she goes ahead and dishes when the topic comes up.

"Okay, so, Viv already knows, but . . . I did it!" She squeals a little and covers her face with her hands, then peeks through her fingers. "I really did."

"Wait," Sara starts, her eyes wide, "you mean you made the newsletters? You organized the bathrobe thing?"

"No, I swear I didn't do that," Lucy insists. "But I just wanted to, I don't know, like, take on the whole vibe."

Claudia sips on her Diet Coke and eyes Lucy like she's not sure she believes her. But she doesn't say anything.

"So why the soccer team?" Meg asks. "You're not on it."

"No, but they're supposed to be so good, right? And they get, like, zero attention. Their uniforms are practically falling apart from what I've heard."

I nod. "Kiera Daniels was telling me they're the same uniforms her mom wore in the '90s."

"That can't be possible," Kaitlyn argues.

"Well, maybe they're not the exact same uniforms, but they are really old," I continue. "And we never do a single thing for them even though they're so great. Marisela Perez made all-state last year and the only reason I even heard about it was because my mom saw some tiny little article in the paper."

"Yeah, it is pretty ridiculous," Sara chimes in.

Claudia shrugs. "I don't mean to be a Debbie Downer or whatever, but how much money can one bake sale raise?" She shakes her Diet Coke can as if she's trying to measure how much is left. No one says anything for a second, and an awkward silence settles over us. Lucy's visible glow of excitement fades just a bit.

"Well, I was thinking we could keep doing fund-raisers for them," she says, not making eye contact with Claudia. "We wouldn't have just one bake sale. I mean, we could keep supporting them all season long. Kind of like what the rally girls and cheerleaders do for the football team."

Claudia nods, her expression still uncertain. But just as I'm about to get really pissed at her, she says, "Well, I can make some lemon bars. They're really good. Viv knows."

I nod enthusiastically. "They are good. Super good. We could charge at least fifty cents per bar. Maybe even a dollar." Geez, I sound spastically psyched about these damn lemon bars.

"Okay, don't oversell the lemon bars, Viv," Claudia says, giving me a look. But she's smiling.

Right after school on Thursday I pull out Meemaw's recipe for Magic Squares. It's a struggle to read her slanty, old-fashioned cursive. When I call her to ask exactly how many cups of butter I need, she practically shouts into the phone with excitement.

"How perfectly ladylike of you, Vivvy! Your mother never liked to bake, you know." Meemaw may be queen of the Stouffer's

163

frozen dinner, but give that woman a pie recipe and she'll make something so good you'll want to slap someone.

"Well, it's for a fund-raiser at school," I tell her. "For the girls' soccer team."

Meemaw pauses. "Well, that's . . . nice. I didn't know there was a girls' soccer team."

"They almost took state last year," I say. I'm kind of enjoying blowing Meemaw's mind.

"Well, bully for them," she says. "Do you want to come over for dinner later? Or do you want me to come over and help with the squares?"

"It's okay, Meemaw," I say, pulling open a bag of chocolate chips and sneaking a few into my mouth. "But thanks."

By the time Mom gets home late from work, the Magic Squares are cooling on the counter. They smell pretty delicious if I do say so myself. My mother gives a little cheer and heads over to grab one.

"One!" I shout from the couch where I'm doing my homework, scaring Joan Jett, who bolts from the den and down the hallway. "They're for a fund-raiser at school."

My mom is already taking a bite as she collapses on the couch next to me like she might faint because the Magic Squares are so good.

"Deeeeeelisssssshhhhh, Vivvy. Seriously."

I smile. Since the awkwardness the morning after John slept over, we've been tiptoeing around each other like parents around a sleeping baby. But right now feels like old times.

"What's the fund-raiser for?" she asks. When I tell her about the girls' soccer team and how no one supports them, my mom's face brightens.

"That is so cool, Viv," she says, leaning over to push some hair out of my face. "Was it your idea?"

Not really, but kind of yes if you think about it.

"It was my friend Lucy's."

"Well, I'm glad you're doing it."

I squirm a bit at the compliment before sliding under my mom's arm, snuggling up close like I did when I was little. She kisses me on top of the head.

"Sorry if I smell like strep throat," she says.

"No, just like hand sanitizer," I reassure her.

"John says there's no way to get the smell off, even if you take two showers when you get home."

I don't want to talk about John right now. And I *really* don't want to think about John in the shower. My mom threads her fingers through my hair, pushing it back off my face. I try to focus on the coziness of it but suddenly my mom's arm seems suffocating.

"You know, I should get ready for bed," I say, forcing a yawn. "I think baking wore me out."

My mom laughs, oblivious to any weirdness between us.

"Okay," she says, letting me loose. "And I really think it's cool about your fund-raiser." She smiles and I smile back, but the old times are gone.

I brush my teeth and get ready for bed.

* * *

Lucy has put up more Moxie bake sale flyers all week long, and I've helped, too. I think Sara put up a couple. But I'm still not sure how many girls will come out with food. Lucy and I make plans to get to the cafeteria right at the start of lunch, and we commandeer the table in the corner that student groups often use for fund-raisers.

"I even filled out the stupid school group fund-raiser form in the office, so we're totally street legal," Lucy says.

"Wait," I say, pulling back the aluminum foil from my Magic Squares, "did you actually put down on the paper that Moxie is a club?"

"Yeah," Lucy says with a shrug. "Well, I mean, I just put my name because you only need one person as club representative. But do you think Principal Wilson or anyone in the administration has even noticed that newsletter or even put together that the bathrobe thing was connected to it? Please."

"I guess," I say, my heart fluttering. Something about Moxie being official—even just on a fund-raiser permission form filed away in the office—makes me anxious. But I can't do anything about it now.

At least I don't have to be anxious about the fund-raiser. Claudia brings her lemon bars and Sara brings banana bread and lots of girls from the soccer team show up with plates of cookies and brownies. Once the sale starts, Lucy grins at every transaction, sliding the dollar bills and coins into an envelope.

Halfway through lunch, Kiera Daniels walks up with her friend Amaya.

"Hey," Kiera says. Both girls eye the spread.

"Hey, Kiera," I say. "Hey, Amaya."

Kiera asks for two lemon bars. She hands over a five dollar bill, and Lucy makes the change while I wrap the bars up in a pink paper napkin.

"So wait," Kiera asks, "are you the girls who made the newsletter thing? With the bathrobes and the hearts and the stars?" She eyes me, confused. She has to be remembering our conversation in the bathroom the day we marked our hands. When I acted like I didn't know anything about it.

"No," I answer, maybe too quickly. "We didn't. But Lucy decided to do this bake sale and just, like, adopt the name, I guess."

Amaya slides the napkin out of Kiera's hands and unwraps the lemon bars. She takes a bite out of one and smiles. "These are so good," she says, her mouth full. Powdered sugar spills down her chin.

Kiera rolls her eyes at Amaya. "You cannot even wait until we get back to the table, can you?" Amaya shoots Kiera a look, but Lucy snorts at Kiera's comment.

"Y'all planning on doing another one?" Kiera asks. "I mean, like another bake sale."

"Yeah, I guess," I say. "I mean, you guys need new uniforms, right?"

Amaya nods vigorously, her mouth full of lemon bar.

Kiera nods, too. She opens her mouth, then closes it, then opens it again. "I guess I was wondering," she starts, "if this club is . . . like . . . open to new members?"

"She means is it just white girls," Amaya says, finishing her lemon bar.

I'm instantly uncomfortable and not sure how to answer, but Lucy doesn't miss a beat. "Well, my dad's Mexican," she says, "so take that for what it's worth." Kiera grins a little when Lucy says that.

"I think everyone should be able to do this," I say. "I mean, it's for everyone. I don't think whoever started Moxie wants, like, a leader. If a girl wants to hold another bake sale, or anything like that, she can just . . . do it."

"And call it Moxie?" Kiera asks, arching an eyebrow.

"Sure, why not?" Lucy answers. A group of freshman boys collects around the table to buy what's left of my Magic Squares, and Lucy turns to help them.

"Well, that's cool," Kiera says. "Okay."

"Okay," I say.

Kiera gives us a small wave, and she and Amaya make their way back to their table.

When the freshman boys leave the table, I whisper to Lucy, "That was kind of awkward."

"What's awkward is how this place is as fucked up when it comes to race as it is about anything else," she tells me, flipping her fingers through the money envelope, doing a quick estimation of how much we've raised. "I mean, look at this cafeteria." She motions at the tables in front of us. The Latina girls who speak mostly Spanish hang out together, and they don't have much to do with the Latina girls like Claudia and Lucy who speak mostly English. And the black girls have their own cliques that I don't fully get. And the few Asian kids and the biracial kids and the kids who don't fit any particular box unless they play a certain sport or something go with whoever will take them. It's messed up.

"At my old school, at least the teachers brought up racial issues in class sometimes," Lucy continues.

I'm glad Claudia's not around to hear Lucy tell us again how advanced life is in the big city. For the first time Lucy makes me feel a little prickly, too. We hardly ever talk about race stuff at East Rockport. Hell, we hardly ever talk about it at home either. The night we watched that documentary about Kathleen Hanna, my mom talked about how Riot Grrrl was mostly white girls, and she was sorry they weren't as welcoming to other girls as they could have been. That it was one of the few regrets she had about the whole thing. But that was as far as she'd gone. East Rockport High isn't just white girls, for sure. I glance over to where Kiera and Amaya are sitting. I think about how in this one way, maybe Moxie could be even better than the Riot Grrrls. Even stronger.

As the bell rings to end lunch, I help Lucy throw out the garbage from the sale.

"We made over a hundred dollars," she tells me.

I frown. "I thought it would be more. That's enough for, like, one uniform."

"Okay, Miss Negative," says Lucy. "We have to start somewhere."

"I know," I answer, my irritation fading a bit. "You're right." Lucy seems so sure of herself. So confident. Standing there in that moment, I can almost convince myself that she's the one who started Moxie, not me.

169

CHAPTER FOURTEEN

THE FEW WEEKS BETWEEN THANKSGIVING AND WINTER BREAK ARE just, I don't know, such an exercise in futility. No one wants to be at school, and that includes the teachers. It's a three-week countdown until a precious, blessed break when we can sleep in, numb out on television, and forget about worksheets and grammar exercises and chemistry labs.

And as far as the girls are concerned, holiday vacation will be a break from the bump 'n' grab.

The bump 'n' grab started not long after the long Thanksgiving weekend. Just like "Make me a sandwich," it started small at first. A few boys did it—boys like Mitchell and Jason and their buddies—and then it started to spread like a match to dry kindling, with so many boys playing along that making it down a hallway was like picking your way through a minefield.

The bump 'n' grab is exactly what it sounds like. A boy bumps you in the hallway. Maybe quasi-gently with a hip. Maybe more forcefully like he's enjoying himself a little too much.

When you stumble, there's a grab. Sometimes you get goosed around the waist. Sometimes you get pinched on the butt. And as quickly as it starts, it's over, and the boy is off down the hall, maybe squawking that he's sorry. Maybe laughing at the top of his lungs.

The whole thing really gets you into the holiday spirit. Ha, ha, ha.

This morning, as I make my way to English, it happens to me. I can't even get a sense of which guy does it, he's so fast, but his fingers manage to make it just under my shirt, cold and rough on my waist.

I want to yell out, chase him down, scream out loud. But I'm frozen from the shock of it, standing so still that some kids behind me whine that I'm blocking the hallway.

My cheeks burning, I make my way into class. With just a few days left before break, Mr. Davies has decided to show the film version of *Romeo and Juliet* (even though we've never read the play, so go figure), and I collapse into my seat, thankful for the cool darkness of the classroom. Lucy leans toward me over her desk.

"You okay? Your face is all red."

At the front of the classroom Mr. Davies seems appropriately checked out, so I lean in and in a quiet voice tell Lucy what happened. She listens, frowns, and then mutters, "Asshole!" a little too loudly. A few kids around us laugh.

"Shhh . . . ," I whisper. But in the same breath, I want to scream *Asshole!* out loud, too.

"I don't get this," Lucy argues. "Is it some kind of game?"

The sappy music from the *Romeo and Juliet* movie drones on. Several kids around us are nodding off, and Mr. Davies's chin is resting on his chest. In a few minutes he'll probably be audibly snoring. Considering permission granted, I explain to Lucy that the bump 'n' grab is one of many games some of the boys at East Rockport like to play.

"Last year, they started this thing where they tried to take pictures up girls' skirts and then posted them online," I explain. "There was this whole point system to it, too."

Lucy mock faints, collapsing into her desk. Then she sits back up again.

"I can't wait for Friday. I need a vacation from this retrograde nightmare."

"Me, too."

"Maybe the *Moxie* newsletter girls will do something about it," she tells me.

"But what?" I ask. It strikes me that I'm open to suggestions.

"Advocate for kneeing them in the balls," Lucy says definitively. "They can call it the knee-in-the-nuts."

I grin back, imagining the scenario. Mitchell Wilson would get it so bad he wouldn't be able to father children. Now that would be a win for human evolution.

After forty more minutes of *Romeo and Juliet*, the bell rings. As we head out of class, I feel a tap on my shoulder. I guess I'm a little jumpy from the bump 'n' grab, because I spin around, a glare on my face.

It's Seth. He blinks his eyes a bit as they adjust to the light of the hallway.

"Hey," he says, pulling back. "Sorry if I scared you."

"Oh," I say, glancing down, embarrassed. "I'm sorry. I thought you were . . . I don't know."

"It's cool."

Lucy gives me a quick wave and a knowing look before ducking into the crowded hallway, and I find myself walking with Seth, my heart keeping double time. At one point we're squeezed up against each other, shoulder to shoulder. He doesn't fall back or pull forward. His shoulder is warm. Sturdy. I didn't know shoulders could be so sexy.

"I listened to that album you told me about," he says.

"Did you like it?"

"Definitely. Especially the lead guitarist."

"Yeah, she's great."

"Are you going anywhere for break?" he asks.

"No, just staying put. Hangin' out with the grandparents."

"Cruising the Sonic?" he asks.

"And the funeral home, naturally," I answer, pleased I don't miss a beat.

"Very funny," Seth says, and we look each other right in the eyes and grin. Seth is super tall like me, but I kind of like the fact that I don't have to peer up at him like I'm some little kid.

We approach my locker, and I tell him I have to stop to get my lunch. He doesn't keep walking, though. He sort of leans up against the locker next to mine, resting on one of his incredibly sexy shoulders. I fumble with my combination and finally open my locker on the second try.

"So . . . what about, like, over the break?" I hear Seth's voice saying as I dig through my stuff for my bag lunch. "What if you let me take you out? Like on a real date? Like eating real food together or whatever. Not just a drive-thru."

Blood pumps in my ears. My hand is clutching my brown bag lunch as if it's the only thing keeping me from collapsing on the tiled floor. I manage to turn to make eye contact with Seth, but as soon as I do he glances past me for a moment and then briefly back at me and then at his shoes.

"Uh, like . . . okay?" I say. "Like, that would be . . . great."

"Cool," Seth says, looking up at me and smiling. I'm still clutching my damn lunch, trying to steady myself. "I'll text you. Or call you. Okay?"

"Okay," I say.

"Okay," he says.

Just as I'm wondering if I should say okay one more time, Seth grins and heads off down the hallway, and I'm feeling all spinny and silly and sure I'm about to pass out. I close my locker and scan the faces around me, looking for Claudia or Lucy.

Bump.

I gasp, catching my breath. It comes from behind, and just as I try to catch my balance, I feel a hand on my back. *Snap!* My bra strap slides back against my skin with a sting.

"What the . . . ," I start, catching a glimpse of what I'm pretty sure is the back of Jason Garza's pointy, pea-brained head as he races off.

"Sorry!" he yells.

A *fuck you* is buried in my throat, but all I can manage to do is make it into the nearest bathroom. I catch a glimpse of a few girls preening at the sinks. I nod at them briefly and slide into one of the stalls, my eyes on the floor, and shut the door behind me. The shock of what Jason's just done makes me want to scream. I think maybe I want to cry, too, but tears don't come out. There's just a buzzing, sharp rage coursing through me. Any good feeling I got from Seth asking me out has been switched off. I can still sense Jason's hand on my back. I can still feel the snap of my bra. I can still hear him shouting out a fake apology.

Outside, the girls' voices are light and lyrical, chatting about Christmas and the upcoming break. I want to make sure I have it together before I leave the stall, and I turn just a bit and take a breath. That's when I see it. Written in black Sharpie on the back wall. Just over the toilet.

MOXIE GIRLS FIGHT BACK!

I don't recognize the handwriting. I don't know who did it. It wasn't me, and Lucy wouldn't have been able to keep it quiet if she'd been the one responsible. That means some girl—a girl I don't even know—has written those words.

MOXIE GIRLS FIGHT BACK!

I take a deep breath and smile at the graffiti as if I expect it to smile back.

That night as I'm zoning out in front of the television, my phone buzzes on the coffee table. I reach for it.

Hey—what's up? It's Seth. I grin.

175

Hey—not much just watching tv

I watch the text bubble pop up and my breathing tightens a little in anticipation.

So about going out . . . what about this friday?

My eyes pop open. That's the very first night of break.

Yeah that would be great

Maybe that Mexican place . . . Los Tios? Went there with my parents a few times right after we moved here

Yeah it's pretty good

I bite my lip. Joan Jett jumps up next to me on the couch and starts pawing at me to pet her. With one hand I reach for her absentmindedly, my eyes glued to my phone.

Listen you probably think I'm an asshole . . .

"Huh?" I say out loud. Joan Jett purrs in agreement.

Uh . . . no . . . should I? I write back.

There's a long pause before a message pops up. My eyes try to take it all in at once, and I have to force myself to slow down and read word by word.

Like . . . I asked you to hang out that one time and then we didn't hang out again . . . I was seeing this girl back in Austin and I felt kind of like a dick hanging out with you when I hadn't really ended things with her . . . which I did recently btw . . .

"Oh," I say out loud, like Seth can hear me. My brain is struggling to process this information. I'm already imagining going through it syllable by syllable when I call Claudia later. Maybe Lucy, too. I take a breath and think of how to respond.

I didn't think you were a dick . . .

Seth responds immediately.

Yeah? Btw I'm worried that last text makes me sound like a fucking player . . . and that is actually not the case

That text makes me smile. I tap out a response.

No it's okay . . . I guess I was just wondering what was up

Pause.

You're going to make me say it?

Reading this text makes me sit up straight, and I accidentally knock Joan Jett off the couch. She saunters away, irritated.

Say what? I type back. My heart flutters.

Pause.

Another pause.

Say that I think you're one cool girl

I blink. This doesn't happen to me. I'm not the kind of girl this happens to.

Yet it is happening.

To me.

I think you're pretty cool too . . . , I type back. I'm smiling so hard my cheeks hurt.

Yeah?

Yeah.

So . . . Friday night?

Yeah . . . Friday night

Okay . . . cool . . . goodnight Vivian

Night Seth

I'm still staring at the phone when I hear my mother's keys in the front door. A few beats later she walks in, throws her purse on the kitchen counter, and opens the refrigerator to look for what I know is an ice-cold Coke.

"Hey, Vivvy," she says, her back toward me.

I think I'm breathing, but I'm not sure. I'm glad my mother isn't looking at me or she'd wonder why I've gone catatonic.

"Hey, Mom," I finally manage.

She fishes a can from the back of the fridge and turns to smile at me.

"How was your day?" she says.

Two asshole guys bump 'n' grabbed me and one not-asshole guy told me he thinks I'm one cool girl. So I guess you could say, it was a day of extremes.

"It was fine."

"That's good," my mom says. Just then her phone buzzes. She smiles at the screen, and I know it's John. She reaches to answer it.

"I'm getting ready for bed," I mouth to her as she presses the phone to her ear and starts talking.

" 'Night, sweetheart," she mouths back, pulling me close to give me a brief good-night hug.

Later, as I slide under the covers, I think about boys. Mostly about Seth, of course, but Jason Garza and Mitchell Wilson and John, too. Some boys piss me off and some annoy me and some of them make my body go electric in the best way ever. I toss and turn and toss some more, and when I finally fall asleep, I dream about driving in a car with John and my mother and Seth around the Eternal Rest Funeral Home until my mom says it's time for Seth and me to go on our date, but when we show up to Los Tios restaurant, Seth turns into Mitchell Wilson, and when I see him, I promptly punch him in the face.

CHAPTER FIFTEEN

THERE ARE A MILLION THINGS I WANT TO KNOW ABOUT SETH ACOSTA, and as we sit in a back booth inside a dimly lit Los Tios, white Christmas lights strung around the windows, queso and tacos in front of us, I keep discovering them like little treasures.

Like he's left-handed.

Like his dad speaks Spanish and German.

Like his dog is named Max after this old jazz drummer his mother loves named Max Roach.

I think it's going to be scary, going on a real date with Seth Acosta. And at first, of course, I'm a little nervous. But soon, it's as easy as the last time we hung out, driving around the funeral home and eating Jack in the Box in an empty parking lot.

From the minute we sit down, we start having one of those conversations where we keep jumping on the ends of each other's sentences.

"And did you read . . ."

"And have you heard . . ."

"And did you ever watch . . ."

And sometimes our knees bump under the table. And once our fingers touch in the chip basket.

And the entire time I'm wonderinghopingthinkingpraying that when this night is over, Seth is going to kiss me.

Please to the God I want to believe in, please let me get my first kiss from Seth Acosta.

After dinner's over, it's still early—not even 9 o'clock.

"What else can we do?" Seth asks as we slide into his car and pull out of the Los Tios parking lot.

"There's a party at this girl's house," I say. "But to be honest, I don't really feel like a party."

"Me neither," Seth says. "What about the beach? Too cold?"

"I brought my jacket."

We head down to the public beach on the bay, right by the Nautical and Seafood Museum of the Gulf Coast and the Holiday Inn. It sounds all romantic and gorgeous to live by the beach, but the Gulf Coast isn't exactly a bastion of moonlit walks on white sand. Seth parks his car and we sit on some ratty old picnic tables on the perimeter of the thin strip of sand, staring out at the mucky Texas water as it laps against clumps of seaweed and a few empty plastic bottles. At least we're the only ones here.

"Kind of sad how there's so much garbage," Seth says, peering at the water line.

"Once in sixth grade our class came down here to do a beach cleanup as a community service project," I say, drawing my knees to my chest, controlling a shiver. It *is* cold. "And my friend Claudia found a condom, but she didn't know what it was, so she asked our science teacher, who was a guy, and he was so embarrassed that he ended the cleanup and we went back to school early."

Seth laughs out loud. I'm not sure if it's weird to bring up a story about a condom in front of Seth, but I feel kind of bold and funny doing it.

"So you want to leave East Rockport or stick around?" Seth asks. "I mean, after next year?"

"I don't know, honestly," I answer. "I mean, I want to go to college, I guess. That's what I'm supposed to say, right? But my mom can probably only afford in-state tuition, so I don't know . . . wherever I go I doubt it will be far from here. What about you? What do you want to do when you graduate?"

Seth tucks a strip of his black hair behind his ear and scratches his chin with his thumb, and it's just the most delicious thing.

"Honestly? I have no idea. Literally zero clue."

"God, that's so nice to hear," I say. "Like, I'm sixteen, right? How the hell can I possibly know?"

"Exactly," Seth answers.

It's quiet for a while, and I get up the guts to ask the question that's been on my mind since Seth asked me out.

"That girl you were hanging out with in Austin. Was she . . . mad? That you ended things?"

Seth glances down at his knees. "I don't think so. I mean, she was a nice girl and everything, and we'd known each other for . . . forever, before we started going out last spring. She was fun to hang out with but it was like we were together because we thought we were supposed to be, I think."

"Oh," I say. "What's her name?"

"Samantha," Seth answers. "She was my first real girlfriend, I guess you could say."

I nod, and I wonder not for the first time if that means he's Done It, but I can't ask that. All I do is say that I think that Samantha is a pretty name.

"Yeah, it's okay, but not as cool as Vivian," Seth answers, and he kind of knocks his body into mine a little and I grin and look down into my lap, reminding myself for the tenth time this evening that this is real and not track number seven of my mental album titled *My Fantasy Boyfriend—Greatest Hits!*

"What about you?" Seth asks. "No boyfriend?"

"Nope," I say, staring out at the dark water. "Never."

Seth draws back and his eyebrows fly up. "You? But you're, like, the Moxie girl."

I flush. "Yeah, well, remember you're the only one who knows about that. And anyway, that's not exactly a plus around here. Most boys of East Rockport would consider that very un-girlfriend material."

Seth shakes his head. "Just proves the guys around here are dumb."

"They're gross, too," I answer, and I start telling him about the bump 'n' grab.

"That *is* gross," he says, "but it's not all the guys, right? I mean, I've found a few guys who aren't complete assholes. Like the guys who hang out in the quad before class. They talk about obscure baseball stats and I literally don't get anything they're saying, but they're not dicks anyway."

"Yeah, but those guys might as well not even exist at East Rockport," I answer, curling up into a tight ball as a brisk wind pushes past us. "Mitchell Wilson, Jason Garza, those dudes. They're the ones who matter. They, like, set the tone."

"So that's why you started *Moxie*."

"Yeah," I say. "I guess that's why I did it. It felt like a way to fight back but quietly. The only way I knew how to."

"Well," Seth says, "just remember that not all guys are like Mitchell Wilson. Not all guys are dicks."

I nod, but I feel prickly. My mouth slips into a little frown.

"Hey." Seth nudges me. "You okay?"

I look at him. He's amazing, but he isn't a girl. I take a deep breath. "I know all guys aren't dicks," I tell him. "I get it. But the thing is, when there are so many dickish dudes around you, it gets hard to remember that, you know?"

Seth nods slowly, like he's chewing over the words.

"Yeah," he says finally, "I hear you."

"But you're not a dick," I say in a rush.

He looks at me and smiles broadly, stretching out his arms wide. "Thank you! I gladly accept the honor of not-a-dick." Suddenly, he pops off the picnic bench and races a few feet in front of me into the sand. "Ladies and gentlemen of East Rockport, I'd like to accept this Not-A-Dick Award on behalf of all the guys out there who recognize it's gross as hell to do the bump 'n' grab," he shouts. "I'd like to thank my mother for raising me with the knowledge that she would disown me if I ever did something like that, and I'd like to thank my dad for backing her up."

He does a couple of bows as I applaud furiously before calling out, "You'd better hurry up, the orchestra is playing you off the stage."

"Just one more thank you," Seth says, like he's trying to fight off some imaginary awards show host pulling him into the wings. "I'd like to thank Vivian Carter for being such a cool girl and agreeing to go out with me, taking a chance that I might be not-a-dick in a town full of actual-dicks."

"Oh, it's nothing," I say, waving my hands in front of me, my face full of false modesty. "Honestly, no need to thank little old me." I'm laughing now, and hard, too.

Seth races up to me, and in the moonlight and the fluorescent lights of the nearby Holiday Inn, I can see his cheeks are red. He's breathing more quickly. He's looking at me in a way he hasn't all night. It's the look Meemaw started warning me about in the seventh grade.

A look that's full of Want.

"Hey." He takes my hand in his, his voice all husky. "Come on." He tugs at me, and I stand up and we head back to his Honda, and I'm not sure if I can make it there without passing out. We slide into the front seats and just after we slam the doors shut, Seth turns to me and says, "Vivian, I want to kiss you."

The small part of my brain that's left to process anything briefly realizes that I always thought my first kiss would happen standing up. But we're in a car, which for some reason seems more grown up.

"So . . . ," Seth asks, leaning in, his dark eyes looking right at me. "Can I kiss you?" His voice is soft, which makes everything he's saying sound dreamier and sweeter, if that's possible. I am memorizing his words. I am already playing them over and over in my mind.

"Yeah," I answer, my heart flooding. My face numb.

And Seth leans in. His hand slides up and around the back of my neck and his mouth is on mine and at first I can't help but think about the mechanics of it. Like the sense of his tongue against my tongue, soft and gentle and alive. Like the subtle *pop!* of our lips pulling apart before they go back together again almost immediately.

But it takes just a few milliseconds before those thoughts escape me and I'm kissing Seth Acosta and how do any two people who like each other not just kiss constantly? How do you do this and stop? Ever?

So the answer is we don't stop. Not right away, anyway. There in that Honda on the first night of winter break in the parking lot of the East Rockport public beach, Seth Acosta and I kiss and we kiss and keep kissing.

Lucy sends me texts full of explosions and firecrackers and little yellow heads with eyeballs bugging out.

Sara writes one long *OMG!!!*

Meg demands every detail including the color of Seth's car (like that matters).

Kaitlyn sends a selfie of herself screaming in joy.

But Claudia?

Nothing.

A full two hours after I get home from my date with Seth, my oldest best friend in the entire universe sends nothing in response to my gushing, excited texts. I eventually call her, but it goes straight to the freaky lady's voice telling me that the number is unavailable.

At midnight I give up, tossing my phone to the side. I sink deep under the covers, replaying all the kissing in my mind—in the car at the beach, and on the drive home when we kissed at the stoplights, and when Seth walked me to the front door and we kissed standing up. But at the back of my skull is a little voice that wonders where Claudia is or if she might be mad at me for some reason.

I can't figure it out. This isn't Moxie stuff, which has been what's seemed to irritate her lately. It has nothing to do with Lucy. And she was happy for me the first time Seth and I hung out and just as happy when I told her Seth and I had plans for Friday night.

Then I realize that Friday after school I never saw Claudia after lunch. I was too tripped up with my own giddiness over my upcoming night with Seth.

I reach around in the darkness until I find my phone on the floor.

Just let me know you're okay . . . I'm scared something's wrong . . . sorry I blabbed on about myself so much

I wait and wait and nothing, and finally I fall asleep with my

186

phone in my bed, my mind alternating between thoughts of kissing Seth and worrying about Claudia.

And then, before I know it, I feel a hand on my shoulder, gently shaking me awake.

"Vivvy, hey. Viv."

I blink, trying to sense what's going on. Sun is streaming in through the blinds.

"Am I late for school?"

I realize my mom is next to me, seated on the edge of my bed.

"No, sweetie, it's Saturday. It's Christmas break."

I rub my eyes, trying to wake up. "Oh, yeah."

"But Claudia's here to see you." My mom looks at me, her face clouded with concern. It's then that I look past my mother and see my best friend since forever standing in my bedroom door. She's dressed in black leggings and an oversized East Rockport Track sweatshirt. Her eyes are rimmed red. Her mouth is a tight line.

"Claudia?" I say, now wide awake. Claudia sniffles a little and holds her hand up in a tiny wave, and my heart breaks for her without even knowing why.

"I'll leave you two alone," my mom says, standing up and giving Claudia a squeeze around her shoulders before shutting my bedroom door.

"Come here," I say, crawling out from under my covers. I pat the bed and in a moment there she is, facedown on my comforter, head buried in my pink cowgirl sheets. She starts sobbing.

"Hey, hey," I say, cuddling up close. "What happened, Claudia? Please tell me what happened." But it's clear that I need to

187

let her cry first—that I need to let her sob—and so I sit and run through a list of horrible, awful things that could make my best friend break down.

Did somebody die? No, my mother would have heard about it already from Claudia's mom or Meemaw or someone else in the East Rockport gossip loop.

Did her parents split up? No, they've been together for a bajillion years and Claudia is always complaining about how they kiss with tongue even in front of her and her brothers.

Did she get in trouble at school? No, Claudia isn't a Goody Two-shoes, but she's not a troublemaker either.

Finally, she sits up and takes a big, shaky breath, then wipes the last few tears away from her cheeks.

"I'm sorry . . . that I didn't text you back last night."

I frown. "Claudia, fuck that! That doesn't matter. Don't apologize. I want to know what happened to you!" I squeeze her hands and then wrap my arms around her. I'm so much bigger than Claudia that I can always get a really good hold on her when we hug, and right now I'm especially grateful for it.

I wait for her to want to talk.

"Okay, so something happened to me yesterday. After lunch." She looks down at her hands. Her cheeks are pink. Blotchy hives are exploding on her neck and chest.

"What?" My heart is hammering.

"Remember how I left the cafeteria early? Because I had to get my gym clothes out of my gym locker to take them home and wash them over break?"

"Yeah," I say, nodding. "I remember."

"Well, when I was walking out of the girls' locker room, I ran into Mitchell Wilson." She sort of spits his name out—all four syllables. Then she shuts her eyes and shakes her head.

Something heavy starts descending over me, and I know I could be an actual giant and I would still feel like I'm being crushed.

"You know that hallway, right outside of the locker rooms?"

The hallway that's not that well-lit. The hallway that's usually empty. The hallway with no classrooms or coaches' offices or teachers hanging out, gossping with each other in the corners.

I nod, starting to feel sick.

"Well, Mitchell walks up to me, just, like, comes right at me, and does that fucking bump 'n' grab bullshit," she says. "Only . . . when he grabs me, he just, like, pins me up against the wall and he actually slides his hand up under my shirt. And he, like . . ." She pinches up her face, wincing. "He, like, grabbed me. Grabbed one of my breasts and squeezed it."

That motherfucking asshole.

"Oh, Claudia," I say, my voice soft. "Claudia, I'm sorry."

Claudia is crying again, and I realize that I'm crying, too.

"It gets worse," Claudia says, wiping the tears sliding down her cheeks with her fingers until she just gives up and lets them fall. "I told him to stop it. That he was hurting me. And he just, like, laughed it off, you know? He just made me stand there like that for what felt like forever, just pawing at me. I could feel his hot breath on my neck. And it hurt. It hurt so much."

My Claudia. The closest thing I have to a sister. The girl I've spent countless hours with collapsing in giggles and screaming

189

in laughter and whispering in hushed voices about our hopes and our dreams and our very worst fears.

"How did you get away?" I ask.

Claudia closes her eyes. "I didn't. He just stopped, eventually. And he, like, walked off." Her brown eyes open, and she looks at me again. "And you know what was so creepy? While he was messing with me, he had this look on his face. This dead look. Like I could have been anyone. Or anything."

I slide my hands around Claudia's again and squeeze them.

"That's not even the end of it," Claudia says. She sniffles.

I stare at Claudia. "Oh my God, did he come back?"

Claudia shakes her head. "No, it's not that," she says. "I went to see Mr. Shelly."

Mr. Shelly, one of the assistant principals. The one who got all over Jana Sykes for her dress-code violation. Principal Wilson's right-hand man.

"And what happened?" I have an awful sense of what the answer will be.

"Well, I went into his office," Claudia says. "I still can't believe I did that. Maybe I was just operating on autopilot, I don't know. But I went in there and I told him, well . . . I didn't go into the details, exactly. I just told him Mitchell had done the bump 'n' grab game to me and it upset me."

"Did you call it that? I mean, like, use that term? The bump 'n' grab game?"

Claudia nods.

"And he, like, knew what it meant?"

Claudia nods again. "Oh, yeah, you could totally tell he knew what it meant. I think they all know. I think they know it goes on and that's what those guys call it and nobody cares." Her voice is flat.

"So what happened after you told?" I ask Claudia.

Claudia twists up her mouth into a frown.

"He looked at me and told me that Mitchell was probably just joking and that I should take the break to relax and forget about it," Claudia answers. She's not crying anymore. She's just still. Mad. "And then he said I should probably take it as a compliment."

"Holy shit," I say.

We just sit there for a moment in silence. My mind can't help but pull back my memories of last night—of kissing Seth, of talking to him and just enjoying being with him. And now this. From so wonderful to so horrible in less than twelve hours. From drooling over an Amazing Boy to fuming over an Asshole Boy overnight.

"Did you tell your parents?" I ask.

Claudia shakes her head again. "No. When I was upset last night I just told them I wasn't feeling well. My mom would flip out and my dad would . . . I don't know what he would do, to be honest."

"You don't think he would want to murder Mitchell?"

Claudia shrugs, uncertain. "Maybe. I don't know. He loves the East Rockport Pirates. He used to play defensive end."

I want to tell Claudia she has to be wrong, that there's no way her dad would choose to support some small-town football team over his own daughter. But how can I even know I'm right?

"I'm tired of talking," Claudia says all of a sudden. "I just want to lie here and not think about anything." She flops back on my bed and stares at the ceiling. "But I feel bad. I should be asking you about your date."

I give her a gentle push. "Stop apologizing. Whatever. I can tell you about it later."

Claudia looks up at me and gives me a soft smile. The first one she's had since she walked into my bedroom.

"Just tell me if he kissed you. And if he was nice."

I grin. "Yes," I say. "And yes."

Claudia smiles a little bigger now. "Good," she says. "That helps."

I crawl off my bed so I can play a song for Claudia. It's another one by Bikini Kill, but it's one of their few slow ones. It's called "Feels Blind" and something about the way Kathleen Hanna's voice cries out—demanding to be heard as she sings about women and hurting and hunger and pain—makes me want to cry each time I hear it. But cry in a way that makes me feel good, like I'm confessing a scary secret. Or abandoning the heaviest load.

As the song plays, I can feel the drums thud in my chest, and I slide back into my bed and lie down next to Claudia. She's still staring at my bedroom ceiling, but I can tell she's listening.

"This song," she says, "it's pretty great."

"Yeah, it is," I say, and I scoot closer and loop my fingers through hers, and I squeeze her hand hard and I hope she feels in her heart that the squeeze means I'll be there for her. Always.

MOXie*

Moxie Girls Fight Back!

Issue #3
FREE!

So.... did you know?

* 56% of girls said they were harassed at least once in the past year

* 1/3 of girls harassed said they were the victims of unwelcome sexual comments or jokes

* 13% said they were touched in an unwelcome way

* 87% experienced detrimental effects from the harassment

- statistics from the American Association of University Women

If a boy bumps 'n' grabs you – TAG HIS LOCKER with a Moxie sticker! ★ ★

If a boy gropes you in the hallway – TAG HIS LOCKER with a Moxie sticker! ★ ★

If a boy thinks he can treat you like an object – TAG HIS LOCKER, TAG HIS CAR, ★ TAG HIS BACKPACK – TAG!!!!!

Moxie girls fight back!

CHAPTER SIXTEEN

I SMOOTH OUT THE PAGES OF *MOXIE*'S NEXT ISSUE ON THE COUCH. The glow of the Christmas tree in the corner of our den casts a soft golden light over the pages.

"Looks cool," Seth says.

"Did I show you what I'm putting inside each one?" I ask, handing him a stack of round, palm-sized stickers.

"Badass," Seth answers, flipping one around in his hands. "As long as one doesn't end up on my locker."

I raise an eyebrow, and my heart starts to race. "Definitely not."

"Like *definitely* not? Or . . . ?" At this Seth leans in toward me, his grin growing. He kisses my neck, just under my ear, and I catch my breath because it feels so good. Then he's kissing my mouth, pressing into me, the warmth of his chest against mine. He smells like spearmint. I can feel our bodies start to shift down into the soft couch cushions.

"Wait," I say, pushing him back a little, "don't squish *Moxie*." I take the issue and toss it on the coffee table. "It's my favorite issue so far."

"Mine, too," says Seth.

"Yeah?"

"Yeah," he answers, grinning. "Now where were we?" Seth says, like a guy in a cheesy movie, and we both start laughing before we start kissing, letting ourselves melt into the couch.

But soon the hoot, hoot of our owl-shaped kitchen clock reminds us that Seth has to leave. My mom will be home from work soon, and even though she knows that Seth and I have been hanging out almost every day over break, I don't think she'd be too jazzed to see us kissing on the couch.

Or does what we were doing constitute making out?

Either way, it would be best if my mother didn't see it.

"I wish you didn't have to go," I say. My lips sting, but in a good way.

"Me, too, but I'll see you at school tomorrow," Seth says, and somehow we stand up and make it to the back door. Seth kisses me one more time before ducking out and walking down the block to where his car is parked, out of sight and sound of

Meemaw and Grandpa next door. I touch my fingers to my mouth as he walks off, like by pressing my lips I can make what just happened even more real in my mind.

I have a boyfriend. An actual boyfriend.

Grinning to myself, I head back to the den and scoop up all the copies of *Moxie* and the stickers I ordered online using the Visa gift card Meemaw and Grandpa gave me for Christmas (along with new socks, a set of fancy pens, and a book of recipes for cakes and cookies—Meemaw is pinning a lot on that Magic Squares incident). I tuck the zines and stickers into my backpack as my mom walks in.

"Hey, sweets," she says.

"Hey," I say, kissing her on the cheek.

"You okay? Ready to venture back to school tomorrow?"

I roll my eyes. "As ready as I'll ever be. You okay?"

My mom sighs and drags her hands through her hair. As she pulls it up off her face, she looks younger for the tiniest second. Then she lets her hair drop, and she's Mom again.

"I just had a little, I don't know . . . argument, I guess . . . with John. He just worked my nerves a little is all." She pulls a pint of ice cream out of the freezer and my heart flutters a little. I shouldn't be glad that my mom is upset with John, but I can't help it.

"What happened?" I ask, hoping that my voice is full of enough real-sounding concern.

She shrugs and carefully peels back the lid of some Rocky Road. "Just this argument about politics. He said he didn't think Ann Richards was that great of a governor."

I stare at her, confused.

"Ann Richards, sweetie. I've told you about her. She was the governor of Texas back in the '90s and she was super tough and super smart." She taps her finger on the bright pink refrigerator magnet that reads, "Ginger Rogers did everything Fred Astaire did—just backward and in high heels."

"Ann loved quoting that line," my mother tells me, smiling faintly.

"Oh yeah," I say. I like hearing about tough ladies, but I'm anxious to make my mother relive something negative about John. "So what did John say?"

"Just that she wasn't the most fiscally responsible governor, which is bullshit, really." She takes another bite of ice cream and puts the pint back in the freezer, dumping the spoon in the kitchen sink without rinsing it. Then she looks up at the ceiling and sighs.

"Well, whatever, he's wrong," I say. "Ann Richards was awesome."

"She most certainly was, baby," my mother agrees.

"So what does that mean for you and John?" There's a hopeful catch in my voice, and I wonder if my mom picks up on it.

But my mother just laughs at me like I'm some kid, which rankles me a little. "Oh, sweetie, John and I are fine," she says. "Adults can disagree about politics sometimes. I mean, he didn't say she belonged in the kitchen barefoot and pregnant or anything."

I shrug. "I guess. But doesn't someone's politics reveal, like, a lot about them?"

My mother grins. "Sure, yes. I taught you that. But reasonable adults can disagree about certain things. John grew up in a very conservative home. He didn't even go to public school until he was a teenager, so he's had different life experiences and that's influenced his views in some ways. Not liking Ann Richards's financial policies doesn't make John evil."

"Okay," I say. "As long as you don't forget you're right and he's wrong."

My mother smiles. "I won't forget. Now get to bed. It's late."

As I slide under the sheets, I think about the copies of *Moxie* sitting in my backpack and Seth's mouth on mine and how cool Seth is about *Moxie*. I'm sure if Seth knows who Ann Richards is, he loves her. And if he doesn't know who she is, I'm convinced he would love her the minute I told him all about her.

It feels so good to tag Mitchell's locker first. Ten stickers. For each one I slap on, I think about Claudia. I think about how humiliated and angry and hurt she was in that empty hallway. I think about Mr. Shelly telling her to forget about it. I think about Mitchell's ruddy face and dead eyes. I think about his daddy letting him do anything he wants.

Slap, slap, slap. I like how loud each slap sounds, my hand making the metal locker reverberate each time I put up a new sticker.

Then I step back and admire my work. I realize my cheeks hurt from smiling.

Mitchell Wilson gets to read that he's an asshole ten times today. Hopefully more.

As the sun starts to stream in the hallway windows, I tag a few more lockers of the boys I know play the bump 'n' grab game. Once, I hear the sound of a janitor coming around the corner, and I duck into an empty classroom. I hold my breath as he walks by, the keys around his waist jingle jangling. His heavy steps are inches away, but he doesn't find me. If he did, I'd be quick with an excuse. I'd smile and come up with something. Because nothing is stopping me today. Especially not some guy.

By the time first period starts, zines and stickers have been distributed throughout all the girls' bathrooms on the first floor and most of the bathrooms on the second floor. By the time I head to history class, everyone is buzzing about it. I catch Jason Garza scowling and trying to peel the sticker on his locker off with his fingers, but he's having trouble.

When I ordered stickers, I made sure to order the kind with the "high bond label."

I smirk to myself.

"Please tell me you saw these?" Sara asks me as I walk into class. I catch Claudia reading the latest issue, a few stickers in her hand.

"Yeah, it's great, isn't it?" I say.

Sara nods, a smile spreading across her face. "It's brilliant."

"Hey, Claudia," I say, and when she looks up at me, I tell her Mitchell Wilson's locker is already covered in stickers.

"Seriously?" she asks, her eyes brightening.

"Seriously," I tell her. "But that doesn't mean you can't add another one. Ask to go to the bathroom during class and do it."

Claudia's eyebrows rise at my boldness. "Maybe," she says.

She tucks the zine and the stickers into her backpack, but half-way through Mrs. Robbins's dull lecture on something dull, Claudia raises her hand and asks to be excused. When she comes back, she winks at me.

That wink is worth everything. All the time spent making *Moxie*. All my Christmas money spent on stickers. Claudia's wink is worth all of that and then some.

All day long, the stickers spread like a contagious rash, black dots spilling out everywhere, more and more each class period. Girls are smart about how they do it, and the teachers are too dense to catch on. Bathroom breaks, trips to the nurse, requests for a drink at the water fountain. All provide opportunity to duck out and tag some boy's locker when no one is looking. After each bell rings, it's like the stickers have been breeding because there are more and more greeting us each time.

Moxie is winning.

And I started Moxie.

And then, on my way to English, my face glowing and my heart racing with pride, Marisela Perez does something magical.

Tim Fitzpatrick—a true asshole sophomore boy who thinks he's hot shit because he plays varsity basketball—decides to bump 'n' grab Marisela as we head to lunch. He gooses Marisela around the waist with his thick, clumsy fingers.

"Wait a minute," Marisela says, grabbing Tim's shoulder, her voice sticky sweet. "I have something for you." Dumb Tim falls for it. He holds still and stares at Marisela, like he's expecting a blow job right there in the hallway.

But Marisela just fishes into the pocket of her jeans, digs out a sticker, and ceremoniously pushes it on him. Right on his chest. She presses down hard enough that Tim actually mutters, "Ouch!" to which Marisela rolls her eyes and walks off, leaving Tim staring at his chest, angrily picking at the sticker that won't budge.

Lucy, who is standing next to me and witnesses the event, grips my arm and squeals as if she's in middle school and her favorite boy band member just strolled by.

"It's like I'm living in a feminist fantasy," Lucy says. "But it can't be a complete fantasy because Roxane Gay isn't here."

I grin and make a note to look up Roxane Gay later, and Lucy and I keep walking toward class when we spot Seth at the door of the classroom. Lucy eyes me pointedly and heads inside.

"Hey," he says, giving me a quick peck on the lips. I'm greeting my boyfriend in the hallway in front of everyone. It makes me feel, like, twenty-five.

"Hey," I say.

"The stickers are all over the place," he says, his voice low. "It's so cool."

"Thanks," I say, grinning at him. "It's catching on even more than I thought it would."

"You're such a rebel, Vivian Carter," Seth says, arching an eyebrow, and I feel like a firework.

In English, Mitchell Wilson and his crew scowl and stew in the back row, and when Mr. Davies picks Lucy to pass back the last round of grammar quizzes at the end of class, Mitchell sees it as a perfect opportunity to be an even bigger dick than usual.

"Hey," he says, eyeing Lucy as she slides his paper on his desk.

It has a 75 on it, circled in red. He probably did worse, but Mr. Davies likes football players.

"What?" Lucy says, her voice sharp.

"You're in that Moxie club, aren't you?" His beady eyes are staring her down, daring her to say yes. I imagine him groping Claudia in that hallway by the locker room, and I think I have enough anger in me to toss my desk over my head and aim it right for Mitchell.

"There's no Moxie club," Lucy says, turning her back on him. She hands out the last few papers and sits down in front of me.

"Yeah, fucking right there's no Moxie club," Mitchell says, raising his voice from the back row.

"Students, language," Mr. Davies mutters from his desk, like all of us have been cursing a blue streak, not just Mitchell. He goes back to shifting papers around in an endless circle on his desk.

Lucy doesn't turn around, but I can hear Mitchell's weaselly voice snaking through the room, threatening everyone with his particular brand of poison.

"You did that queer-ass bake sale for the girls' soccer team," he says. "You organized it. I saw you."

Out of the side of my eyes, I catch Seth watching the exchange. I notice Lucy's shoulders hunch up closer to her ears, like she's trying to protect herself. My heart is hammering, and I'm trying to figure out what to do. I glance at the clock. Five minutes left.

"You and your little man-hating, lesbo baking club," Mitchell continues under his breath.

My stomach churns. I want to smack Mitchell Wilson. I want to punch him right in the face.

I clench my fist. I shut my eyes for a moment.

Suddenly my hand is stretching out, up into the sky.

"Um, Mr. Davies?" I never talk in class. Ever. It's like when you hear your voice on a recording and it sounds totally bizarre to your ears, like it can't actually be you. That's what it's like to hear my voice out loud in a classroom.

"Yes, Viv?" Mr. Davies says, looking at me, surprised.

"I was wondering if you might be willing to review that last grammar concept?" I start, not caring that my cheeks are pink. Only caring that, for the moment, Mitchell has shut up. "I was a little lost on the . . . what did you call them, the gerundive phrases?"

And then, from across the room, Seth's voice.

"Yeah, me, too, Mr. Davies. I was a little lost, and we have five pages of homework on them, don't we?"

I glance at Seth, my eyes grateful.

Mr. Davies groans and runs his hand through his buzz cut like he'd rather not, but he eases out of his desk and starts lecturing again, and his presence in front of us is enough to shut Mitchell up. When the bell rings, Lucy turns to look at me.

"Thank you," she whispers.

By the end of the day, Moxie stickers are everywhere, and when I get to my locker to gather my stuff, I'm feeling more than proud of myself. That's when I spot Claudia darting through the hall-way with determination.

"Viv, did you hear?" she says, breathless.

"What?" I ask, slamming my locker door shut.

"Well . . . ," she says, but then she shakes her head. I can't tell if she's happy or scared or both. "You have to come see."

She tugs me by the wrist and drags me out the side door toward the faculty parking lot. As I follow, I hear the distinct buzz of voices building. Snippets of students saying, "No shit?" and shouts full of the giddiness that comes with good gossip. With the excitement of Something Finally Happening.

And there the something is, in the front row of the faculty lot. Right under the RESERVED FOR PRINCIPAL sign.

There, on the bumper of Principal Wilson's bright red, late model, extended cab Ford truck are four Moxie stickers, lined up one right after another like floats on parade.

YOU'RE AN ASSHOLE xoxo MOXIE   YOU'RE AN ASSHOLE xoxo MOXIE   YOU'RE AN ASSHOLE xoxo MOXIE   YOU'RE AN ASSHOLE xoxo MOXIE

CHAPTER SEVENTEEN

THE ASSEMBLY IS MANDATORY. AND GIRLS ONLY.

We file in during first period on Tuesday, and it hits me that I've never been in a space with so many girls before and no guys. Even though I'm sure we're about to be punished, something about it feels special, exhilirating even. It's just us. Just girls. I remember seeing some of my mom's old Riot Grrrl zines and flyers—how they advertised girl-only spaces and girl-only shows, or how they wouldn't let the boys come to the front of the stage when their bands were playing but reserved that space just for ladies, so all the women would feel safe.

But right now the East Rockport High School auditorium doesn't feel safe, especially with Principal Wilson standing on the stage, his arms crossed in front of him, his mouth a firm line.

"File in quickly, you're going too slow," he commands into the microphone.

"So what's going to happen to us?" Lucy says, tucking an arm into mine. "Will we be threatened with the gallows? Or burned at the stake? It's all going to go down very Salem Witch Trials. Mark my words."

Claudia's in front and she turns around, her face anxious.

"He does seem pissed, doesn't he? You don't think they know who did the stickers, do they?"

"*We* don't know who did the stickers, remember?" Lucy says. "Don't worry, Claudia."

"But I . . ." Claudia's voice drops to barely there levels. "I put one on a locker."

We continue getting jostled down the aisle of the auditorium as Lucy puts her arm around Claudia. "Claudia," she says, "I'm betting half of the girls in this room put one on a locker. Did you see the school yesterday? I'm sure Wilson is just going to blow off some steam and give us all a warning."

"But what if they have cameras?" Sara pipes up.

"They don't, so don't worry," I say. It's one thing I checked on before I distributed my first copies of *Moxie*. East Rockport High spends more money on football than security.

Still, my friends' nervousness is contagious. Maybe someone did spot something. Maybe somehow something has been traced back to somebody, namely me. Maybe Frank at U COPY IT is some undercover spy for Principal Wilson.

Stop it, Viv, you're being ridiculous.

As we take our seats, I notice Emma Johnson walking across the stage, taking the one empty seat next to Principal Wilson, who is standing at the microphone. She has her hands folded in her lap, her slender fingers wrapped around several index cards. She crosses her feet at the ankles and gazes out at all of us, like a warden at a women's prison.

"What is she doing up there?" I ask, but no one gets a chance to answer because Principal Wilson raises his hands to get our silence.

"Ladies of East Rockport, your attention, now," he barks, and my stomach burns at the sound of his voice. His beady little eyes remind me of a snake's. And of his son's.

We shift in our seats as Principal Wilson waits for total silence. Even after he gets it he waits a few beats more, his mouth turning into a small frown. Finally he starts talking again.

"Girls, to say I'm angry would be an understatement," he begins. "I'm livid. There are stickers all over boys' lockers and reports that girls are placing stickers on boys' shirts." I'm surprised he doesn't mention his truck. I hope it's because he's too embarrassed. "This destruction of school property must stop. This bad behavior must stop. Immediately. The cost to remove these stickers will eat into the school budget, so in the end, you're only hurting yourselves." I imagine the football budget won't be touched, but Principal Wilson's expression is so angry, his voice so stern, that I'm almost scared to think something rebellious for fear he might read my mind.

"Now it's my understanding this Moxie club has been doing bake sales in the cafeteria for the girls' soccer team," he continues, and my cheeks flood with heat. I work up the guts to glance at Lucy. Her name is on the club paperwork in the main office. But she just stares ahead, her expression icy.

210

"Raising money for an athletic team is a noble goal and is allowed on school grounds, but now that this graffiti has become such a problem in our fine school, I have no choice but to ban the Moxie club from any future activities," continues Principal Wilson. "Any girl who is caught defacing school property or using this Moxie label will be suspended immediately and I will move to have her expelled."

The audience of girls breaks into whispers.

"Can he really do that?" Sara murmurs.

But no one needs to answer her. We all know Principal Wilson can do whatever he wants.

"For those of you applying to college, I don't have to tell you what that kind of consequence will look like on your transcript, but let me spell it out for you," he adds. "No school would accept such a girl." I think about the college fund Mom has been building for me since I was in kindergarten. I remember the years she worked Christmas Eve and the times she pulled double shifts to be able to sock away some extra money.

"Now in conclusion, I would like to have your class vice president, Emma Johnson, share a few words with you," Principal Wilson says. At this, Emma tosses her hair over her shoulder and steps up to the microphone. She gazes down at her note cards for a moment, but she never uses them as she speaks. Instead she looks toward us, but I can tell she's using that public speaking trick of talking at the tops of our heads. She's not really making eye contact with any of us.

"Y'all, Principal Wilson asked me to talk with you today about the importance of being a lady," she begins, her voice soft and even. She pauses and looks out, then takes a breath and keeps going.

"Being a lady means acting in such a way that you show respect to other people and places, too. Places that should be close to your heart, like our school. East Rockport High is our home away from home, and we need to treat it as such when we're here. So I'm asking you, girl to girl, to please stop all this nonsense with the stickers and remember to hold yourself to the standards of a Texas lady." She gives us a little nod to punctuate her speech, then steps back and sits down. There's a smattering of applause from a handful of girls in the front row—Emma's friends. But mostly I want to squirm. To see one of our own—even someone who always seems to have it all—shilling for the administration is super gross and weird. It's almost enough to make me feel sorry for Emma, but not quite.

Then Principal Wilson steps back up to the microphone.

"I hope you take those words to heart, girls, and I hope you take my warning very, very seriously," he says. "Now you're dismissed. Get to your first period classes immediately."

Quietly, we file up the ratty red carpet that covers the aisles. Girls are looking at each other with wide eyes and open mouths. The buzzing and sense of possibility that I felt yesterday has fizzled into fear. My heart sinks.

Up ahead Assistant Principal Shelly is standing by the main doors of the auditorium, watching us exit.

"Lucy Hernandez?" he says as my friends and I head toward him.

"Yeah?" says Lucy. Not yes, but yeah.

"Try 'Yes, sir,' next time," Mr. Shelly says, scowling. Girls coming up the aisles glance at us as they pass by, then start whispering to each other. Claudia is standing just behind us with Sara and the others, and when I turn to check on her, her face is strained.

"I need you to come with me," Mr. Shelly says, curling his index finger toward himself like Lucy is a misbehaving toddler and he's about to send her to the naughty chair.

"For what?" Lucy asks, and the tiny little tremor in her voice tells me that her level of bravado has fallen a notch or two.

"We'll discuss it in my office," he says. And just like that, Lucy is spirited away down the crowded halls of East Rockport.

"Shit," I say once they're out of earshot, and I turn to look at Claudia, Sara, and the others.

"I wonder if she did make those stickers," Claudia says, frowning.

"I really believe she didn't," I say, turning my focus toward the direction where Mr. Shelly went with Lucy. I should go after them. I should at least tell Mr. Shelly that I helped plan the bake sale. But my feet don't move. Shame courses through me.

"What do you think's going to happen to her?" Sara asks.

"I don't know," I answer.

Claudia bites her bottom lip. "Even if she did make those stickers, she doesn't deserve to get in tons of trouble," she says. "I think girls used them for a reason. Not just to mess with school property."

"Yeah," I say, and as my eyes meet Claudia's, I know that she's a Moxie girl now for real. But given Principal Wilson's warnings, being a Moxie girl can only mean danger.

We don't see Lucy in any of our classes or at lunch. When I text her, she doesn't respond. All day long I can't sit still, constantly checking my phone, willing it to buzz with some message from Lucy telling me she's okay. Guilt keeps building inside me, leaving me half-queasy.

"I'm worried," I tell Seth when he meets me at my locker at the end of the day. "She's going to take the fall for everything because she put her name on that club form to do the bake sale."

Seth scratches the back of his neck and frowns. "But they can't prove anything, right?"

"That doesn't matter here," I say, my voice barely a whisper. "If they want to pin it on her, they will."

Seth shakes his head. "You make this place sound like it's run by the Russian mob or something."

I can tell he doesn't get it. "Sometimes it feels like that," I say, my voice tight.

Just then, at last, I get a text.

Can you please please please come over? To my house? I'm home now. Do you remember where I live? 9762 Memorial? I really need to talk

"Oh, good, it's Lucy," I say, holding up the phone as proof. "She's at home. Maybe the school sent her home early? God, I hope she wasn't suspended." Before Seth answers, I text Lucy back that I'm on my way.

214

"I need to see her. Think you can give me a lift?" I ask, lugging my backpack over my shoulder.

"Yeah, no problem," says Seth, but he doesn't sound like it's no problem.

We trudge out to the parking lot, dodging other students. It's weirdly quiet between us. "Thanks again," I say, eager to fill the space. "I just want to make sure she's okay."

"Yeah, I get it," Seth says, clicking open his Honda. "So when do you want to watch the documentary we were going to check out this afternoon?"

"Oh, yeah, that," I answer, sliding into the front passenger seat. Suddenly I feel like the subject of one of those stupid quizzes in the teen magazines that I used to read in middle school. ("Are You a True Blue BFF or a Fair-Weather Friend?" "Is It Love or Lust?" "Do You Put Your Guy or Your Gal Pals First?") Lucy needs me. I promised to hang out with Seth. I don't want either one of them to be disappointed in me. I want to see Lucy and find out what happened to her today. And I want to kiss Seth again. I *really* want to kiss Seth again.

But I also want him to get how much trouble Lucy could be in, and how much that matters to me. And I don't know that he does.

"I'm sorry, I just feel like everything that's happened to Lucy is all my fault . . . which it is."

"No, no, I'm being a dick," Seth insists. "You don't have to apologize. You should be with your friend." He nods his head, like he's trying to prove to me how he really feels. And maybe to himself, too.

"We can hang out tomorrow? And every day this week? And maybe this weekend?" Why is everything I say coming out like a desperate question? Having a Real Boyfriend is so much more complicated than having a Fantasy Boyfriend.

"It's cool, Vivian," Seth says. "I should probably make some more guy friends around here. Maybe start brushing up on my obscure baseball stats so I fit in more with the guys I eat lunch with." He shoots me a warm smile. The kind of smile that makes me want to evaporate into a mushy, crushy girl puddle. Then he asks for directions, and it's not long before we pull up in front of Lucy's grandmother's house.

"Thanks for the lift," I say, turning toward him. "And I'm really sorry we couldn't hang out."

But Seth doesn't say anything. Just leans in and kisses me, all soft and warm and perfect, and my head is dizzy as I make my way up the front walk to the door.

"Hey," Lucy says, pulling open the door in one swift motion just as I make a move to knock. "I was watching for you. Thanks for coming." Her face looks a little pale, and she's not smiling.

As I walk in, I realize how little I really know about Lucy's life outside of school, and how much you learn when you see where someone lives. Lucy's grandmother's house is crammed with large pieces of dark wood furniture and tons of knick-knacks, like a collection of ceramic sewing thimbles on the coffee table and a shelf full of nothing but conch shells. The walls are decorated in gold-and-white-striped wallpaper, and there are framed photographs everywhere. The smiling eyes of people I can only guess are Lucy's relatives watch my every move. I focus on a few that must be of Lucy as a little girl, complete with an infectious grin and smiling eyes.

"Are you here by yourself?" I ask.

"No," she says. "My grandmother and little brother are in the den watching television. Wanna say hi?" She doesn't wait for an answer as she leads me toward the back of the house, where a woman with salt-and-pepper hair is curled up with a little boy on the couch. They're watching PBS Kids. Lucy's brother never breaks his gaze from the television screen.

"Hey, Abuelita," Lucy says, waving. "This is my friend from school? Vivian?"

"Hi, dear," the woman says to me, nodding. "Are you here to help keep our girl out of trouble? She's never been sent home early from school before." She pitches an eyebrow up high, and Lucy just sighs and rolls her eyes.

"Abuelita, I told you it's not like that," she says, and she drags me by the wrist out of the den and up the stairs.

"God, I love her, but I really, really want us to get our own place," Lucy says, leading me into a tiny room the size of a walk-in closet. She shuts the door behind me, and I let my backpack slide to my feet. Lucy kicks off her shoes and I follow.

"This is where I sleep," she says, motioning her hand around. "At least I get my own space. My poor brother sleeps on the couch downstairs and keeps all his stuff in my parents' bedroom."

Lucy sits down on the unmade twin bed that's tucked into the corner and motions for me to join her. It's really the only place to sit since the floor is covered in books and papers and schoolwork. The rest of the room is covered, too, with every inch of wall space decorated in postcards and music posters and ripped-out pages from magazines. Along the side of the one tiny window next to Lucy's bed is a series of bright-yellow Post-its. Each one has a single word on it, spelling out the vertical message YOUR SILENCE WILL NOT PROTECT YOU. When Lucy catches me glancing at it, she tells me it's a quote from a poet named Audre Lorde.

"Cool," I say. "I like it."

"Yeah, she was a badass. She died a long time ago, though."

"How long until your family gets its own place?" I ask.

"Well, my mom just got a job doing medical billing at the same retirement home my dad works at," she says, "so it's looking up. Maybe by the end of next month."

"That's good," I say, nodding my head. I'm trying to act supportive and casual, but suddenly, I feel like I'm going to cry. I keep picturing mean Mr. Shelly marching Lucy down the hall. I keep imagining her all alone with him.

"So," she starts, dragging her long hair up and tying it effortlessly into a knot on top of her head, "do you want to know the gory details?"

"Please tell me you're not in huge trouble," I say.

"Well, I'm not going to be named student of the week anytime soon, that's for sure," Lucy says, her voice softening. "Mr. Shelly hauled me into his office, wanted to know all about the Moxie club. He said everything I told him would be reported back to Principal Wilson and they're all watching me." At this, Lucy's cheeks flush, and she stares down at the bedspread. "I told him I had nothing to do with the stickers. I mean, I left out the part about putting them on lockers, which of course I did. But I didn't make them."

"Did he believe you?" I ask, my heart fluttering.

"Maybe," says Lucy, still not making eye contact with me. "It was hard to tell. But I wasn't lying, Viv. I really didn't make them. You believe me, don't you?" She finally looks up. The half-queasy feeling I had earlier is a full-on wave of nausea now.

"I believe you," I insist. God, I'm a shithead.

"Mr. Shelly said if I do anything Moxie related, I'm suspended and probably expelled," Lucy continues.

"And then what happened?" I ask.

"Then he sent me home early," Lucy says with a shrug. "He said it wouldn't go down as a suspension on my record *this* time, but he still wants me to take it as a serious warning or whatever." She scowls, but then, out of nowhere, her eyes glass over and a tear or two tumbles down her cheek.

"Fuck it," Lucy says, wiping the tears away. "I'm sorry, I hate crying in front of people."

"No, it's okay," I say, looking around the room for a tissue or a napkin or even a semi-clean piece of laundry for her to wipe her eyes with.

"Don't worry about it," she says, shaking her head and sniffling. "I'm fine. I'm . . . fine."

I can't remember the first time I saw Claudia cry or the first time she saw me do it. It was always something we knew we could do in front of each other, but with Lucy, our friendship still feels fresh. Fragile even. I'm not sure if I should hold her in

219

my arms like I did the morning Claudia came over to tell me about Mitchell. Lucy's eagerness to shut down her crying makes me think she wouldn't like that, so I just scoot a little closer to her and rub her shoulder a bit.

"I'm sorry, Lucy," I say. "I'm sorry this happened." *Because of me.*

Lucy wipes at her red eyes with the edge of her black T-shirt. "You know what pisses me off the most?" she asks, and without waiting for my answer, she keeps going. "In Houston I never got in trouble. Ever. I was, like, a super nerd in my school. I was a kick-ass student and in, like, twenty clubs. I was even on the student advisory board. Teachers liked me. The principal fucking loved me!" Lucy moves her hands in the air as she talks, emphasizing her points.

"They had a student advisory board?" I ask, my eyes widening at the idea.

"Yes!" Lucy says, half-wistful, half-angry. And with that she slumps down and curls up in the corner of her bed. "I know I come off like some tough girl here or whatever because I actually care about social issues and stuff," she continues, "but honestly, I really just want to do well in school and go to college. I can't get into serious trouble because that could affect stuff like admissions and scholarships and everything."

"I know," I say, nodding. "I really know. And I'm really, really sorry you had to deal with all this." I reach out tentatively and stroke the top of Lucy's dark curls. She looks up and manages a half smile and the two of us sit there, quiet except for Lucy's occasional sniffles. I lean my head against the cool glass of the tiny

220

bedroom window and peer down at the front yard. Lucy's little brother is racing his scooter up and down the sidewalk, his dark hair flying out behind him, not a care in the world. At last Lucy says, "You're a good friend, Viv. I'm really glad I met you."

"I'm really glad I met you, too," I say. But my stomach churns. A good friend would tell Lucy the truth right now. A good friend wouldn't let her carry the weight of everything.

I open my mouth. Then I shut it.

Maybe I'm not a good friend. Just a chicken.

"You know, Moxie has been a total saving grace for me," she says, taking a deep breath, "but I kind of hope it takes a break for a bit. Until shit calms down."

It stings to hear those words, and it hurts to see Lucy so defeated. If I had the guts to admit I started Moxie, maybe Lucy would want to keep the fight going. The only trouble is, I think part of Moxie's power is that it *is* a secret who started it. Would it be as powerful if everyone knew it was my idea?

"I wonder if whoever started it got freaked out enough by Principal Wilson to stop," I wonder out loud, to see what Lucy will say.

"Whoever started Moxie doesn't seem like they'd get too frightened too easily," she answers. "But I'm scared. I definitely think the administration is going to be keeping a super close eye on all us girls. I don't know. I hate to say it, but I really do think Moxie should take a hiatus." She frowns.

"Yeah, probably," I say, trying to shake the empty feeling that's come over me. Did I really just decide to stop Moxie?

Just then my phone buzzes, and I slide it out of my pocket.

Hey how's Lucy doing?

"Ooh, is that your guy?" Lucy says, kicking me gently in the shin.

I shoot her a look. "Maybe."

"Well, if it isn't, he better not know about whoever it is whose texts make your face go all goofy like that."

"Look, he just wants to know how you are," I tell her, showing her the screen.

"Wow, an East Rockport guy who isn't a dick," Lucy says. "He should be, like, bronzed or something."

I laugh out loud and text Seth back.

She's doing okay considering but we're still hanging out . . . can I call you later?

A second later Seth writes back.

Yeah sure . . . just don't forget your pathetic lonely boyfriend over here

I blush briefly. Boyfriend. It's the first time Seth's used that word with me.

I won't forget you . . . I promise

"Okay, enough, lover," says Lucy. "Let's go downstairs and see if we can raid my grandmother's Klondike bar collection in the freezer." At that she pulls herself off the bed and heads for the door of her bedroom. I slide my phone back into my pocket, my head spinning at the idea of a cute boy who calls himself my boyfriend and my heart aching at the feeling that all of a sudden Moxie has stepped on the brakes. I'm not sure how I'm supposed to make sense of it, but I guess it would be asking too much for 100 percent of my life to be 100 percent awesome 100 percent of the time.

CHAPTER EIGHTEEN

I'M MAKING OUT WITH MY BOYFRIEND.

Even though Seth and I have been going out for almost two months—since Christmas, really—sometimes I have to stop (briefly) in the middle of a make-out session and consciously recognize that yes, Seth Acosta is my boyfriend. And I get to make out whenever I want.

The way he kisses that place right behind my ear.

The way he can't stop touching my hair, running his fingers through it over and over until I get goose bumps.

The way he looks at me with his dark eyes, his cheeks flushed, before he collapses into me and we kiss again.

Only normally this happens in his car or by the beach or in my living room before my mother gets home from work. To-night it's happening in his house—in his house decorated full of strange paintings and sleek, shiny furniture—the total opposite of Meemaw's country kitchen vibe. (There's not a damn rooster knickknack in sight, that's for sure.) Making out in this house makes the making out seem more grown-up somehow. Or at least more sophisticated.

Finally, we pull apart, catching our breaths.

"My parents are going to be here soon," he says, blinking. Trying to steady himself.

I peer at him from my end of the couch. I really want to attack him again.

"Yeah," I say, "I don't want my face to look all, like, make out-ey when they get here."

"I didn't realize *make out-ey* was a word," Seth says, grinning.

"It totally is." A smile breaks out on my face, and I lean in and kiss him again.

It's a testament to how super crazy I am about Seth that I would even risk making out with him in his house so soon before his mom and dad are set to arrive with dinner. I've never even seen them before, but Seth's mom insisted I come over today, Friday—the weekend before Valentine's Day—so we could meet in person.

"She's just, like, into knowing who you are, since we've been hanging out," Seth explained to me a few days ago when he asked me if I would mind coming over.

"Are you blushing?" I'd asked him.

"No," Seth had answered, even though he totally had been.

Finally, Seth and I manage to stop messing around and it's a good thing, too, because just moments later his parents come through the door carrying white plastic bags full of takeout from the House of Beijing, the one Chinese place in the entire East Rockport area. Delicious smells float in with them, and my stomach growls just a little.

"Vivvy?" a female voice asks, and I stand up from the couch and see Seth's mom. Long graying hair in a tight ponytail. Beautiful face with a slash of red lipstick in the middle of it. Black jeans and a black T-shirt with a silver scribble running down the middle. Silver and turquoise bangles line both wrists. She walks right up to me and hugs me without warning. She smells of baby powder.

"I've *so* been looking forward to meeting you, honey!"

"Hi," I say, anxious about getting this woman to like me and wondering what the right thing is to say. It turns out I don't need to say anything. Seth's mom introduces herself ("Please call me Zoe. And please call Seth's dad Alejandro, okay?") and then she doesn't stop talking. Like, at all. Not as she takes out the bright green Fiestaware from the cabinets to set the table. Not as she slides out her phone and taps at it for a moment or two. Not as she slips an arm around Alejandro and kisses him on the cheek in a way that feels a little more intimate than I'd expect from people who've been married for a hundred years.

She talks about Austin and East Rockport and art and politics and the weather and the lack of good ethnic food in the area and soul music and manicures and how she likes my boots. She talks about how she just found and ordered a vintage Italian parasol online that she really loves, and she talks about how she thinks she's just had a breakthrough on her recent commissioned piece. ("I just need to keep listening to it sing to me, you know?")

Her voice is knowing and lilting and sure of itself, and by the time all of us sit down at the groovy modern all-white kitchen table and chairs, I'm not sure if I should be smiling or nodding or laughing at everything Zoe Acosta says. But I'm pretty sure I'm exhausted.

That's when Alejandro offers me some wine.

"Red or white, Viv?" he asks, a bottle in each hand. He's younger than Zoe. Handsome like Seth. A tattoo of a snake slides down his left arm and wraps itself around his wrist.

I thought my mom was cool, but honestly next to Seth's mom and dad, she looks like the president of the PTO.

"Oh," I say. I glance at Seth, who's sitting across from me, calmly scooping moo goo gai pan onto his bright green plate.

"You don't have to have any, sweetie, but we're okay with Seth having a little bit of wine with his dinner," Zoe says.

"I don't want any," Seth says, not looking up. He seems tense, somehow, but I'm not sure if I'm imagining it.

"I'm . . . okay, too," I say. My mom has let me have a sip of her wine in the past when I was curious ("Don't tell Meemaw, okay?") and I've had my fair share of crappy semi-cold cans of beer at stupid parties when people's parents were out of town, but I've never been offered alcohol by an adult in a way that felt so casual.

Alejandro doesn't offer me wine again, and he and Zoe spend the rest of the meal chatting among themselves, with Zoe inserting a simple question or two directed at me every so often, like was I born in East Rockport and what do I think I want to study in college and so on. I manage simple, to-the-point answers and then sit back and listen as Zoe picks up from where she left off before she asked me anything, sliding back into conversation about her favorite topic: herself.

As Alejandro starts clearing the table and Zoe begins to brew coffee, Seth shoots me a look that clearly reads desperate. His eyebrows arched, he carefully mouths, "Let's go." I shrug, scared of appearing rude. But Seth just stands up, clears his dishes and mine, and says, "Well, look, I think I've got to be getting Vivian home."

"But you just got here!" Zoe shouts, turning and walking toward me, clutching my hands in hers like I'm about to journey into the woods with no plan to ever return.

"She and her mom have a thing," he answers, outright lying.

Zoe performs an exaggerated pout, her mouth sliding down into a severe upside-down U.

"Well, we'll let you go only if you and your mom come by one night for dinner, all right, *preciosa*?" Her Spanish accent is awful. She puts her hands on her hips and Alejandro comes over from the kitchen sink and scoots his arms around her waist and kisses her on the neck.

"You and your mom should definitely join us one night," Seth's dad says, lifting his gaze and smiling at me. I notice he has tiny diamond earrings—one in each ear.

"You ready, Vivian?" Seth says, pocketing his keys off the counter.

"Sure," I say, standing up and offering Zoe and Alejandro my most polite smile. "It was so nice to meet you. Thanks for a delicious dinner."

227

"Thank you for being the cutest thing ever," Zoe says, slipping out of Alejandro's grip and swallowing me up in one last suffocating hug.

Outside in Seth's car, he slides his key in the ignition, but instead of starting the engine, he just looks at me and slumps against the driver's seat.

"And those were my parents," he says, sounding like a sideshow barker who's been introducing the same carnival act for years.

I smile and try to think of what I want to say.

"They were . . . nice. Really."

"They drive me nuts," Seth says, starting up the car. "Wanna go to the beach? It's not too cold."

"Yeah, sure." I pick out a song by this all-girl band from Louisiana that I just found out about and Seth nods approvingly, but I can tell he's still feeling off about the dinner. "Your parents really are nice, they're just . . ." I search for the word. "They're intense."

"I mean, they're fine," Seth says. "It's not like I've got any reason to complain. They bought me a car. They kind of let me do what I want. They're not assholes or anything. I mean, I think they're fundamentally, like, decent people. It's just that they're really, really into being themselves. Especially my mom."

I nod, peering out the window of Seth's car, watching East Rockport at night zip past. I think about my mom moving back to her hometown after my dad died. Working hard to put herself through school. Raising me as a single parent and always letting me know in big and small ways how much I matter. She always put me first, to the point where I think maybe she forgot to have her own life.

"I wonder if my mom hasn't been into herself enough," I say.

"Yeah? What do you mean?"

I'm still working it out in my head, so I speak slowly. "Well, she basically hated living here when she was a teenager and she had this whole plan to leave East Rockport, and she did it. Then because of me she had to come back and live next door to her mom and dad. She works long hours to make ends meet and does it all on her own. This guy John that she's dating, he's only the second boyfriend she's had in my whole life."

Seth pulls the car into the public beach parking lot. I can see a few other cars here, parked down the row. It's prime make-out territory tonight.

"Wanna get out and walk for a while?" he asks.

"Yeah."

We maneuver by a few empty beer cans and an abandoned green-and-yellow beach towel, and Seth takes my hand in his. The lights of East Rockport twinkle at us from the other side of the bay. If you can ignore the fishy smell in the air, it's almost romantic.

"So you think your mom will ever leave?" Seth asks. "After you do?"

I shrug. "Who knows? I think at this point she's probably pretty settled. Honestly, things with John seem pretty serious." I pause, and Seth waits for me while I think. "I know I complain about him because he voted Republican, but the truth is, she really seems to like him and he does actually seem okay.

I guess it is good for my mom to do something that makes her happy."

"I'm sure my parents will head back to Austin after this crazy small-town Texas experiment is over," he says. "They always follow their whims."

I'm seized by a horrible feeling. "But not right away, right? I mean, you don't think they'll get tired of East Rockport anytime soon?" I try to make my voice sound casual.

But Seth grins. "Why, would you miss me or something?"

"Shut up," I say. "And yes."

"I think their East Rockport performance art piece will probably last until I finish high school at least. So I'm not going anywhere."

Now it's my turn to grin. We walk to the picnic tables and sit down next to each other. Seth squeezes my hand. I lean my head on his shoulder.

"I liked meeting your parents," I say.

"Well, I'm glad they didn't totally overwhelm you," Seth says. "They're just weird. God, this one time my mother actually . . ." He stops, like his brain just caught up with his mouth. "Forget it."

"Now you have to tell me."

"It's embarrassing."

"What?" I insist, elbowing him a little.

Seth looks out at the bay as he answers. "My mom literally bought me a box of condoms for my sixteenth birthday after I started going out with Samantha," he says. "She wrapped them in fancy wrapping paper and put a bow on them and everything."

Seth owning condoms. Seth having sex with Samantha. Seth wanting to have sex with me. Seth and me having sex. Condoms, sex, Seth, sex, sex, and sex. That's essentially what runs through my mind in the seconds after Seth speaks.

"Did you have to unwrap the present in front of her?"

"Yes!" Seth says, shouting and laughing at the same time. "She put the box on my dinner plate. My dad took a picture. I can only hope to God it's not online somewhere."

"You are not serious."

"I am serious."

"Holy shit."

"Exactly. My mom told me it's what the Dutch do and she thought it was, I don't know, progressive or something."

"Wow," I say, but my heart is hammering. I muster up the courage to ask. "So you and Samantha . . . ?"

Seth shakes his head no, just slightly.

"We never did. I don't know . . . I mean, I was . . . *interested*, I'm not going to lie. But she wasn't sure. So it just, like, never happened."

I tuck some hair behind my ear, suddenly feeling bold.

"So you've never, like, done it?"

"No," he says. His voice drops to almost a whisper. "You?"

"No!" I say, incredulous. "I told you I've never even gone out with anyone before."

"Okay, okay," he says, squeezing my hand again and laughing a little. "I was just wondering."

I rub my thumb over one of Seth's knuckles. I breathe in the minty, yummy smell of him.

231

"I think if you like someone a lot, like, a *lot*, and you really care about them, and you've been together for a while, it's okay, though," I whisper, my body humming. It's what I've always believed to be true. Even before I met Seth.

"Yeah," Seth says. "Me, too." Bubbles are exploding under my skin and my cheeks are warm and I'm a little dizzy. I lean into Seth and we kiss and somehow it's like a new kind of kissing. Kissing full of even more possibility, which is both scary and exciting.

Eventually I have to be getting home, so after one final kiss we pry ourselves apart and head back to his car. As Seth drives toward my house he says, "Valentine's Day is coming up."

"Okay," I tell him, shooting him a look, "but I'm not having sex with you next week."

Seth bursts out laughing. "I know! I was just pointing it out. Like that this thing, this societally approved day of romance, is occurring next week."

"Yeah, Wednesday. Please don't buy me a stuffed teddy bear from the Walgreens."

"What?" Seth says, raising an eyebrow. "Oh, have we just met? Hi, I'm Seth."

"The couples at East Rockport get really into Valentine's Day in this super-cheesy way," I say. "Lots of teddy bears that say I Wuv U on the tummies. Lots of cheap chocolate and grocery-store roses."

"I could never do that to a Moxie girl," Seth says, pulling into my neighborhood.

"Ugh, don't say that, it makes me depressed." I frown at my reflection in the passenger window.

"I'm sorry, I didn't mean it to," Seth offers.

"It's okay," I say. "I just wish things were different." The heady, awesome day that the girls tagged the school with Moxie stickers seems like a million years ago. Since Principal Wilson's threats at assembly and Lucy getting into trouble, things have gone back to East Rockport's version of normal. Mitchell and his friends still ask girls to make them a sandwich. There was a brief but vicious streak of dress code checks at the end of January. We haven't even tried to have another bake sale for the girls' soccer team because doing it under a different name just isn't as exciting.

"It's cool you tried, but it's hard to believe anything will ever permanently change that school," Seth says, his headlights illuminating my street. "At least you know you have one more year and then you're out of there."

I frown, a little irritated. "Maybe, but it's not like there aren't going to be girls left behind after I leave. I didn't do Moxie for me. I did it for girls." I shake my head a little. "Forget it, that sounds like I have some huge crazy ego or something."

"No, I get it," Seth says, pulling into my driveway. I look up and see the lights are on. My mom's home.

"I don't know if you could really get it," I say, sighing. "Not until someone plays the bump 'n' grab game with you."

"You can always play the bump 'n' grab game with me, if that helps," Seth says, and the tiny part of me that wishes he wouldn't make a joke of it disappears as soon as we press our lips together.

"See you later," he says with a grin, and I melt for the millionth time that night.

When I get inside, my mom is curled up on the couch, watching television.

"How was dinner?" she asks.

"Okay. Seth's parents are these artists from Austin and they're a little . . . I guess you could say intense."

"Oh man, I know the artist-from-Austin type," my mom says.

"I'm gonna get some ice cream," I tell her. "You want some?"

"Sure, I'd love it." She seems pleased. Maybe because we haven't hung out like this in a while.

As I scoop out two bowls of chocolate and join her on the couch, I tell my mom about Zoe and Alejandro and even do an impression of Zoe, including her bad Spanish accent. My mother laughs hard.

"Don't laugh," I tell her. "They want both of us to join them for dinner one night." My mother rolls her eyes but she keeps on laughing, and I'm glad. It's been too long since we laughed together, talked over our days together, cuddled on the couch together. I wonder if John makes her laugh as much as I do sometimes. I hope he does.

We each take a few mouthfuls and then my mom says, "So it seems like you and Seth are getting kind of . . . do people your age say 'getting serious' anymore?"

"Mom, please."

"I'm just saying you're spending a lot of time together. I want to make sure you don't have any questions."

I think about Seth's mother gift wrapping condoms and leaving them on his dinner plate. My cheeks redden just a bit.

"Mom, I promise you, if I have any questions, I will ask them. But no, it's fine."

"Fine?"

I give her a pointed look. "I really like him. A lot."

My mom swallows a spoonful of ice cream and smiles. "Just asking. Don't attack me."

I decide I need to change the subject.

"Where's John? I thought you'd be going out."

"He had the late shift. I might meet him for breakfast tomorrow. Wanna come?"

I shrug. "Maybe. You want me to?"

"It would be nice."

"Yeah," I say. "Okay."

My mom puts her ice-cream bowl down on the coffee table and leans in closer. Her long hair tickles my cheek.

"Thank you. I know you're not a fan of John," she says, her voice soft. A little sad.

"No, it's not that, Mom . . . ," I begin. I think about Seth's mom and how she makes her life all about her, and about my mom and how she makes so much of her life about me. I slide my own bowl of ice cream next to my mother's and nuzzle under her arm. "Mom, do you ever regret getting stuck here in East Rockport because of me?" It's easier to ask this since I'm not looking her directly in the eyes.

"No, of course not," my mother answers. "I got away for a bit. I saw the world. I had lots of fun." I think about the MY MISSPENT YOUTH box.

235

"Do you ever wonder what would have happened if my dad hadn't died?" I ask.

There's a pause, and I can feel my mother's chest slowly rise and fall. "Of course," she says, and her voice cracks just the tiniest bit. "But in this life you have to deal with what happens. You have to take what comes at you. And coming back here . . . I was able to finish school. I made my peace with Meemaw and Grandpa. They got to see their granddaughter grow up. Those are good things."

"Yeah," I say. "That's true."

"I know John isn't who you expected me to end up with—if you even imagined me ending up with anyone at all," my mother says, reaching over and running her gentle fingers through my hair. "Truth be told, when I was your age, I wouldn't have expected me to end up with him either. But I really like him, Viv. I really enjoy being with him."

I peer up at my mom, so she can see my eyes. I want her to know I mean it when I say, "I'm glad, Mom. I'm really glad. You deserve someone nice."

My mom's smile cracks her face wide open, and she kisses me on the forehead.

"You're my best thing," she says. It's one of the things she likes to say to me. When I was little, she always said it when she was tickling me or braiding my hair or swinging me around in her arms.

"I love you, Mom," I answer, snuggling up a bit closer.

"I love you, too, my sweet peanut."

"You haven't called me that in ages."

"I know. It's a little girl's nickname. And you're not really my little girl anymore."

"Oh, come on, Mom," I say, "don't be cheesy." But something about it makes me feel warm all over, like when I was tiny and my mom would wrap me in a fuzzy towel after my bath and snuggle with me.

"Aw, you never let me be cheesy," she says.

"Fine, okay," I say. "But just for tonight."

"All right," she says. "Whatever you say, sweet peanut."

And we cuddle together for a while, not even needing to talk.

On Wednesday, Valentine's Day, I show up at school and see girls carrying bags of cheap red-and-pink candy to hand out to their friends, and boys holding Walgreens teddy bears and sad, already-fading carnations. I know it's a stupid, manufactured holiday, but I can't help wondering if Seth is going to do anything for it. In my backpack is a book of Shirley Jackson short stories since we'd talked about "The Lottery" that one time in class, and Seth had seemed to like the story. I confess I feel pretty cool giving Seth a book of short stories by a horror writer for Valentine's Day. It's so not East Rockport.

But I can't find Seth all morning. There's nothing on or in my locker. I do get a text from him that reads *Happy Walgreens Teddy Bear Day* followed by a bunch of red heart emojis, and I wonder if Seth is just too cool for Valentine's Day. Not even Shirley Jackson cool, but a completely different level of cool where the holiday just doesn't exist.

My heart sinks a little with disappointment. And this makes me feel stupid.

But then it's time for English. I walk in, and my stomach twists with nerves because I know I'm about to see him. Around me a few girls clutch their drugstore prizes of teenage love. A few of them are comparing gifts.

Then, as the bell rings, Seth walks in wearing a black hoodie over a black T-shirt. He slides into his seat and looks over at me, smiling.

He is so cute I really can't breathe sometimes.

With a shrug of his shoulders he takes off his hoodie, letting it fall onto his desk chair. His T-shirt underneath is sleeveless and there, in black Sharpie marker on his left arm, is a carefully drawn heart, big enough for me to spot it clearly from my seat on the other side of the room.

And inside the heart—in coal-back, painstakingly drawn letters—reads the word VIVIAN.

Among the whispers of the rest of the class, Lucy turns to me and says, "Oh my God," but I can't see what her face looks like because I am staring into Seth's dark, laughing eyes and I am grinning at him so hard and I am certain that I'm the first person on Earth to ever feel this awake and alive.

CHAPTER NINETEEN

IT'S CLAUDIA'S IDEA TO HAVE A SLUMBER PARTY AND INVITE everyone, including Lucy. She tells me about it as we walk home from school one early March morning, just the tiniest hint of Texas humidity in the air, a signal of what's to come.

"It can be like when we were younger, in middle school. We can watch a bunch of scary movies, make sundaes." She smiles at me.

"Look at you, Miss Nostalgia," I say, smiling back.

"I just thought it would be fun," Claudia answers. "Unless you're too busy with your man."

"No, not too busy," I answer, blushing, but just a little. It's getting easier for me to talk about Seth with my friends. Since his public display of Sharpie affection on Valentine's Day, we are definitely an item at East Rockport High. And the highs I'm getting from our relationship (making out, hanging out, making out, hanging out) are enough to dull the mix of anger and sadness I feel when I think about how Principal Wilson managed to stomp out Moxie in one threat-filled assembly.

So the first Friday in March finds Lucy, Sara, Meg, Kaitlyn, and me huddled in Claudia's bedroom, listening to music and eating chocolatey, salty snacks while Lucy puts temporary tattoos on our hands and all of us discuss the latest gossip.

"You know, this is way fun," Meg says, peering at her temporary tattoo of Wonder Woman. "It's been forever since we did something like this."

"It reminds me of that slumber party scene in the movie *Grease*," says Kaitlyn. "Let's do mud masks."

"Let's not and say we did," Lucy mutters, and we all laugh. Claudia laughs the loudest. For a moment we are this perfect bubble of girl happiness and nothing can mess with it.

Until Sara stops scrolling through her phone and says, quite plainly, "Oh, shit. March Madness."

March Madness. How could I forget?

"Let me see," says Kaitlyn, scooting over to peer at Sara's screen.

"What is March Madness?" Lucy asks, frowning. "You mean like the college basketball thing?"

"No, not like the college basketball thing," Sara says with a sigh.

And so, sitting in a loose circle, we take turns filling Lucy in. March Madness at East Rockport is, in fact, inspired by the college basketball championship because it involves brackets and competition, but that's the only similarity. It's so gross that I half expect Lucy to break a window or scream in rage. But she just sits there as we tell her about this charming East Rockport High tradition.

Tradition implies something of value being repeated, I guess, but East Rockport High's March Madness is empty of anything resembling values—not any decent ones, anyway. It's a system of brackets with sixty-four junior and senior girls, about a quarter of the girls in each class. The rest aren't included because they're not deemed ballot-worthy. The brackets are created by the upper-classmen guys who rule the school—the jocks and the popular guys. The Mitchell Wilsons of our world. Over the course of a couple of weeks, they use some complicated system of voting and personal testimony to pit girls against each other as the brackets lead to one girl in the junior or senior class. The final girl is referred to—casually and frequently—as East Rockport's Most Fuckable.

And the boys share everything online. Every bracket update and every girl's name.

Lucy eyes Sara's phone. I expect her to start raging as only Lucy can, but she just shrugs her shoulders.

"What can you expect from this place?" she says. "I need more Doritos." She crawls away from Sara's phone and digs her hand into a blue Tupperware bowl full of chips. There's something about the defeated way she says it that makes me feel half like crying and half like raging myself.

"Claudia, look, you're on it!" Sara gasps, using her fingers to enlarge the picture.

"What?" Claudia asks, but we all can see it's true. Claudia's made the first bracket. The only one of all of us who has. She blushes, and I wonder if she's thinking about Mitchell in the hallway before Christmas break. I wonder how much that gross incident affected her placement.

"Remember when we were freshmen?" Meg asks. "We wanted to be on it. And we were jealous of the older girls who were."

"Yeah," says Claudia, like she's trying to recall it.

"And now?" I ask, eyeing Claudia carefully.

Claudia just shrugs. "It's gross. But I'm not going to lie. Now it's like I'm tempted to check it. To see if I'm advancing or not."

"That's fucked up," Lucy says from over by the Doritos. I tense up, but Claudia just looks at her and nods.

"Yeah, it is," she says.

"We could make a pact," I say. "That we're not going to look at it again?"

Kaitlyn shakes her head. "That's only going to work if we all agree to bury our phones in Claudia's backyard and stay off the Internet for the next month. You can't escape it." I know Kaitlyn's right, so I don't respond. The only sound is Lucy chomping on her Doritos.

"Hey," says Claudia, finally breaking the silence. "I think my mom has an old bottle of red wine hidden in the kitchen that she's forgotten about. Everyone's asleep. Do you want to see if we can find it?"

"Yes, please," says Lucy. "Red wine goes well with fake cheese, or so I hear."

In no time we are sipping wine out of flowered juice glasses and laughing at our red-stained lips and teeth, and everything's okay again, but the truth is that the March Madness brackets never leave my mind, not really. The picture on Sara's phone has burrowed its way into my brain, and the idea of the girls of East Rockport being measured and ranked and compared on nothing more than their asses and breasts and faces makes it difficult to fall asleep, even after all the other girls—including Lucy—are sleeping peacefully around me, their light snores punctuating the quiet.

Later that week as I'm walking toward school, shuffling formulas I need to know for an upcoming math quiz through my mind, I spot Kiera Daniels sitting on the stoop of the school's side entrance, fooling around with her phone. It's still pretty early, and there aren't many other students around. The sky is overcast, and it's chilly, too.

"Hey," I say.

"Hey," she answers, peering up at me. "What's up?"

I shrug. "Not much. What about you?"

Kiera shakes her head. "Just looking at this March Madness thing."

I exhale. "Yeah."

"I'm on it," Kiera says flatly, holding the phone out toward me as if I need proof.

I think maybe it's okay for me to sit down next to her, so I do, the cold cement of the stoop seeping through my jeans.

"Should I say . . . congrats?" I ask, uncertain. But Kiera just scowls.

243

"It's stupid," she announces. "It's totally fucked on multiple levels."

"I know," I say, glad to be able to talk about it. "But it's just this . . . this thing that happens. And nobody questions it."

Kiera doesn't answer. Just bites her bottom lip and stares at her phone again before clicking it off and tossing it into her backpack.

"You know what's so infuriating to me?" Kiera says. "My boyfriend actually thinks it's cool I got picked. Like it makes him cooler, which is just gross. And what's also gross is it's always a white girl who wins, anyway. And all the girls who aren't white get pissed about it and it's like, wait, isn't it screwed up that anyone *wins* this bullshit in the first place?"

I frown. "I never thought about it like that. That a white girl always wins."

"Well, no offense," says Kiera, eyeing me, "but you're white, so you wouldn't have." But then she offers a wry smile, so I think it's okay. I smile back.

Kiera and I sit there for a bit, not talking. The weedy, sad patches of grass that make up East Rockport High's poor excuse for a campus lawn stretch out in front of us. It's a chilly, gray morning, especially for March in Texas, and I'm in a lousy mood.

"I wish we could do more bake sales, like maybe under some name that's not Moxie," Kiera says finally. "Soccer season is upon us, and my uniform isn't getting any newer, you know." She scowls a bit. "But maybe not even that is safe with Wilson watching."

"Yeah, I've thought the same thing," I say. "It would be great

244

to do another bake sale, but my friend Lucy, who planned the first one, got sent home on the day of the assembly. She wasn't even the one who made the stickers, but they sent her home anyway. It just seems too risky. Even if we don't call it Moxie."

Kiera nods. "I get it. It just sucks that whoever the girls are who did that newsletter have stopped altogether."

"Yeah," I say, deflated. It's almost like it was some other girl who made the *Moxie* zines, and she doesn't exist anymore. Not since she got replaced by a girl who has a super cute and nice boyfriend and spends her free time making out at the beach and thinking about when she should have sex for the first time.

That girl is great, too.

But she misses Moxie.

A breeze makes it way past us, kicking up a few cigarette butts and dead leaves. Then Kiera says, "Maybe something off campus would work. Like a place where Wilson couldn't get to it."

It is an idea, and one I haven't thought of before. But where and how it could happen? It seems like so much work and risk that I don't feel fired up about it.

"Yeah, maybe," I say. I don't want to hurt Kiera's feelings, so I quickly add, "It's a good idea."

Kiera nods slowly, then looks across the lawn and points.

"There's your man," she says, and I see Seth heading toward us.

"Yup," I say, and as excited as I am to see him—I'm always excited to see him—there's a part of me that wants to sit here and keep talking to Kiera. To try to work out this Moxie thing, even if I can't tell her I'm the one who started it all.

But Kiera stands up and brushes off the back of her pants. "I'm taking off."

"'Kay," I say as Seth gets closer.

"Good talking to you," she says, walking away.

"Good talking to you, too," I tell her. But before she gets too far, I call out to her. "Kiera!"

"Yeah?" she asks, turning to look at me.

"Fuck March Madness," I say.

A wide grin spreads over Kiera's face.

"Fuck it!" she shouts, popping both middle fingers in the air for good measure.

I stand as Seth approaches, and we share a quick kiss.

"What were you talking to Kiera about?" he asks.

I fill him in on March Madness and tell him Kiera made the first bracket.

"Oh, I saw stuff about that online," he says. "It's stupid."

"Yeah, really stupid," I add. "But I'm still depressed about it, I guess."

"Well, just remember," Seth says, and he sneaks an arm around my waist, pulling me in for another kiss, "not all guys are like that."

Before I even realize I'm doing it, I ice up and pull back a bit.

"What's wrong?" Seth asks, frowning.

"I just . . . ," I exhale. More and more kids are starting to walk up toward the building. I lower my voice.

"I just miss Moxie, that's all," I whisper. "I miss finding a way to fight back against all the bullshit in this school. And you telling me not all guys are like that doesn't really help me feel better. Because some guys *are* like that. A lot of them, actually."

Seth's eyes go wide. I can't tell if he's hurt or surprised.

"But Vivian, there are guys at this school who don't do March Madness," he says. "The guys I sometimes eat lunch with . . . the guys who are into baseball stats and shit. They're not that kind of guy. I'm not that kind of guy. It's not like this place is all awful. I mean, we've got each other here, right? And anyway, you're going to graduate eventually and you'll leave. I just don't want to see you get so upset."

I take a deep breath. How can I make him get it? He doesn't understand that Moxie isn't—wasn't—just a fun thing I did to be cool or different like his old hipster friends in Austin. I sincerely wanted to change East Rockport High School. Maybe I was naïve to think I could, but deep down I believed it might happen.

"What?" Seth asks.

"What what?" I answer.

"Are you . . . like . . . what's up?" he asks, stepping back from me, his brow wrinkling in confusion.

"Nothing," I say, shaking my head. "Just forget it." I'm frustrated with him, but I'm also frustrated with myself. That I can't find the words to explain it to him. I'm totally sure he's not doing it on purpose, but Seth is a guy, and he can't ever know what it feels like to walk down a hallway and know that you're getting judged for the size of your ass or how big your boobs are. He'll never understand what it's like to second guess everything you wear and how you sit and walk and stand in case it doesn't attract the right kind of attention, or worse, attracts the wrong kind. He'll never get how scary and crazy-making it is to feel like you belong to some big Boy Monster that decides it can grab you and touch you and rank you whenever and however it wants.

The first bell rings long and loud. By now kids are streaming in all around us, bumping into Seth and me as we stand there and stare at each other, awkward for the first time since we met.

"Can I walk you in, or is that not okay?" Seth asks, and his voice has got the tiniest edge to it.

"I don't want to fight," I murmur, looking down at my feet.

"Me neither," he says. "I really like you, Vivian. Like, a lot."

I nod. "I like you, too," I say.

"So let's go in? Maybe talk about this later?"

I nod again, and Seth and I walk up the steps into the main building. As I head inside, I get smacked with the scent of industrial cleanser mixed with Axe body spray. I hear the shouts of voices—mostly boys' voices because nice girls don't shout—and catch words like *March Madness* and *dumb bitch* and *she's so hot*.

I clench my fists. I feel like a match about to be lit. Or like the first crack of thunder before the storm. When Seth turns to tell me goodbye before heading to his first-period class, I jump, almost like I forgot he was there.

moxie shines a light on the sexist bullshit at ERHS. moxie won't give up!
Moxie WILL WIN!

Did you ever stop & think...

That March Madness is just one more way for certain boys at ERHS to treat girls like objects? PLUS it pits us girls against one another. It creates competition where there should be unity. It idealizes one type of beauty (white & thin) over all others. It shames us and humiliates us. It's sick, gross, and essentially condoned by the school and community.
   MARCH MADNESS
IS FUCKED UP.
DON'T FORGET IT.

Remember...

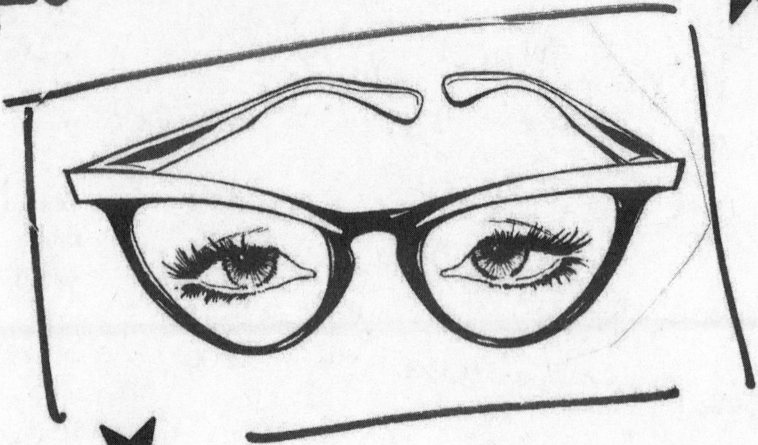

Moxie is always WATCHING

CHAPTER TWENTY

LUCY'S FACE IS EAGER AND OPEN WHEN SHE FINDS ME THE MORNING after the fourth issue of *Moxie* makes its debut.

"They're back!" she shouts, almost collapsing into me, clutching a copy in her hands.

I yawn and blink. I made the fourth issue last night in an explosive rush of anger. By the time I got it all done and biked down to U COPY IT, it was almost 10:30 at night. My mom had been on an overnight shift, so I wasn't worried about beating her home. Frank the copy guy insisted it was "the coolest issue yet" and I was on a high by the time I biked home, so nervous and hyper that I'd stayed awake until almost one in the morning, watching old Bikini Kill videos on YouTube and reading the fourth issue over and over. Each time Principal Wilson's threats from the assembly started to worm through my mind, I played the next video even louder. The risks I'm taking with this issue—the chance that it could hurt Lucy, the chance I could get caught and be expelled—were ever present in my head as I cut and glued and folded. But I'm done with Principal Wilson. I'm done with East Rockport High School bullshit. No more fun and games.

"Yeah, I saw it, too," I answer.

She flips the zine over and peers at the back, then opens it, her eyes scanning the words and images I carefully chose while listening to Bratmobile and Team Dresch.

"This issue is . . . I don't know how to describe it. I think it's more intense than before."

"You think?" I ask, peering over Lucy's shoulder like I'm taking it all in for the first time. But Lucy's right. When I made this issue of *Moxie*, I felt rage coursing through me like steam. Like a venomous snake. And when I slipped on a hoodie this morning before distributing the copies, I felt like a soldier on a dangerous mission, determined to succeed no matter what. The anger was enough to make me almost forget what a treacherous position I was putting myself in. And Lucy.

"It's much more aggressive, I think," she says, her eyes still on the issue of *Moxie*. "Only there's no call to action. No stickers or bathrobes or whatever. It's just . . . angry."

"Well," I say, slamming my locker shut, "there's a lot to be angry about."

"Yeah, obviously," Lucy answers, and we join the wave of students filing to class, their voices echoing off the walls and their shoes squeaking on the tiled floor. "You know, I'm wondering if that girl Marisela Perez made it."

My eyebrows shoot up, and I immediately try to cover up how surprised I must appear.

"What makes you say that?" I ask.

"Remember that morning we saw her put her asshole sticker on Tim Fitzpatrick?" she asks. "She just seems like she'd have the guts to do this."

"Huh," I offer. "Yeah, well, she's as good a guess as any."

"I just hope I don't get hauled into the principal's office over it," Lucy says, and my stomach knots up.

"There's no way he can know who it is," I say. "You just thought it was Marisela."

"Yeah," Lucy says, shrugging. "You're right." But I can tell she's a little worried.

We part ways with promises to see each other in English class. I scan the halls for Seth's face. After our conversation outside school yesterday morning, things have felt a little strange between us. A little awkward even. I'm not sure. I didn't even tell him about this latest issue of *Moxie*. I'm worried about what it means that I didn't feel the urge to share it with him.

That afternoon I head over to Meemaw and Grandpa's for dinner. After some Stouffer's mac and cheese and a salad of iceberg lettuce doused in ranch dressing, I join them in the TV room to work on my homework while they watch *Wheel of Fortune*. As I listen to Meemaw blurt out nonsensical answers (*"The Nile River!" "Bridge on the River Kwai!" "'Old Man River!'"*), I let my thoughts drift back to the fall, back before Moxie started. When

I started making the zine, I felt like I was cracking something open. Telling a secret that needed to be told. And for a while it was amazing. And then came Seth, who was—*is*—smart and cool and nice. That was great, too. But Moxie fell by the wayside.

But since March Madness started something has changed again. With this fourth *Moxie* zine, I'm itching for something but I'm not sure what.

"You okay, sweetie?" Meemaw asks during a commercial break, tilting her head a little in concern.

"How come you're asking?"

"Well, for starters, you've been sitting there staring at the wall for the whole last round of the *Wheel*," Grandpa offers. "You look as confused as a goat on Astroturf."

I blush slightly and look down at my math spiral. I'm holding a pencil, but I've only done one problem.

"Just stuff on my mind," I say. "Nothing serious."

"Anything you want to talk about?" Meemaw asks. I think of trying to explain Moxie and Seth and March Madness to my grandmother. As much as I love her, I know she wouldn't get it. Meemaw and Grandpa see the world one way. You go to church on Sunday, you don't wear white after Labor Day, and you always say "Merry Christmas," not "Happy Holidays."

"I'm really fine," I say, forcing a smile. "Just tired, I guess."

Meemaw smiles back. This is an answer that makes sense to her, and it seems to reassure her and Grandpa. They go back to watching television, and I go back to trying to focus on my math until a few moments later when my phone buzzes.

Hey you mind if I come over later? Is your mom home?

Seth. I didn't really speak to him much at school today. I know he saw the zine because he told me so after English. He said it was "cool," and that it was "cool" that I was making *Moxie* again. But we didn't really have a long conversation.

I text back that I'm at my grandparents', but I'll be home in a few minutes.

Cool, he writes back.

My heart starts to hammer. Is this Seth's version of the "we need to talk" line that always comes before breakups in stupid rom coms and television sitcoms?

I tell Meemaw and Grandpa that I need to head home and give them each a kiss on the cheek. Grandpa walks me to the door and watches until I make it to our house.

"Love you!" he shouts.

"I love you, too, Grandpa!"

I sit in the living room so I can keep an eye out the front door. Seth knows to park down the street to avoid being spotted by my grandparents. When I catch a glimpse of him making his way down the sidewalk, his hands in his jeans pockets, his head bowed low, my first thought is *He is so crazy cute*. I watch as he slips through the alley between my house and our other next door neighbors' before coming in through the back door, which I've already unlocked.

"Hey," he says, sliding his hoodie off his shoulders. "I always feel like a secret agent when I sneak in like this."

I grin. In truth I bet my mom already knows Seth comes by when she's not here. But it's just a little bit easier if we can keep Meemaw and Grandpa out of it.

257

"Sorry," I say. "But you really don't want my grandparents to see you. My grandpa owns a shotgun."

"Of course he does," Seth says.

This would normally be the moment when Seth kisses me, when we collapse onto the couch and start making out, and I start wondering if and when we'll go further than we have the time before. But this time he just stands there, and I hear myself blurt out, "Are we breaking up?"

Seth's eyes pop open, genuinely surprised. "No! What?" He blinks once, then twice. "Not unless you want to break up with me."

I'm blushing, embarrassed. I feel like I'm playing the part of the anxious girlfriend, and I hate it. I just shake my head and look at my feet.

"It's stupid," I say. "But I just feel like . . . since that morning when you saw me talking to Kiera . . . we've been awkward."

"You wanna talk?" Seth asks.

I nod, and we end up on the couch together.

"So what's up?" Seth starts.

I bite my lip and try to find the right words. "I don't know . . . I don't even know what I'm trying to say," I start. "I just felt like you were . . . trying to make me think things weren't so bad. With the March Madness thing. Because you aren't that kind of guy. And I was frustrated because of course, like, I know you're not that guy. But there *are* those guys at East Rockport. There are . . . so many of them."

Seth nods, scratches the back of his head.

"Yeah, I can see that," he says.

"I'm not upset because there are no good guys at East Rockport. I'm upset because there are so many assholes. When I get upset about March Madness, it's not about you."

"Yeah," he answers, exhaling. "I guess I was being kind of a dick."

"No, not a dick," I say. "You were just kind of . . . unaware. Defensive even?"

"I feel like I can't say the right thing here," Seth says.

"No, you are saying the right thing. It's okay."

Seth gives me a half grin. "I promise I'll try to be . . . more sensitive about stuff." What that might look like to Seth I'm not exactly sure. I think he could just be saying it because he hopes it's the right thing to say. Honestly, I'm not even sure what I want Seth to say. Maybe there isn't a right thing.

"I did like the latest issue of *Moxie*," he says. "I wasn't just saying so earlier. It was different this time."

I pluck at a loose string on my jeans, recalling what Lucy said about the issue. "Different how?" I dare to look up at Seth.

"Maybe a little more intense," he says. "Not that that's necessarily bad or whatever. I liked the art you chose. I just think it's cool you're doing it again. Plus it makes you happy, right?"

I'm not sure I would describe the feeling of making *Moxie* as happy. Important, maybe. Necessary? Definitely. But I just smile and nod. At this, Seth reaches out and runs his thumb over my knee, sending an electric shiver up my body. I give him a knowing look.

"Oh, do you want to fool around or something?" I ask, acting like I'm surprised.

"I don't know, do you?" Seth asks, his voice casual, like we're talking about what we want to watch on Netflix.

"Shut up," I say, throwing a couch cushion at his head.

"When does your mom get home?" Seth asks, his voice dropping a little. Getting all whispery. My breathing quickens just a bit.

"Like in an hour or so," I say.

"Okay," Seth says, nodding. He's close to me now, and I can smell his soap and aftershave and the peppermint Tic Tacs he must have popped in his mouth just before coming over. His dark eyes stare into mine.

I want to attack him right there. So I do, reaching over to kiss him and letting myself fall into him, forgetting all my mixed-up feelings and ignoring the sense that the conversation we just had didn't really change anything at all. That it was just a make-nice before the make out.

But in this moment, with Seth's hands reaching up my back and his lips making their way to that spot on my neck, I will myself not to care much.

Not long after I put out the fourth zine of *Moxie*—maybe a week or so—I'm surprised to find Kiera Daniels waiting for me by my locker one Monday morning. She nods at me as she sees me approach.

"Hey," I say.

"Hey," Kiera says back. She peeks over her shoulder and then in a hushed voice says, "Even though nothing bad happened after that last newsletter came out, we have to keep this quiet at school. To be safe." She presses a piece of paper into my hand. I feel like a spy in an old movie.

I look down and unfold the paper.

I look up, smiling.

"You came up with this?"

Kiera grins. "Yeah, me and Amaya. After you and I talked . . . and after that last issue of *Moxie*, I got to thinking that I really wanted to make something happen. I know we have to be careful. But it just seems . . . worth it."

"This is so cool," I say, and I realize I'm smiling so hard that my cheeks are aching a little. "How'd you get the hall?"

"My grandfather is a Vietnam vet," Kiera says. "I told him it was a girls' club to talk about how to support the football team." She smirks.

"You didn't!"

"I really did." At this she laughs out loud, and I do, too. I flash back to those elementary school days, to when Kiera and I would try to make our own *Diary of a Wimpy Kid* books together. We even had sleepovers at her house a few times when my mom had an overnight shift. Standing here, talking to her in the hallway, it seems crazy that we didn't stay friends.

"You know what?" Kiera says. "I broke up with Marcus."

My eyes open wider. Kiera had been dating Marcus Tucker—the center for the East Rockport Pirates—since the beginning of high school. They were a Serious Couple.

"I'm sorry," I say.

"Don't be," says Kiera. "I didn't like how he was treating me.

MOXIE
ARTS AND
CRAFTS SHOW

Proceeds go to girls' soccer team

Food and Drink   *Music and Dancing*

Crafts for sale   *GIRLS ONLY*

TALK TO KIERA AND AMAYA IF YER INTERESTED

DON'T POST JUST SPREAD THE WORRRRRRRD!

ALL GIRLS WELCOME!!!!!

THIS SATURDAY!!

VFW HALL

$5 ADMISSION

Acting like he was God's gift just because he played football. Him getting excited about me being on March Madness was enough to make me realize I was done."

I nod. "Good for you, then."

"Yeah," Kiera says. "It hasn't been easy, exactly, but I just decided to throw everything into organizing this"—she motions to the flyer—"and that's helped."

"You need me to do anything?" I ask.

"Just spread the word to any girls you think would be cool with it," she tells me.

I grin. "That I can do. This will be the perfect way to cleanse ourselves from March Madness."

Kiera rolls her eyes. "You see Emma Johnson won?"

"I've actually been trying to ignore all that shit, but yeah, I saw. I'm not surprised they picked her."

"Me neither," says Kiera. "Okay, I got to get to Spanish. But see you Saturday?"

"Yes," I say, my heart fluttering with excitement at the thought of it. "See you Saturday."

I think about Emma Johnson winning Most Fuckable Girl when I see her in English, sitting at her desk taking notes as Mr. Davies speaks. I think about inviting her to Kiera's thing and it's like thinking about inviting a debutante to a drunken tailgate. Emma hangs with the elite, with the coolest football players and the most popular cheer squad girls. And she was the one who spoke out against Moxie at the assembly.

The reasons for not inviting Emma are good. But a passage from one of the Bikini Kill album liner notes about all girls being

263

soldiers in their own way, even the girls with the big hair who go out with jocks, sticks in my mind. I unfold Kiera's flyer again and see the words ALL GIRLS WELCOME. As the bell rings, I think about tapping Emma on the shoulder and saying, "Hey, I know we never talk and you barely know I exist, but I was wondering if you wanted to come to this thing for girls who are pissed about all this shit at East Rockport High that actually seems to work to your advantage?"

But I don't say anything. I just catch the flip of her honey-blond hair as she makes her way out of class.

CHAPTER TWENTY-ONE

I PULL OPEN THE HEAVY DOOR OF THE VFW HALL AND AM IMMEDIATELY overtaken by the scent of stale cigarette smoke.

"Phew, it smells like our den before my dad quit," says Claudia, wrinkling her nose.

Lucy, Sara, Kaitlyn, and Meg are with us, too. We all blink as our eyes adjust to the semi-darkness of the wood-paneled room that hasn't been renovated since the 1970s at least. Old Lone Star and Shiner Bock beer signs hang in the corner by an empty bar.

"Hey," says Amaya, walking toward us. I look around. There are about twenty girls here. My heart sinks a bit. That's a really small number of girls considering the size of East Rockport. But I remind myself that it's still early.

"Five dollars," Amaya says, opening a shoe box. We all pull out our crumpled bills, and Amaya thanks us for coming and tells us we can put the baked goods we brought with us on the bake sale table.

Most of the girls here are on the soccer team. Music thumps, and my friends and I clump together as we awkwardly walk the perimeter of the hall.

"Hey, there you are," Kiera says, coming up. She's dressed in dark jeans and a bright pink top. She's wearing pink lipstick to match. "Glad you made it."

"This is cool," says Lucy, even though nothing is really happening. I know she wants Kiera to like her. To be glad she's here.

"Thanks," says Kiera. She looks at her phone. "I'm hoping a few more girls come. I just heard from my friends Maci and Charity that they're on their way."

"Cool," I say, nodding.

Kiera smiles and heads off, and my friends and I walk around, clutching our paper plates full of lemon bars and chocolate chip cookies.

Around the room, girls have different stuff for sale, their wares spread out on card tables. Marisela Perez has dozens of tiny charm bracelets she's made by hand, each for sale for five dollars. They're delicate things, with tiny colored plastic beads lining them like gum drops.

"These are pretty," says Claudia, reaching out to touch one.

"Thanks," says Marisela, picking up one of her creations. "I just make them for fun and sell them to my cousins. This is the first time I'm trying to, you know, sell them to other people. But it helps me, too, since I'm on the soccer team."

"I'll buy one before the night is over," Claudia says, and Marisela grins.

After we drop off our bars and cookies at the bake sale table, we keep exploring. We see jewelry, magnets, and stickers for sale. My heart wants to burst when I see a bunch of the *Moxie* zines—all the way back to the first one—laid out on a table in careful rows, free for the taking. I guess that Kiera made copies of existing zines because the images are a little blurrier and softer than in the copies I made.

I recognize Kiera's table immediately. It's full of her drawings— a row of leafless trees in winter, stretching out to the horizon. Two hands clutching each other, their fingers laced together. A single eyeball, staring steadily back. Her sketches are all black and white and really remarkable. She's come a long way since our *Diary of a Wimpy Kid* days.

"This is . . . so *cool*," says Lucy, barely able to contain herself. "It's reminding me of my old GRIT club in Houston." Claudia and the other girls seems a little less certain, but we decide to walk the perimeter in our awkward clump again— Claudia wants to get one of Marisela's bracelets—and by the time we've made it around, a few more girls have spilled in. They look like underclassmen, uncertain and nervous. I lift a hand and smile hello, and they smile back.

The door keeps opening and more girls keep coming in, enough that we have to start shouting over the music. It starts to grow stuffy and hot, and Kiera and Amaya open the windows because the air conditioner isn't working so well, but our thin sheens of sweat start to make us all glow a bit. My friends and I decide to go for some lemonade.

"Do you want regular or . . . fortified?" the girl behind the table says, eyeing us.

"Fortified?" Claudia asks loudly, and the girl shoots her a look. I recognize her as one of the soccer players. I think her name is Jane.

Lucy nudges Claudia with an elbow and all of us notice a paper bag on the floor with a slim bottle in it.

"Vodka," Jane whispers. She winks.

"Fortified, please," Lucy says without hesitation as she forks over her money, and soon we are clutching plastic cups of special lemonade. It's not long before Claudia starts bopping around to the beat of the music, a sly smile spreading over her face.

"Claudia is way fortified," she says to us, and we laugh. At this point the room is close to full, girls from almost every group at East Rockport High moving around and in between each other, handing over babysitting dollars and Sonic carhop dollars and weekly allowance dollars to buy Marisela's bracelets and Kiera's drawings and stickers someone made that read BOSS BITCH.

We yell hey and hi and ohmygod at each other, and we hug and we kiss on the cheek and we catch up with each other, for once ignoring the unspoken dividing lines of race and class and grade and popularity that we've always lived by. Some girls are dancing in the corners, moving their bodies with the freedom that comes when no boy is watching you. It feels buzzy and dizzy and sweaty and so, so, so joyful. I think this is the closest I've ever come to feeling like a Riot Grrrl, like my mom from way back when, but this is even better because it's my own thing. It's *our* own thing. The girls of East Rockport High. It's Moxie, and it feels so real and alive and right now.

An hour or so into it, Kiera makes her way to a tiny stage at the back of the room, and she grabs a microphone and taps it.

"Uh, can I get your attention, please," she asks. A lazy smile slips across her face and I'm pretty sure she's had a fortified lemonade or two. I take a sip from my second one. My lips feel semi-numb.

The room quiets down and we all turn to face Kiera. When she has our attention, she leans into the microphone.

"Uh, first of all . . . ," she starts, taking a more than dramatic pause, "Moxie girls fight back!" To my delight and surprise, the girls around me cheer and scream and a few hold up their red Solo cups. Kiera keeps going. "This is a kick-ass lady event, and we've raised a ton of money for the girls' soccer team, enough that we can buy uniforms from this century, I think. So thanks for coming. That's it. Turn up the music."

Everyone cheers again, and soon we're dancing, our bodies moving, one big mass of girls having fun. As I watch Lucy spin and knock her dark curls around, and as I listen to Claudia laugh and sing along (badly), it occurs to me that this is what it means to be a feminist. Not a humanist or an equalist or whatever. But a feminist. It's not a bad word. After today it might be my favorite word. Because really all it is is girls supporting each other and wanting to be treated like human beings in a world that's always finding ways to tell them they're not.

After another hour or so, it's starting to grow dark outside, and Kiera makes another announcement into the microphone that they have to lock up the hall. Girls boo until Kiera promises to organize another Moxie meet up later, which gains more cheers. She reminds girls to walk home if they've had too much "grown-up lemonade" and to walk in groups.

"I'm okay to drive," says Sara. "I didn't drink."

Kaitlyn and Meg go with her, but Claudia and I agree to walk home with Lucy, who doesn't live too far from the hall and who walked to get here.

"Maybe we should try to help clean up a little bit first?" Claudia asks, pointing at Kiera and Amaya and a few other girls folding up card tables and dumping cups into big black trash bags.

"Yeah, that would be nice," Lucy agrees. As she and Claudia busy themselves, I offer to lug some of the garbage bags to the Dumpster.

When I push the back door open, the hot, sticky night air surrounds me like a too-tight hug. There's a scraping sound as I shove the door open over the gravel parking lot.

"Oh, hey," a female voice calls out from nearby. I look up and blink my eyes, trying to adjust to the darkness, and spot Marisela and Jane pulling apart from what I can only guess was something more than just a friendly hug. Jane tugs down her T-shirt. Marisela coughs. I've stumbled onto a secret, and if it weren't so dark, Marisela and Jane would be able to see just how much I'm blushing.

"I was just trying to throw these out," I say, pointing weakly at the bags by my feet. "I'm sorry I interrupted y'all." I hope my voice reads *it's cool*. There are two boys who are out at East

Rockport, both of them seniors and both of them involved in the theater department. They hang out together and even though I don't think they're *together* together, everyone assumes they are, and they're the regular butt of stupid jokes and promises that they'll be prayed for. I can only imagine that they each have a calendar counting down the days before they can leave this place.

But I don't know of a single girl who's come out in all my time at East Rockport High. I mean, there have been rumors, obviously. But that's all they've been. Rumors.

"You won't tell anyone, right?" Marisela says, leaving the thing I'm not supposed to tell unspoken but obvious. I shake my head no and say, for emphasis, "I won't tell anyone. I promise." And I know that I won't. Not even Lucy or Claudia. Because in a town like East Rockport, what Marisela and Jane have going on is the sort of thing you can't risk too many people knowing about.

"Thanks," says Jane. She crosses her arms in front of her, avoids eye contact, and my heart cracks a little for her, and for Marisela, too.

"Here, let me help you," says Marisela, and she grabs one of the garbage bags, and we haul them into the big blue Dumpster behind the hall.

"Okay," I say. "Well, I'm heading back in."

"'Kay," says Marisela. Then, after a beat, she says, "Tonight was fun. I think this is the best night I've had in maybe my entire life." Her voice is soft and slow, like she's had her fair share of lemonade. When Marisela says this, Jane looks right at her and smiles so big you can see her gums.

"It was a pretty cool night," I say, grinning back.

By the time Claudia and I walk Lucy home, we are yawning and dragging our feet on the sidewalk. It feels later than it is.

"You can spend the night if you want, or I can drive you home," Lucy offers. "I only had one cup of that lemonade, and that was hours ago." We take Lucy up on her offer of a lift since our parents are waiting up, and we don't have any of the stuff we need for a sleepover. I text my mom that I'm on my way. By the time Lucy drops me off, Claudia is half-asleep in the backseat.

"'Night, Claud," I murmur over my shoulder.

"Hmmph."

"I'm so glad Kiera put that together," Lucy says. "If it wouldn't scare your mom and your grandparents, I'd honk my horn out of happiness."

I reach over and honk Lucy's car horn twice—*toot toot*.

"What the hell?" says Claudia, sitting up suddenly, blinking and rubbing her eyes. Lucy laughs, and I do, too.

"Moxie!" I yell, getting out of the car.

"Moxie!" Lucy yells back. She toots the horn one more time before pulling out of the driveway.

My mom greets me at the front door.

"Viv, what's going on? Are you okay?"

I smile at her and pull her in for a sweaty hug. "Sorry, we were just being stupid."

"You stink!"

"Thanks a lot," I say, opening the refrigerator to hunt down something cold to drink. I pour myself some orange juice.

"So how was it?" she asks. I'd told my mom I was going to a

272

girls-only fund-raiser for the soccer team, but I'd been vague on the details.

"Mom, it was so fun," I tell her, "but I'm so tired." I want to get to bed while my memories of the night are still fresh so I can fall asleep replaying them in my head.

"Did a lot of girls show up?" my mom asks, leaning against the kitchen counter, watching as I down the entire glass of juice in a few gulps. I hadn't realized how hot and thirsty I was.

"Yeah," I say, setting the glass in the sink. "Lots."

"That's great," my mom answers. "I love that the girls wanted to do that. Who organized it, exactly?"

My head is starting to ache a little bit. Maybe from the lemonade. I rub my temples and close my eyes.

"It was just the girls on the soccer team and some other girls," I say, edging my way down the hall.

"I ran into Claudia's mom, and she said it was some group called Moxie? She saw Claudia's flyer for it?"

I pause at my bedroom door, my back to my mom. "Oh, yeah," I say, surprised Claudia didn't keep the flyer better hidden. My heart starts racing. Should I tell my mom about Moxie? She would probably think it's cool, and even have good advice for me about how to keep it going.

But it suddenly hits me that Moxie isn't all about me. And it's certainly not about my mom. It belongs to all the girls at East Rockport High School. The heartbeat of the VFW hall is ours and ours alone.

"Are you involved in it?" my mom says, not giving up. "Moxie, I mean. It's a cool name."

273

"Well, I went to this thing tonight, so yeah, sort of," I say, stripping off my sweaty clothes and searching for my pajamas. "Mom, I'm going to bed, okay? I'm just so sleepy. There was dancing and stuff, and I'm all achy. Can we talk more tomorrow?" I finally work up the guts to turn around and face her.

"Sure, yeah, let's talk tomorrow," she says, but her eyes look a little sad, her voice sounds just the tiniest bit wistful. "It just seems like you had fun. You *look* like you had fun, you know?"

"I did have fun, Mom, I promise," I tell her, giving her a kiss on the cheek. After she leaves, I check my phone as I collapse into bed. There are a few messages from Seth. The last one reads, *How was it? Fun I hope.*

I tap out one quick answer.

sooooooo fun thanks for asking more tomorrow I'm sleepy! xo

Then I toss the phone on the floor, and as I slide into sleep, my mind is full of images of girls dancing together and smiling and holding hands, taking up all the space they want.

The meet up at the VFW hall changes the energy at school—and in a good way. Girls who normally don't have much to do with each other say hi in the hallways, smiling at each other when they pass. I mean, it's still the same in a lot of ways—I hear guys arguing about whether Emma Johnson deserved to win March Madness even though she's still a junior, and Mitchell and his friends still tell girls to make them sandwiches and try to bump 'n' grab—but still, there's something about those first few days

274

after Kiera's event that feel different. Like we're all just a little bit more aware. Awake.

"I wonder if whoever is making the *Moxie* newsletter is a senior," Claudia says as she and I meet up with Lucy outside school before the first bell. "When they graduate, maybe it will stop."

"Yeah, but even if it is a senior making the newsletters," says Lucy, pulling her curls up into a ponytail, "it almost doesn't matter. After Saturday, doesn't it feel like Moxie could just keep happening no matter what?"

"So you don't think Kiera started it?" Claudia asks.

Lucy shakes her head. "I don't think so. Kiera's flyer had a different feel to it than the newsletters. Just like my bake sale flyers had a different look. Because I didn't make the newsletters either."

"I think Lucy is right," I say.

"That Kiera didn't make the newsletters?" asks Claudia.

"Well, yeah," I answer, "but also that it doesn't matter who made them at all, even if they're graduating. Because Moxie is a thing that's everyone's." I glance at Claudia, hesitating, then say, "I mean, I think it belongs to girls who care about being feminists."

Claudia doesn't respond. Just nods, like she wants to think it over. At that moment, my phone buzzes.

Come to the front doors of the school you won't believe it

"It's Sara," I say, peering down at the text. "Something's going on around front."

We make our way around to the front steps of East Rockport

High. A crowd is gathering around the stairs that lead to two sets of large, gray metal doors. But you can barely see the doors because they're covered in bright pink flyers. The buzz of students' voices grows louder with each passing moment.

Sara spots us, races over with a flyer in her hand. Breathless, she hands it over and we stare.

"Holy shit," says Lucy.

Because really, that's all there is to say.

MOXIE WALKOUT!!!

THIS FRIDAY
AT THE ATTENDANCE BELL

I am tired of being silent.

Mitchell Wilson tried to rape me at a party.

I won't be quiet anymore.

Principal Wilson and the administration of ERHS

REFUSED TO LISTEN TO ME

If you support this walkout

You support all girls

You support a movement

THAT REFUSES TO TOLERATE
VIOLENCE AGAINST GIRLS

CHAPTER TWENTY-TWO

OF COURSE, IT'S ALL ANYONE CAN TALK ABOUT. BUT WEIRDLY, EAST Rockport almost feels quieter than normal. Because people are so stunned by the flyer that they are whispering, speaking in hushed voices. Not even opening their mouths so much as staring at each other with can-you-believe-it? looks on their faces.

Here and there, I catch snippets of conversation.

"Has anyone seen Mitchell?"

"Who do you think did this?"

"Do you think it's true?"

Lucy has to leave us to head to first period, but Claudia and I walk to history class together, Claudia's hand clutching the paper, her eyes scanning the words over and over.

"Claudia, watch out," I say, tugging on her elbow. "You almost ran into a wall."

"Huh?" Claudia says, looking up at me at last. "Oh. Sorry."

"You okay?" I ask.

Claudia frowns and shakes her head. She doesn't have to talk for me to know what she's thinking as she stares at the flyer. *This could have been me.*

Claudia heads into history class, but just as I'm about to walk in, Seth comes around the corner, holding a flyer like everyone else. He leans in to kiss me, but I freeze up. I don't feel like kissing.

"You okay?" he says, pulling back. A hurt expression crosses his face. I pretend it's not there.

"Yeah, I'm okay," I say. "Just . . . that flyer. It's disturbing."

"I know," he says. "You have any idea who did it?" But I shake my head no.

"You think it's true?" he asks.

Now it's my turn to pull back. My throat tightens up. My chest feels heavy.

"Of course it's true," I say. I look around and then, practically mouthing the words, I say, "I told you what he did to Claudia."

Seth nods, like he'd forgotten all about Claudia. Maybe he has. "Yeah, of course. I mean, I know he did that. And it's gross. But this girl"—he holds the flyer up—"she's saying he tried to rape her."

"I know," I say. "And?"

"Just that that's a really big accusation to make against a guy, that's all."

I don't even know what to say. I stare at Seth. I want him to be on my side. Defending this girl with me.

"Look, I'm not saying it's not true," says Seth, flustered. "Just that this is a pretty big accusation and I'm just, like, surprised she put it out there like this instead of letting the school handle it."

"But she said they didn't listen to her, and when Claudia went to the school they told her to use winter break to forget about what happened," I say. I can feel heat radiating off my face. I tug on the shoulder straps of my backpack and hug it closer to me. "Look, I'm going to be late."

"Okay, fine, I was just making a point," Seth says. "I'm not saying it didn't happen."

"I guess it kind of sounded like you *were* saying that," I snap.

"Look, Vivian, calm down," he says. "I'm not . . ."

"Let's talk later," I say, angry. "And don't tell me to calm down."

Seth steps back, like I've just punched him hard in the gut.

I walk into class, blinking back tears I didn't know were threatening to spill out.

"You okay?" Claudia asks as I take my seat in front of her.

"I just got into a . . ." I search for a better word, but there isn't one. "I got into a fight with Seth. He was saying he wonders if the girl who made the flyer is even telling the truth."

Just then the bell rings, but our teacher, Mrs. Robbins, isn't there. Everyone around us is talking about the flyers, but Claudia leans in toward me, her face concerned. "I'm sorry, Vivvy. What happened?" But I don't get a chance to answer because suddenly Mrs. Robbins walks in with more purpose than she's exhibited all year. Clapping her hands together, she barks at us to pay attention.

"I've just come from an emergency faculty meeting," she says,

280

acting as if an emergency faculty meeting is the equivalent of high-level nuclear disarmament talks. "Principal Wilson is about to make an announcement. All of you need to listen *very* carefully." She stares at all of us, but it feels like her icy gaze lingers longer on the girls.

A few moments later, the intercom makes a tinny beep. Then Principal Wilson's gruff voice begins talking, his twang thick with anger.

"Students of East Rockport, it has come to my attention that a flyer is making its way around the school calling for a walkout tomorrow afternoon," he says. I imagine him standing in his office, talking into a microphone like he's the dictator of a small country.

"Any student who walks out of this school will be suspended immediately, and I will begin the process of expulsion immediately," he says. At this heads turn and whispers start, but Mrs. Robbins claps her hands agains and shouts, "Listen up, people!"

"Regarding the situation in the flyer itself," continues Principal Wilson, "please know the administration is looking into the allegations. Safety for our students is a top concern, of course." The words are so perfunctory and laughable I can't help but turn in my seat and roll my eyes at Claudia and Sara. I don't care if Mrs. Robbins sees.

"Now let's get back to learning," he says. "Our custodial staff is in the process of removing the flyers. Any flyer found will be confiscated."

I sit at my desk, burning with rage. He's looking into the allegations involving his own asshole son. A visit from Martians during lunchtime is more likely.

Mrs. Robbins tries to run class, but all of us are distracted, and my mind keeps spinning in circles, thinking about both Seth and the walkout. When the bell rings, Claudia asks Sara and me if we're going to participate on Friday.

"I think I want to do it," I say as we maneuver through the hallway. It surprises me as soon as it's out of my mouth. But it's the only possible answer. The only one that makes sense.

"You're not afraid of getting expelled?" Claudia asks, twisting up her mouth in concern.

A girl I don't know all that well—she's only a freshman, I think—overhears us.

"Look, Wilson can't expel us if we *all* walk out," she insists. "Moxie girls fight back, right?" I remember her from the VFW hall, and in this moment I know for sure that Moxie is out of my hands. It's thrilling and terrifying at the same time.

Just then Claudia's phone buzzes. She looks down and gasps.

"What?" Sara asks, alarmed.

"Check your phones," she says. "Meg texted us."

Wilson pulled Lucy out of first period . . . she never came back. He was PISSED

"Shit," I say. "Why did she have to be so by the book and fill out that form for the bake sale?"

"But *she* didn't make the flyers, right?" Sara asks.

"No, but Wilson only wants someone he can pin this on," I say. I remember Lucy crying in her bedroom, worrying about college scholarships. My stomach knots up. "God, I hope he only brought her in to question her."

But by English no one has spotted Lucy, and she doesn't show up for class. Neither does Mitchell Wilson, for that matter, which causes another round of whispers. When Seth walks in, he doesn't look at me and I don't look at him. I swallow hard and try to ignore the ache in my throat. I bite the inside of my cheeks to keep from crying. Everything feels so fucked up.

Before Mr. Davies starts class, I text Lucy for the tenth time.

Where are you????? Please tell me you're okay

Nothing.

Finally, at the end of the day, Lucy texts back.

I got suspended. I'm a mess. . . . can you please come over? But just you, ok? I can't take a hundred million questions from everyone.

I text back right away.

I'll get there somehow I promise

I dart through the halls looking for Claudia, hoping she borrowed her mom's car to drive to school like she sometimes does. When I see her, I tell her what's happened and ask if she can take me to Lucy's. She says yes without hesitating.

As we drive to Lucy's house, I tell Claudia that Lucy only wants me to come in.

"I hope you understand," I say. I think back to earlier in the year. To the times when Claudia acted a little bit irritated by Lucy.

Claudia nods. "It's okay. I get it." She pulls up to Lucy's grand-mother's house. "Tell her I'm sorry, though, okay?"

I smile at my best friend since forever and start to open the car door.

"Hey," Claudia says, stopping me. I turn back to find her looking at me intently. She bites her bottom lip.

"What is it? Are you okay?"

"It's just . . . ," she starts, her voice a little shaky, "I kind of feel like I want to do the walkout. I know it's crazy, maybe. But part of me really wants to do it. Because screw Mitchell Wilson and his dad."

My smile grows bigger, and I reach out to hug Claudia. "I think you're a badass," I whisper into her ear. "And a really good friend." Her hug feels like everything good and warm and familiar.

"I love you, Viv," she whispers back.

"I love you, too."

When I knock on Lucy's front door, Lucy's grandmother greets me, her mouth turned down in a tight frown.

"I'm not sure if I should let you in," she says. "Lucy never got in trouble at the school before. Suspended? *Qué barbaridad!*"

"Abuelita, please let her in!" comes Lucy's voice from the top of the stairs, strained and tight.

Lucy's grandmother rolls her eyes slightly and then steps back, and soon I'm in Lucy's cluttered room. My friend is curled up on her bed, her eyes red from crying.

"I'm so fucked," she says, reaching for a relatively clean Kleenex from the mountain of crumpled tissues spread out before her and dabs her eyes.

"Oh, Lucy, I'm so sorry," I say, sinking onto the bed. All the guilt I felt when Lucy was sent home after the assembly about the stickers starts to build again, making me sick to my stomach. "What happened?"

In long, rushed phrases punctuated by half sobs and sniffles, Lucy tells me how she was hauled out of first period and taken directly to Principal Wilson's office ("It's like a shrine to the football team in there, in cases you're wondering") and how Principal Wilson accused her of making the flyer since the Moxie name was on it. When Lucy denied it and refused to provide any information, Principal Wilson told her he didn't believe her.

"So he thinks you accused Mitchell of trying to rape you?" I say.

"That's the thing," Lucy says, sitting up, rubbing her eyes. "It was like he knew the flyer wasn't about me—which it isn't—but he was still accusing me of making it."

"So you think he knows who Mitchell tried to rape?"

Lucy shrugs, takes the tissue in her hand, and squeezes it into a tight ball before throwing it off the side of her bed. "Yeah," she says. "I mean, the flyer said the girl went and told him, so he must."

"So now what?" I ask, frowning.

"I'm suspended tomorrow," she says. "He's not expelling me, but he says he's going to contact every college I apply to next year, to let them know what I did." I expect her to start wailing at this, but instead she just slides back against her bedroom wall and stares out numbly at the space in front of her. "I wish I knew who started Moxie," she says. "I would ask them what the hell to do next."

My heart starts to pound, then journey up to my throat. I open my mouth, then close it.

I can't do it. But I have to do it.

"So I won't be at school tomorrow," Lucy continues. "He made sure that I wouldn't be there for the walkout. Since he thinks I'm the leader of Moxie, I guess he assumes that if I'm absent, I'll be less of an influence."

Once I say it, there's no going back.

I look down at my hands. They're gripping Lucy's lavender-flowered bedspread so tight the veins in my knuckles are popping out.

"I have to tell you something," I say, and now it's too late to stop for sure.

"What?"

I swallow hard. I take a deep breath.

"I made *Moxie*," I say out loud. At last. "I made the zines. Everyone keeps calling them newsletters, but they're zines. I made the stickers, and I started the bathrobe thing and the stars-and-the-hearts-on-the-hands thing. It was me. I got inspired by my mom's Riot Grrrl stuff from the '90s. The only other person who knows is Seth, but I think maybe now we've broken up or something, so . . . I don't know. But I did it. I started it." My throat starts to tighten up. I swallow and feel my face start to flush.

Lucy stares at me and then, slowly, her body slides off the bed until she collapses into a lump on the messy floor.

"Lucy?" I say.

She looks up at me and says, slowly and deliberately, "You. Are. Shitting. Me."

"No," I say, shaking my head. "I really did it." My heart is still hammering, trying to catch up with what I've just done.

"But you didn't do the flyer this morning?" she asks, concerned.

"No," I say. "And Kiera did the VFW hall thing and you did the bake sale. I have no idea who made the flyer. Or who put the stickers on Principal Wilson's car."

"Holy shit, Viv!" Lucy says, standing up.

"Are you mad at me?" I feel tears start to fight their way out, but I hold them back. I can't be the one who's upset here. Lucy should be mad at me. I lied to her so much.

"Why would I be mad at you?" She's almost shouting. "And why am I standing up?" Then she falls back down on her bed with a flop.

"I can't let you take the fall for this, Lucy," I say, my voice cracking a bit. "I can't let you get in trouble for the walkout when you didn't even start Moxie." I imagine turning myself in to Principal Wilson. Meemaw and Grandpa will be scandalized. I'm not sure how my mom will feel. But it's the right thing to do. "I'm sorry I didn't tell you earlier. I probably should have. The whole thing has just gotten out of control."

Lucy sits up. "Oh, Viv, it's okay. I mean, I guess I am a little hurt you didn't tell me. But the truth is, Moxie was almost more powerful because it didn't have a leader, you know? Like, I can see why you did it that way." Then she shoots me a rueful grin. "And anyway, maybe it's better I didn't know. I always have had trouble keeping my big mouth shut."

I manage a smile. It's nice she's taking it so well. But still.

"I need to go in to talk to Wilson," I say. "I have to."

"I don't know," she answers. "I'm already in trouble for putting my name on the form. Wilson probably won't even believe you. And he'd rather blame some Mexican girl from the city than a nice white girl like you who's been here all her life."

I flop back on Lucy's bed. There's a tiny crack running across the ceiling. I trace it with my eyes until the tears finally come. I let them stream down my cheeks, not even trying to stop them.

"Viv?" Lucy says.

"Everything is so screwed up," I say. "Moxie's gotten out of hand. And now Seth and I are in a fight, and you're in trouble, and it's all messed up. And what does it matter? Nothing is going to change. Nothing. I should have just done what my mom always planned for me to do and kept my head down and got into college and gotten out of here."

"No, Viv, no," says Lucy, shaking me. "Are you kidding me? Moxie has been worth it. Think about last Saturday. Think about the fact that the girl Mitchell attacked wouldn't have spoken up without Moxie. Hell, at the very least, acknowledge that Moxie is the reason you and I became friends."

I peer up at Lucy and smile. Behind her, I spy the bright yellow Post-its with the Audre Lorde quote on them.

YOUR SILENCE WILL NOT PROTECT YOU.

"Should I do the walkout?" I say.

Lucy looks me dead in the eyes. She nods firmly. "You know the answer," she says. "I don't even care if I take the blame for all of it. It's worth it to me if it happens. I'll write an essay about it for my college applications. If nobody does the walkout, it's like I got suspended for nothing. It's like Wilson wins."

I nod, and I know Lucy is right. "Who do you think made the flyer?" I asked.

"I don't know," she answers. "The messed-up thing is it could be almost any girl. But whoever it is, she's telling the truth. I believe her with all my heart."

I curl into myself, remembering Seth's doubt. I tell Lucy about my conversation with him earlier in the day.

"Sometimes I think even the best guys have a hard time getting it," Lucy says, her voice sad and soft. "And I think Seth is a really great guy. I do. But if he hasn't lived it, he just can't know, I guess."

I sniffle a little. "You think he's a good guy?"

"Yeah," she says. "I do."

"Lucy," I say, my voice cracking, "I'm so glad we're friends."

Lucy grins. "Me, too," she says. "And I still can't believe you made those newsletters."

"Zines. They're called zines."

"Okay, *zines*," she says, rolling her eyes. She reaches out to hug me. A good, strong hug. The kind of hug that says, "I get it." The kind of hug that says, "I'm here."

Lucy's grandmother won't let her drive me home, so I have to make the long walk to my house from hers, and halfway home my phone buzzes with a text from my mom.

Just got one of those robocalls from your school . . . something about a walkout?

Damn it. Wilson is pulling out all the stops.

Yeah it's a long story . . . a girl accused Mitchell Wilson of trying to rape her. And some girls are organizing a walkout to protest that the school isn't doing anything about it.

I choose to leave out the part about me actually starting the movement that sparked the walkout to begin with.

My phone rings mere seconds after I send the text. I stop in the middle of the sidewalk to answer.

"Mom?"

"What is going on at that school?" she asks, not even saying hello. In the background I can hear voices shouting and the hustle-bustle sounds of the urgent care center.

"Exactly what I said in my text," I tell her.

"God, it's like nothing's changed in all these years," my mom mutters, her voice full of exasperation.

"What did the robocall say?" I ask.

"Just that a walkout had been planned and if anyone participated they would be subject to suspension and possible expulsion."

Principal Wilson isn't messing around if he's gone so far as to call parents. I stand there, the mid-April heat surrounding me. I stare at the house in front of me, wishing it were mine so that I would already be home and hiding under my covers.

"What time are you coming home tonight?" I ask, and suddenly I feel like crying again.

"I have a date with John," she says. "Do you need me to cancel?"

"Yeah," I say. Now I'm definitely crying again.

"Vivvy, are you okay? You need me to come home now?"

"Mom, I think me and Seth broke up," I say. Tears are pouring down my face. "Everything is so messed up."

"Oh, honey, I'm leaving right now."

I squeeze my eyes shut and try to calm down. "No, no, it's okay. I'm not even home yet. I'm walking home from Lucy's. Just come home as soon as you can, okay?"

"Okay," my mom answers. "You're sure you don't want me to leave right now?"

"Yes," I say, taking a deep breath. "I'm okay."

She makes me promise to text when I get home and to head over to Meemaw and Grandpa's if I get too upset, but the truth is the only place I want to be is in my bedroom all by myself. I want to turn Bikini Kill up as loud as it will go and curl up in my bed and let my body absorb all the lyrics until I have enough strength to deal with whatever is going to happen next.

My mom finds me in bed, my throat raw from the crying I did at Lucy's house and the crying that started up again as soon as I got home.

She wordlessly curls up next to me, still dressed in her scrubs, and hugs me. She doesn't say anything for a while. Just rests next to me. Even Joan Jett joins us, like she knows I need the company. She balls up next to my stomach and purrs like a diesel engine.

"Wanna talk?" my mother says at last.

"Yeah," I say. Staring at tacked-up posters of bands I used to like in ninth grade, I give her the basics about the flyer and the walkout and then, my voice cracking, I tell her about my fight with Seth.

"I feel awful," I say, turning toward her.

My mom sighs and sits up, undoes her ponytail and does it up again.

"How did you end things again?" she asks.

"I told him to stop telling me to calm down," I say. "I feel bad that I said it, but at the same time, I don't. Because I meant it."

My mom nods. "You know one thing I loved about your dad?" she says. My eyebrows pop up slightly. We hardly ever talk about my father. "Well, I mean, there were a lot of things I loved about him, but one thing I loved about him more than anything was that I knew that I could say anything to him, and we would be okay. I could snap or get mad. I could get frustrated. And he got frustrated with me, too. That's what happens in relationships. People aren't perfect. But at the core, I knew he loved me for me. I knew he accepted me for who I was. He was a good man because of that."

I think about what Lucy said earlier. "Seth is a good person," I say.

My mother nods again. "He seems to be, so far as I can tell."

"But he didn't get it. About the flyer. About what Mitchell did."

292

"He's still learning," my mother offers. "The thing is, guys are indoctrinated with the same bullshit."

"I guess I never thought about it that way," I say.

My mother pulls me toward her and kisses me on the top of the head. "Vivvy, you'll work it out. I bet you really will."

I shrug, not so sure. "Even if we do or don't, it doesn't really answer the question about the walkout." I gnaw on a thumbnail.

"So it was this Moxie group that called for the walkout?" my mom asks, her voice full of concern. My mouth goes dry. It was okay to talk about Seth with my mom. That felt okay. But now we're venturing into trickier territory.

"Yeah, it was the Moxie name on the flyer," I say, glancing back up at my posters, avoiding eye contact. "But, I mean, no one knows the exact girl who made the flyer."

I could tell my mom about Moxie. Like I told Lucy. I could. But my entire mouth has turned into sandpaper.

"So, I'm confused," my mom continues. I glance at her and feel my cheeks redden, so I look away again. "Is this Moxie group like a club or what? With a president and everything?"

"Not exactly," I say.

If only she knew.

I roll to my side, my back to my mother. If I tell my mom I started Moxie, it will be like giving it to a grownup, almost like taking it away from the girls of East Rockport.

"Well, a walkout is a pretty big statement, don't you think?" my mother asks, reaching out to stroke my hair. It's a kind gesture, but I find myself freezing up.

"Yeah, it is," I answer, still facing away from her. I decide to test the waters. "You think I should do it? Even though Principal Wilson is threatening to expel the girls who do?"

There's a pause. "This is some sort of karmic thing, isn't it?" she says at last.

I turn and look over my shoulder, peering up at her. "What do you mean?"

"All the times I insisted to Meemaw and Grandpa that all my crazy stunts in high school were just my way of fighting The System—capital *T*, capital *S*," my mother says, shaking her head. "And now you're asking me for permission to participate in civil disobedience."

"I guess that is some irony for you," I say.

"It's blistering." She sighs and rubs her eyes.

"You still haven't told me what you think I should do."

She takes a deep breath. "The mother I thought I would be when I was nineteen wants to tell you to do it," she answers. "And the mother I've morphed into wants to tell you I'm afraid. Afraid that you could get expelled. Afraid for what that might mean for your future. For college. I don't know, Vivvy."

My stomach sinks. Because I know that in the end the only person who's going to be able to decide what to do when it comes to the walkout is me. I tug my bedspread over my face.

"You wanna be alone for a little while?" my mom asks, her voice muffled.

"Yeah," I answer. But then I peek my eyes out. I don't want to end our conversation like this. My mom's mouth has turned into a soft, anxious frown, like she's searching for the just-right words.

"Viv, I love you," she says finally. "And whatever you decide . . . whatever happens . . . I'll always love you, and I'll always stand with you."

The knots in my gut give way a bit. But not enough that I want to tell her about Moxie. I love my mom. I just don't think she could handle it.

Her expression still uncertain, she slides off the bed and leaves my room, Joan Jett following her. I hide under the covers with my phone and find lots of stuff online about the walkout. Girls are debating back and forth about whether they should do it, and most boys are saying it's stupid. I text Claudia and my other friends and ask them if they're going to do it and they all write back variations on the same thing.

I think so. But I'm scared

Marisela posts that she's tired of boys at East Rockport acting like assholes and treating girls like property. People agree with her but some boys start posting that she's accusing all boys of being jerks, and a huge debate follows. Kiera posts a picture of Wonder Woman and a quote by a woman named Angela Davis. "When one commits oneself to the struggle, it must be for a lifetime." I look her up and read about how Angela Davis was a black feminist who was imprisoned for fighting for her beliefs. It makes a walkout look pretty minor in comparison, to be honest.

I fight the urge to text Seth.

He doesn't text me.

After a little while, my mom brings me some reheated lasagna from dinner the night before. I make myself eat a few bites.

"I feel like going to bed," I say.

"It's not even nine o'clock."

"Yeah, but if I go to sleep, I don't have to think about any of this," I answer.

My mother nods and clears the plate, and soon I'm in my pajamas in the dark. But it's a long time until I drift off, my mind unsettled and my heart pumping steadily as it circles back to tomorrow, tomorrow, tomorrow.

CHAPTER TWENTY-THREE

THE WALKOUT IS SUPPOSED TO BE MIDWAY THROUGH MY ENGLISH class. According to the flyer, we should get up and leave when the bell rings to alert teachers to take the daily attendance.

It's a loaded class for the walkout to happen. Not only will Seth be in there, but Mitchell will be there, too. Lucy would be there, of course, if she weren't suspended.

It's literally all everyone is talking about, and as my friends and I gather on the front steps to discuss it, we all get texts from Lucy.

When the walkout happens send me pics. I have an idea

When, not if. My hands go numb, but I manage to text back.

What's the idea?

You'll see—just send pics of all the girls walking out

"Think it's gonna happen?" says Sara.

"I think something's going to happen," Claudia answers.

"Some girls were posting some really intense stuff last night that made it sound like they're committed."

"So you're going to do it?" asks Meg.

"I think so," I answer. But now that it's here, my stomach's a rock. I think about getting suspended. Maybe even expelled. I picture myself standing in front of the school with five or six other girls. Then I remember the words of that freshman girl the other day.

"Wilson can't expel us if we *all* walk out."

The first bell rings and we all head in, but my mind is blank as we listen in class and go to our lockers during passing period and make eye contact in the hallways. The school feels electric. On edge. The teachers are all standing in the hallways in little clumps, whispering to each other. It's the most engaged I've seen them all year.

I look for Seth but don't find him.

I spot Mitchell Wilson and his fellow apes hanging out like every other day. Their loud boy voices, laced with Mountain Dew and the knowledge that the world belongs to them, ring through the halls, echoing off the walls, making my skin crawl.

If they walk, they're gonna be so fucked.

They won't do it. They don't have the guts.

Finally, English class. Mr. Davies passes out a worksheet and clears his throat, then glances at the clock.

The seconds tick by.

I peer over at Seth, who walked in at the bell. When I look away I think I feel him looking at me, but I don't look back.

Five minutes until 11:15.

"Can I get someone to read the passage?" Mr. Davies asks. He folds and refolds his arms. He grimaces and stares out at all of us, his expression sour.

No one volunteers. Finally, Mr. Davies calls on one of Mitchell's friends, who starts reading some short passage in a halting voice.

"John . . . Steinbeck was an American author . . . who wrote . . . many novels. He is best known for his . . . Pulitzer Prize—winning masterpiece *The Grapes of Wrath*."

Tick tick tick.

"Setting is an important part of . . . Steinbeck's novels. Most of his stories . . . are set in . . . central and southern California."

Tick tick tick.

My heart starts to hammer. One minute left. I want to scream the tension is so heavy.

"In 1962 . . . John Steinbeck won . . . the Nobel Prize in Literature. Steinbeck's works regularly . . . touch on the concepts of . . . injustice."

BUZZ.

There's a collective jump, and Mr. Davies moves toward his computer to input attendance, like he expects nothing. Everyone is watching everyone else. I want to get up. I want to stand up. But I'm frozen. I look out into the hallway, hoping to see a ponytail floating by. I'm desperate to hear the sounds of girls' voices as they gather together and march out of the building.

Mitchell Wilson snorts under his breath. Mitchell Wilson, who is almost certainly a rapist.

Get up, Vivian. Get up!

My leg muscles tense and then, just as I start to stand, I'm cut off.

By Emma Johnson.

Queen Emma. Cheer squad Emma. Vice president of the student council let's-all-act-like-Texas-ladies Emma. *That* Emma.

She stands up, whips a Sharpie from her pocket, and—her china doll cheeks flushed with what I quickly perceive to be rage—she writes the word *MOXIE* down her left forearm.

Her hand is shaking.

Then she looks toward the back of the classroom. She stares at Mitchell with eyes full of a fury so awesome her face reminds me of Kathleen Hanna's voice.

"Mitchell," she says, her voice clear and cutting. "Fuck you."

And she walks out.

She's not two steps out the door before I get up and follow, my skin buzzing, my heart on fire. In that moment I don't even care if any other girl is following me. All I know is that I won't let Emma walk out alone.

She is halfway down the hallway before I catch up to her. There are a few other girls standing by the lockers, looking around a bit aimlessly, not sure what to do.

"Are you okay?" I ask Emma. She's crying now, tears running down her cheeks. Her perfect eye makeup is smudged. Two tiny coal-black streams slide down her face. She wipes them away.

"I'm okay," she says. "But what happens now?"

"It was you, wasn't it?" I say. "Who made the flyer?"

"Yeah," says Emma, nodding.

My first impulse is to hug her, but I'm not sure she wants to be touched.

"Let's go out," I say, my voice rising, so the other girls will hear. "Let's head out toward the front steps of the school. We can figure it out there."

"Thanks," she says, sniffling.

The girls in the hallway follow me, and as we walk, more and more classroom doors start to open. I spy Kiera and Meg and Marisela and Amaya and Kaitlyn, their faces uncertain as they step out, then smiling as they see they're not alone.

I see Claudia. She sees me. She sticks her tongue out, she's so excited.

Our numbers start to grow, and quickly, too. At least half of the girls in East Rockport are walking out. Maybe more. As soon as other girls inside classrooms hear noises, they venture out. Teachers step into the hallways, shout at us that we're going to be expelled.

Look, Wilson can't expel us if we *all* walk out.

I see that freshman girl, too, grinning so big her face looks like it might split in half.

We keep marching, our feet trampling over Principal Wilson's threats and our teachers' warnings. We are marching because those words deserve to be run over. Steamrolled. Flattened to dust. We are marching in our Converse and our candy-colored flip-flops and our kitten heels, too. Our legs are moving, our arms are swinging, our mouths are set in lines so straight and sharp you could cut yourself on them.

Maybe we hope you do.

We don't speak as we march. We don't even whisper. We just move, our eyes on the ones in front us. Blond hair in ponytails and black hair in braids and brown hair and red hair, too. Hair cut pixie-style or held back with cheap barrettes or carefully styled into loose spiral curls that still smell of that morning's dose of hair spray.

The only sound is the squeak of our feet on the floor. But if you listen hard enough, you can hear our heartbeat.

Now there's the *cha-chunk* of the school's heavy metal front doors opening. We see the light from the outside streaming into the main hallway, and we squint a little but we don't stop marching. We don't stop walking. We don't stop heading outside.

We don't back down.

As all of us gather on the front steps of the school, I lean into Emma.

"Do you want to say something?" I offer. "About why we're here?"

"Yeah," she says, and I see a bit of that vice principal of the student council in her starting to come out. She's composing herself, taking deep breaths. "But will you stand with me?"

"Yes," I say. "Of course."

Girls watch as Emma and I take the top step. They gather in a tight knot around us.

"Hey, listen up!" I shout. "Emma's got something to say!"

That's when I see him. Seth. Off to the side by the front of the campus, apart from us girls. He's standing there with a handful of other boys—some of the guys he sometimes eats lunch with. When he sees me looking at him, he nods. Then he gives me a thumbs-up, which is the corniest thing he's ever done. I smile in return, then turn my attention back to Emma.

Emma looks out at the sea of girls in front of her and when she tries to speak, her voice cracks. I place my hand on her shoulder, and she looks at me, her eyes grateful.

"First I want to say thanks for coming out here," she begins. "And I want to say that I didn't want it to come to this. When Mitchell Wilson tried to assault me at a party last weekend . . ." Her voice breaks again. Then, from the back, I hear a girl shout, "We believe you!"

Emma squeezes her eyes shut, collects herself, then continues.

"I was able to get away. But then later when I tried to tell Principal Wilson, he wouldn't listen. He told me that I'd imagined it! That it was nothing and to forget it. Well, I won't forget it! And I don't want the school to forget it either!"

Girls shout their approval at Emma's words. They holler and clap and yell. I spy Claudia in the crowd, and her eyes are red from crying. My heart feels like it's going to explode.

Suddenly we hear shouts behind us, and we turn to see Principal Wilson and Mr. Shelly and all the other administrators heading toward us like a snarling pack. Mr. Shelly has a clipboard, and he's trying to write and walk at the same time. His jowls are shaking and his face is sweaty and red.

Principal Wilson has a fucking bullhorn in his hands.

"Girls, I order you to form a straight line so your names can be collected by Mr. Shelly," he shouts into the bullhorn. "I am moving forward with suspensions for all of you as well as the process of expulsion." He storms over to Emma and me.

"Emma," he says, dropping the bullhorn to his side. "I told you this would be handled."

"But you *didn't* handle it, Principal Wilson," Emma yells back, her hands balling up into fists. It's jarring to see perfect Emma Johnson shout at authority like this.

And it's pretty amazing, too.

I glance at the crowd of girls. Several of them are taking pictures with their phones.

"Am I to understand that you're responsible for this Moxie group? Along with Lucy Hernandez?"

Emma frowns, confusion crossing her face.

"I planned this walkout, yes," she says.

"And you were behind all the other Moxie activities?" Principal Wilson asks. "Along with Miss Hernandez?"

Emma shakes her head no, and I know it's finally time. I turn and look Principal Wilson right in the eye, grateful for my height. I open my mouth and say as loudly as I can, "I started Moxie, Principal Wilson. I made the zines and the stickers, and I put them in the bathrooms. It was me."

Emma's eyes grow wide, and I hear a ripple of talk spread out among the crowd of girls. I know I've just doomed myself to never graduating from high school, but in that moment it's all so worth it I wish I could say those words again for the first time.

"Wait," says another voice, and my head turns to see Kiera moving up to the top of the steps. "Viv wasn't the only girl behind Moxie. I helped organize it, too."

Principal Wilson peers down at Kiera like he's looking at a bug or smelling a fart. Kiera stares at him, unmoved.

304

"Kiera and Viv weren't the only ones," comes another voice from the crowd. I can tell without looking it's Marisela. "I helped start Moxie."

"Wait," says another girl. "They aren't the only ones. I helped, too." It's that freshman girl. The one who said Principal Wilson couldn't punish all of us.

"I helped, too!" shouts another voice from deeper in the crowd. It's Claudia.

"Me, too!" yells another. And another. And one more and then another until each admission of guilt—each admission of proud ownership—trips over the next, and Principal Wilson is starting to lose his cool. He huffs loudly, snapping his gaze toward Mr. Shelly.

"Are you getting these names down?" he barks, and Mr. Shelly nods as he scribbles furiously on his clipboard.

"Look, Principal Wilson," Emma says, raising her voice, "you don't get it. We won't be quiet anymore!" It's then that I remember she's the head of the cheerleading squad and the perfect person for this moment. She turns to face the crowd and cups her hands to her mouth.

"We are Moxie!" she shouts, her voice deep and rich. "We are Moxie!"

In an instant we are following along, clapping our hands 1-2-3.

"We are Moxie! We are Moxie!"

My palms are slick with sweat from the April sunshine and nerves and joy, but I clap and I shout, and I don't care that the principal is steps away. And I know right now that if I live to be a hundred, I'll always remember this.

I clap harder. I shout louder.

Principal Wilson grabs his bullhorn and starts shouting directions. We shout back, drowning him out. Our voices are so loud. So big. So much.

So beautiful.

Principal Wilson scoots over to the side to confer with Mr. Shelly and the other administrators. He points and gestures with his hands, desperate-seeming, and we keep shouting. We keep clapping. Finally, he grabs his bullhorn and yells at the top of his lungs.

"School is canceled for the remainder of the day. We will be moving forward with expulsion procedures for all of you. Exit the campus now!"

At this we erupt in a roar. It feels like a victory. We've won even if Principal Wilson is trying to get us to think we've lost. I turn and look at Emma Johnson, a girl I've hardly spoken to in almost three years of high school. A girl I always thought I had nothing in common with.

But really, she's a girl from East Rockport. Just like me.

"Thank you, Vivian," she says. And she reaches out to hug me. I hug her back, hard, and Principal Wilson's desperate orders to disperse become background noise. Honestly, I can barely hear him.

CHAPTER TWENTY-FOUR

WE SCATTER FROM CAMPUS AS PRINCIPAL WILSON BARKS OVER AND over into his bullhorn that school is canceled. I lose sight of Emma in the crush of people. I lose sight of Seth, too. But Claudia grabs my hand and leads me to her Tercel. As soon as we shut the car doors, she turns to me, her car keys still in her hand.

"You made those issues of *Moxie*?" she asks, her eyes wide, like she's seeing me for the first time even though she's known me practically since birth.

"Yeah," I say, the giddiness and chaos and shock of the afternoon still zipping through me.

"Wow," she says, turning to stare out the front windshield, watching girls heading home, some of them still chanting about *Moxie*, still clapping their hands.

"Please don't be mad I didn't tell you," I say, gripped with worry that Claudia won't understand. "I didn't tell anyone. Well,

Seth knows. But only because he caught me putting the zines in bathrooms. And I did tell Lucy yesterday. But that's only because I felt bad that she was taking so much of the blame for everything."

Claudia turns her gaze back at me. I stop babbling. "Were you worried that I wouldn't get it?" she asks. "Is that why you didn't tell me?" I can't tell if she's hurt or curious.

"Maybe a little," I admit. "But also I thought the more people that knew about it, the riskier it was."

Claudia nods. "I get it. And really, back when you put out that first issue . . . maybe I wouldn't have gotten it. At all."

"So you're not mad?"

"No," Claudia says, shaking her head. "Just . . . stunned. But also . . . sort of proud. No, not sort of. Really proud." And she gives me the biggest, most glowing smile.

"Even though maybe I've just gotten us all suspended? And maybe expelled?"

Claudia rolls her eyes. "Did you see how many girls were out there today? More than half the girls in the school. Hundreds of us. I don't care how good Mitchell can throw a football. His dumb daddy isn't going to get to kick us all out of school."

I burst out laughing. "Look at you and your tough talk," I tease, but really I'm just so relieved. Relieved that the secret's out, that Claudia understands, that she thinks we won't get in trouble.

Claudia shrugs, full of false modesty. "Want to head to your house? You can help me figure out how to spin this to my parents."

"Yeah, my mom's at work. Let's go."

Not long after we're camped out on my bed with sodas and our phones and Joan Jett curled up between us.

And that's when we realize Lucy Hernandez has gone viral.

Using the girls' pictures and videos from the walkout, Lucy has crafted a blog post not just about this afternoon but about everything that's happened at East Rockport High School over the past year. Everything from the over-the-top expensive pep rallies to the bump 'n' grab game to the crazy, arbitrary dress code checks. She tracks all of Moxie's activities from the bathrobes to the stickers to the walkout. She even includes pictures of the zines I made. And then she shares the post on every social media outlet possible.

Not only that, she also sends it to all of these feminist blogs and websites she likes—blogs and websites run by cool girls in New York City and Los Angeles. Girls who seem like they exist in some other alternate universe that is nothing like East Rockport, Texas.

But they start to pick up Lucy's story.

And they share and reblog and repost.

By dinnertime, Moxie isn't an East Rockport phenomenon. It's not even a Texas phenomenon. It's spreading so fast it doesn't feel real.

SMALL-TOWN TEXAS GIRLS STAND UP TO
SEXIST PRINCIPAL [WITH VIDEO]

MOXIE GIRLS FIGHT BACK—AND TELL THEIR
SEXIST PRINCIPAL WHERE TO SHOVE IT!

EAST ROCKPORT HIGH SCHOOL PUTS THE GRRRRRR INTO GRRRL POWER

"Damn," says Claudia as she reads the latest headlines. By now we've eaten a frozen pizza and moved on to ice cream straight from the container.

"Claudia says 'damn,'" I tell Lucy over the phone, taking a spoonful of chocolate. "And she's smiling really big."

"Tell her thanks," Lucy says. "Can you believe this?"

"Given how this year has gone, I guess sort of yes and sort of no," I say. "Are you still grounded?"

"Yeah," says Lucy. "Thank God my parents didn't take my phone away. It's how I shared all of this."

"What's going to happen next?" Claudia asks out loud, scrolling through her phone.

"Claudia wants to know what's going to happen next," I ask Lucy.

"I don't know," she answers. "But I do hope all this attention means Principal Wilson and Mitchell don't get away with what happened to Emma. Or to anyone else."

"Lucy," I say, smiling into my phone, "you're a hero."

"Oh, whatever," she says. "You're the one who started Moxie."

"I started it, but we all did it," I say.

"Okay, I admit it. I'm a hero," she says. "But now I have to go help clean up the kitchen."

"I can't believe you're sitting there in your room and your parents aren't even aware that you've become a global phenomenon."

"Maybe just an American one," Lucy argues.

"No, some girls in England are talking about you," I say.

"Oh, shut up," she says. But I hear pride in her voice. And amazement. "I'll see you later."

"Can't wait."

After Lucy and I hang up, Claudia stops studying her phone and tosses it aside. She takes a few more mouthfuls of chocolate ice cream and asks, "So what *is* going to happen next? With Wilson, I mean. I don't think he's going to expel us, but do you think he's going to pretend this never happened?"

"I don't think he can," I say, checking my phone. "Hey, look. It's starting to get picked up by local news stations." I catch a glimpse of Seth in one of the shots on a local news site, and I scroll through my texts, hoping for one from him. But there's nothing.

Claudia and I venture into the den with Joan Jett following, and that's where my mom finds us not much later, sitting on the couch and flipping through the local channels, listening to the big-haired news anchors talk about what they're referring to as "a major protest" at East Rockport High.

"I just heard something about this on the radio," my mom says, her eyes focusing on the television screen. "Vivvy," she says, her mouth opening, her eyes widening. "Sweetheart, is that you on TV?"

Mom sets her phone down on the kitchen counter and rubs at her ear.

"Well, I think I finally convinced Meemaw and Grandpa that you're not going to prison," she says. Curled up in a corner on the couch, I eye my mom, who's been very quiet since I admitted to starting Moxie by making the zines—something that sparked Claudia's urgent need to go home.

"Are they mad?" I ask, my voice small. Mom doesn't answer, just walks over to the cabinet where she keeps a small bottle of bourbon. She drops two ice cubes into a juice glass—plink, plunk—and then pours a decent amount of amber liquid over them. Only after she takes a generous swallow does she answer.

"I don't think they're mad, Vivvy. Just shocked." She heads into the den and curls up next to me on the couch. "The Vivian they know wouldn't do something like this."

"Are *you* mad?" I ask.

Sip. Another sip. My heart pounds.

"I think," she says, her voice soft, her words carefully chosen, "that I'm finally realizing that you're more my daughter than I ever realized. And that the Vivian I know is . . . growing up."

I hug my knees to my chest. "Is that . . . a bad thing?" My voice cracks a bit, surprising me.

At this, my mom's eyes turn glassy almost immediately. She presses her fingertips up to her eyes, then gives up. A few tears snake their way down her face.

"Mom, please don't be mad," I say, scooting toward her. I guess I didn't expect my mom to be thrilled. But I didn't expect her to be acting like whatever this is.

"Oh, Vivian, I'm not mad," she says. "I mean, maybe, like, 10 percent mad. That you kept it all such a secret." She pauses, her voice a little wounded. "You didn't feel like you could tell me?"

"Mom, I'm sorry," I say, shifting with guilt. "It's not that I didn't think I could. It's just . . . something I wanted to do on my own. But it's not because I didn't think I could trust you with it."

"Okay," she whispers. "Just so long as you always feel you can tell me anything."

"I know I can, Mom," I say. And then, maybe to make her feel like she was involved all along, I tell her, "I got the idea from your box of Riot Grrrl stuff, you know."

"I knew I should have hidden that box in the attic," she says, rolling her red-rimmed eyes.

"So you're not crying because you're mad?" I ask.

My mom shakes her head. "No, I'm crying because . . . because . . . hell, I don't know why I'm crying. Because I'm proud and surprised. And because I'm old and you're young— but not so young anymore, it seems. Because life is weird sometimes, and just when I think I have it figured out something weird happens again."

"So you're really . . . proud?" I ask, twisting my mouth into a hopeful smile.

She eyes me over the glass of bourbon.

"Truthfully?" she says. "Yeah."

My hopeful smile grows bigger.

She nods and takes another swallow from her glass. "Honestly," she says, "I almost want Principal Wilson to try and expel you and all the other girls." She laughs out loud all of a sudden, so loud she sends Joan Jett running out of the den. "If that asshole thinks he's going to get half the girls in the school kicked out because he tried to cover up an attempted rape, he's going to have to deal with me!" She punches an arm in the air, giddy.

"Okay, Mom, settle down," I say.

My mother is about to answer me when the doorbell rings. It's almost 9 o'clock at night.

"Is it John?" I ask, peering over my shoulder toward the front of the house.

"No, he's still at work," my mother says, heading toward the door. A few moments later she walks back into the den.

Seth is with her.

This fucking day.

"I'm sorry it's late," he says, glancing first at my mom, then at me. "I just really wanted to talk to Viv. In person."

My mouth is dry. My arms have goose bumps. And Seth is standing there, looking at me with his dark eyes. I remember his thumbs-up from the walkout earlier today.

"Hey," I say.

My mother's eyes ping-pong between us until she finally speaks.

"Look, I might be a semi-cool mom or whatever, but you're staying here in the den and I'm going to my bedroom," she says. "I'll have my door open halfway, by the way." She gives me a knowing look and starts heading down the hallway before running back to grab the bottle of bourbon.

314

"So, hey," Seth says after my mom leaves at last. He slides his hands into his jeans pockets.

"You want to sit down?" I ask him, and it hits me that I want him to sit down next to me so much. Like, I want him to sit down next to me for a really long time.

So Seth takes a seat on the couch, but he leaves a good foot or two of distance between us. He's wearing the Black Flag T-shirt I like so much. He jiggles his knee. He gazes at our television even though it's turned off.

I think he's nervous.

"So . . . ," he says. "Some walkout, huh?"

"Yeah," I say. "It was pretty crazy."

"Really crazy. But really cool, too."

I scoot a little closer to him. I nudge him gently with my shoulder. He manages to look at me.

"Thanks for walking out with us," I say.

He nods slowly, slides his mouth into a soft grin, remembering.

"You should have seen Mitchell after you followed Emma out and other girls got up to join you," he says. "He looked like someone had just puked up rotten eggs right in the middle of his lap."

"I really wish I could have seen that," I tell him. I inch the teeniest bit closer.

"If I had to describe it, I would say it was the look of someone who's always been told he's untouchable finally fucking realizing that he isn't," says Seth. "It was pretty glorious. And after that I just got up and walked out."

I slide my hand toward Seth's. I graze his knuckles with my fingertips.

"Is this okay?" I ask.

"Yeah," says Seth.

I snake my fingers through his. His palms are sweaty. I don't care. Every follicle on my scalp perks up as our hands touch. My heart speeds up. I glance at him and smile, and he smiles back.

"I'm sorry if I acted like a dumb ass," Seth blurts out.

I smile. "You're not a dumb ass," I say.

"I shouldn't have doubted what the flyer said. I should have tried to understand better what Moxie was all about."

"Well," I say, "I shouldn't have expected you to be perfect."

"Nobody is," says Seth. "Especially not me. But I promise that from now on I'm going to try to listen better about the stuff I can't totally understand because I'm a guy."

"See, there you go," I whisper, our eyes meeting. "You say you're not perfect, but that answer makes me think you're pretty close."

We are millimeters apart now. I can smell his boyness. I can count the three freckles on his right cheek. I reach out with the hand that's not holding his and touch them. Then I lean up and kiss them, too.

"Your mom's in the back bedroom," Seth says, his voice husky, his dark eyes glancing over my head for a moment.

"Okay," I say.

"Okay what?" Seth says.

"Okay then we'll have to kiss very quietly," I tell him.

"Like super stealth quiet?" he asks, leaning into me. My cheeks warm up, and my body thuds with anticipation.

"Like super intense, extra level stealth quiet," I answer. Or rather, I try to answer. Because by the third or fourth word Seth is kissing me, and I'm kissing him, and all I can hope is that my mother stays in her bedroom for a while, because from the way Seth's kisses make me feel, I don't know how we're ever going to stop.

CHAPTER TWENTY-FIVE

THE LAST DAY OF SCHOOL IS ALWAYS A HALF DAY, SO THE LAST CLASS of my junior year of high school is English with Mr. Davies, who has announced this week to extremely little fanfare that this will be his final year at East Rockport High School. He's told us that he's retiring to spend more time fishing.

I didn't realize they allow fishing at Hunter's Pub, which is where everyone in town knows Mr. Davies hangs out. But anyway.

So due to his impending retirement, Mr. Davies is spending these last hours packing up a few boxes and letting us talk and count the minutes to summer break. Lucy, Seth, and I have pushed our desks into a loose circle.

"God, how much longer?" Lucy announces as she doodles hearts and stars all over her hands with a blue ballpoint. "Hey, Viv," she says, holding her hand up, "take you back?"

I grin a little and so does Seth.

"Yeah, it does," I say. "I still remember how excited I was when I saw your hands that day."

"What about me?" asks Seth, wounded.

"Oh, she flipped out about you doing it, trust me," Lucy chimes in, and Seth cracks up and I roll my eyes.

The intercom crackles to life and Mr. Henriquez's voice comes through the speaker. We half listen as he reminds us about cleaning out our lockers and leaving the school in a timely and orderly manner at the final bell.

"I want to close by thanking you once again for welcoming me to East Rockport High during these last few weeks of school, and I look forward to leading our school community in the fall," he says. "Now go on and have a safe and productive summer!"

Amid a few sarcastic whoops and forced applause from our classmates, Lucy asks whether we think he's really coming back.

"At the very least, Wilson won't be back," Seth says. "We know that much."

After all the news coverage and Moxie becoming an Internet sensation, not to mention Principal Wilson's actual attempt to expel more than half the girls in the school, it didn't take long for the school board to get involved. Two weeks later, the fair citizens of East Rockport discovered the principal of their fine high school had spent the past few years funneling funds into pet projects like the football program and away from things like updated chemistry lab materials and sports equipment for girls' teams. Some deal was struck and the details were kept hush-hush, and all we knew was that by mid-May Principal Wilson

319

and Mitchell Wilson were both long gone. Mitchell deserved to have charges to be pressed against him, but they were never investigated, which pissed us all off. Overnight, the Wilson house was emptied out and a FOR SALE sign sprouted up in the front yard. The morning my mom walked into my bedroom reading the news that Principal Wilson was being replaced, I jumped up off the bed with such excitement I actually fell off. I didn't care. I just laughed.

Of course, there had been the grumblings in school and around town about how the events probably ensured a losing football season this fall. But it was easy to ignore them with so many girls on Moxie's side. And when Meemaw and Grandpa told me they were proud of me, I considered it an especially hard-won victory.

Mr. Shelly quit, too, along with a few other administrators who'd been close to Principal Wilson. And then Mr. Henriquez, the principal of one of the middle schools, was brought in to finish the year. So far he seemed okay. No dress code checks at least.

"Just five more minutes," Lucy says, eyeing the clock. She caps her pen and shoves it in her backpack. "I have to go home right after school and finish boxing up my room." Lucy's mom and dad have finally found a place of their own, and Lucy is already planning a Moxie sleepover for the following weekend. She was sure to invite Kiera and Amaya, too, and Marisela and Jane and a few other girls. Lucy said she wanted to strategize for next year. Even if Mr. Henriquez turned out to be as okay as he seemed, she said, it was important to be prepared. "I mean, the patriarchy is more than one guy, right?" Lucy informed us at

320

lunch. Claudia agreed and offered to bring lemon bars to the sleepover.

As the classroom clock ticks down the final moments, I glance at Emma Johnson sitting in her desk reading a paperback novel. Since the walkout, in many ways she's still been Emma Johnson. Still gorgeous. Still perfectly groomed and organized and high achieving. The MOXIE she wrote down her forearm in Sharpie eventually faded, and she kept quiet for the last few weeks of the year. But I noticed that not long after the walkout she wasn't eating with the cheerleaders as often, sometimes choosing to sit on the outskirts of some other group. After the accusations against Mitchell were swept under the rug, she seemed to distance herself even more.

When Emma saw me in the hallways or in class, she would look me in the eyes. Smile. We'd even said hi once when we ran into each other in the bathroom. But after that heady, explosive moment on the front steps of East Rockport High, we'd retreated to our own camps, not really talking to each other much again.

Emma must sense me looking at her because she meets my eyes. I blush slightly, but Emma raises her hand a little in a brief hello and smiles. Something inside tugs at me.

Then, with only seconds left, a few students start a countdown. "10 . . . 9 . . . 8 . . . 7 . . ." and soon the room is erupting in cheers.

"Want to go eat somewhere?" Seth asks, getting up from his desk.

"I think I want to go talk to Emma," I say. "Okay?"

"Yeah," says Seth. "Let's hang out tonight maybe?"

"Definitely," I say with a smile, and after giving me a quick kiss, Seth offers to drop Lucy off at her house. I scoot between the desks and hurry out the classroom door to catch up with Emma. When I call her name, she turns to look at me.

"Hey, Vivian," she says. Some guy pushes past her in the crowded hallway, jostling up against her shoulder. She frowns and presses herself against the wall.

"Lately, I'm not sure if that's on purpose or by accident," Emma says. "There's a certain faction that's pretty pissed about what I did."

"Yeah, I'll bet," I say. I ignore the part of me that finds it odd to be talking to a girl I once considered so elite that I imagined her locker to be lined in gold. "You okay?"

Emma's cornflower-blue eyes peer up at the ceiling for a moment, then back at me. Her eyes are glassy. She blinks and one fat tear escapes. She catches it with a perfectly manicured finger.

"I've been better," she says. "I mean, I'm not falling apart or anything. But I've been better, too, you know?"

"Yeah," I say. "I know what you mean."

The squeaks of shoes on cracked linoleum floors, the slams of locker doors, the shrieks and shouts of teenagers finally acquiring freedom after months of imprisonment—the noises surround us as we stand there, looking at each other.

"I have to head to my locker, do you?" Emma asks.

"No, I cleaned mine out already," I tell her. "But I'll come with you if you want."

"Okay," she says, her lips parting into a smile. "Thanks."

Emma's locker is mostly empty, but she has a neat stack of pastel-colored spirals and loose papers on the top shelf. She pulls a mirror with a pink frame off the inside of the locker door and places it on top of the stack, then takes everything out. My eyes spy the first issue of *Moxie*.

"Hey," I say. "I recognize that."

"Yeah," says Emma, "I have them all."

My face must read incredulous because Emma says, "I was curious. I was too chicken to admit it at first since my crowd wasn't really into it."

"So you didn't want to speak to all of us at that assembly after the bathrobe thing?"

Emma wrinkles her nose. "No, I didn't. But Principal Wilson sort of bullied me into it, I guess. Just like he'd bullied me into running for vice president instead of president of student council the year before."

"Wait, are you kidding me?" I ask. But Emma shakes her head no, then tells me how Principal Wilson told her having a boy as head of student council would give the council more authority overall.

"He said vice president was perfect for a female leader," says Emma. "And I didn't want to cause trouble, so I did what he said." Then a tiny smile works its way onto her face. "I did something else, though," she adds.

"What?" I ask.

"I was the one who put the Moxie stickers on his truck."

She grins wide, revealing her model-perfect teeth. My own mouth drops open in shock.

"You seriously did?"

"I really did!" she says, giggling. "And the asshole never found out either."

Witnessing Emma Johnson curse reminds me of the one time I overheard Meemaw say *shit*. (She'd dropped an entire Stouffer's chicken enchiladas dish on the floor and it had spilled everywhere.) It's equal parts weird and hilarious and awesome.

Emma closes her locker. The hallways have cleared out by now, and we start heading down the mostly empty main hallway toward the front doors. It's the same hallway we marched down side by side, weeks ago during the walkout. I remember Emma and me walking together, tears flowing down her face, my heart pounding, something really happening.

"You got plans for the summer?" I ask.

"I'm lifeguarding at the pool again," says Emma as we walk. "And working on my college essays. What about you?"

I shrug. "Not sure, really. I might help out at the urgent care center where my mom is a nurse. They need someone to work in their records room. It's a little extra money anyway."

"And you'll spend time with your boyfriend, yeah?" Emma asks, raising an eyebrow.

"Yeah," I say, grinning. It's easy to talk to Emma Johnson, I realize. She's just a nice girl who goes to my high school. That's probably all she's ever been.

We finally reach the main doors of East Rockport High, and my skin gets goose bumps like it can still sense the energy of the walkout all these weeks later. Like the energy has been caught in the school's atmosphere. Like Kathleen Hanna and the Riot

Grrrls said, it's an energy that is a revolutionary soul force made by girls for girls.

I hope like hell it's here to stay.

I push on the heavy door, and Emma and I head out. "Hey," I say, shielding my eyes from the Texas sun, "next weekend my friend Lucy is having a sleepover at her house." We're standing on the front steps now. Emma slides a pair of fancy sunglasses out of her purse and slips them on.

"Lucy's the new girl who put everything online, right?" Emma asks.

"Yeah."

"I like Lucy," says Emma, grinning.

"She likes you," I say. "Anyway, we were wondering if maybe you want to come? There's going to be some other girls there, too. Girls who were involved in Moxie this year. We're going to, like, figure out a way to keep things going next year. I mean, even though Wilson's gone . . ."

"Oh, yeah," says Emma, nodding like I don't even need to finish the sentence. "Just because he's gone doesn't mean there isn't still work to do."

"So you'd be into it? Coming to the sleepover?"

"You want me there?" Emma says. "Even though I'm, like, head cheerleader?" And the way she asks it—the way her voice is full of longing and doubt and just a touch of self-deprecation—is all I need to predict that Emma Johnson and I are going to become good friends.

"Totally we want you there," I say. "Moxie is for every girl. Cheerleaders, too."

"Okay, cool," says Emma. "That would be really cool. Actually, to be totally honest, I have some ideas if you want them."

"You mean Moxie ideas?" I ask.

"Yeah," says Emma, her cheeks reddening. "But whatever. You can hear them at the sleepover. Or never. I mean, well, when I was planning the walkout, I made, this, like, Excel spreadsheet with some basic plans."

Of course she did. She is Emma Johnson after all.

"I would love to see this spreadsheet," I tell her, grinning.

"Yeah?"

"I really would," I say.

"Well, I have my mom's car," Emma says, motioning toward the student lot. "You want a lift? Maybe we could go eat. I mean, if you have time."

I smile at Emma. Of course I have time. It's the summer, with long, lazy days ahead of me. Ahead of us. Perfect for dreaming. Perfect for scheming. Perfect for planning how Moxie girls fight back.

NOTE FROM THE AUTHOR

Dearest Reader,

When I first became interested in feminism and the women's movement back in the dark ages of the early to mid '90s, the Internet was not available to the average person. Were it not for *Sassy* magazine (look it up!) and my college experience, I might have remained clueless for too long about how inspiring, rewarding, and, yes, how *joyful* it can be to live your life as a feminist.

Now we have the Internet, which, in addition to providing many cute videos of kittens and puppies who are BFFs, also provides info about feminism. Following, in no particular order, are some resources I personally love. I have taken care to choose resources that support an intersectional feminist viewpoint and welcome all ladies, including girls of color, girls with disabilities, queer girls, and transgender girls.

feministing.com   bust.com

rookiemag.com   thefbomb.org

bitchmedia.org   scarleteen.com

therepresentationproject.org

If you want to get a good old-fashioned book in your hands, I highly recommend Jessica Valenti's *Full Frontal Feminism: A Young Woman's Guide to Why Feminism Matters* and Chimamanda Ngozi Adichie's *We Should All Be Feminists*. If you want to watch an interesting documentary, I recommend *She's Beautiful When She's Angry*.

And if you'd like more info about Riot Grrrl, check out the documentary *The Punk Singer* or read Sara Marcus's *Girls to the Front: The True Story of the Riot Grrrl Revolution*. There's lots of fun stuff online that's easy to find, too, including interviews and videos. Just search for Riot Grrrl.

If you're interested in living your life as a Moxie girl and meeting other girls like you, check out moxiegirlsfightback.com or send an email to moxiegirlsfightback@gmail.com.

And finally, if you or someone you know needs information about sexual assault, please call the National Sexual Assault Hotline operated by RAINN (Rape, Abuse & Incest National Network) at 1-800-656-HOPE. You can also go to rainn.org for more information or to use the online hotline.

Thank you, dear reader, for taking the time to get to know Viv and her friends. Always remember that Moxie Girls Fight Back!

xoxoxo,

Jennifer Mathieu

ACKNOWLEDGMENTS

I would like to thank my mother for buying the book *Girls Can Be Anything* by Norma Klein and reading it to me when I was little.

I would like to thank all the Moxie girls and women I have met along the way who inspire me daily.

Thank you to Kathleen Hanna and Bikini Kill for creating songs that I love as much at forty as I did at twenty. Especially "Rebel Girl" and "Feels Blind." xoxoxoxo

A million thanks to my wonderful editor, Katherine Jacobs, for her continued brilliance and care.

I am forever grateful to my amazing agent, Kerry Sparks, and the entire team at Levine Greenberg Rostan for always looking out for my best interests and moving mountains when necessary.

Thank you to the entire team at Macmillan and Roaring Brook Press, especially Mary Van Akin and Johanna Kirby, two of the Moxiest ladies in the publishing business.

A big thanks to the faculty, staff, and students of Bellaire High School for their encouragement and support of my second career. I am Cardinal Proud!

Un abrazo muy fuerte for the lovely Domino Perez for reading over portions of an early draft.

Many thanks to Dee Gravink for his small-town Texas stories, including the one about cruising the funeral home.

So many thanks to all the friends who support me on this writing journey, especially Kate Sowa, Jessica Taylor, Julie Murphy, Christa Desir, Summer Heacock, Tamarie Cooper, Karen Jensen, Leigh Bardugo, Ava Dellaira, Emmy Laybourne, the YAHOUs as well as Valerie Koehler, Cathy Berner, and all the lovely people at Blue Willow Bookshop in Houston.

Thank you to my family members who continue to be my biggest fans, with an extra special thank you to my wonderful husband, Kevin, who knows that when a father takes care of his own child, it's not called babysitting. I couldn't do any of this without you. Texas-sized love to you and Elliott forever.

GO FISH

QUESTIONS FOR THE AUTHOR

JENNIFER MATHIEU

What did you want to be when you grew up?
When I was very young, I used to say architect because I liked the sound of the word. Honestly, that's why I chose it. But I was terrible at math—it would have been an awful profession for me. I knew I wanted to do something with writing from a very young age—from elementary school, really. I didn't know what, but I knew I would make my life from words somehow.

What was your favorite thing about school?
When I was little, my favorite part of school was library time. I had a wonderful elementary school librarian named Mrs. Long. We would go down to the library as a class and sit around her feet on a carpet, and she would read these books to us. Her voice was just magical. Sometimes, we girls would play with each other's hair while she read, and she would always say in this gentle way, "Girls, this isn't a hair salon." It was so cute. I just adored those moments sitting crisscross applesauce and listening to stories. As I got older, my favorite thing about school was being good at it. I was a very focused student. It was important for me to do well, and I actually enjoyed organizing my work, doing my homework,

and pushing myself on projects and papers. What can I say? I was and am a total nerd.

What were your hobbies as a kid? What are your hobbies now?

Like Kelsie in *The Truth About Alice*, I loved making shoe-box dioramas. I had a dollhouse and I was heavily into making up stories with the characters and acting out different voices for the different dolls. I made little dioramas for the characters to explore: a restaurant, a store, a chapel, and so on. I was into it well into junior high. With a husband, son, full-time teaching job, and my writing, I have very little time left for hobbies. I mainly read! If social media counts as a hobby, I could definitely claim that one, too.

What was your first job, and what was your "worst" job?

I started babysitting around my neighborhood when I was eleven or twelve, but my first actual job where I received a paycheck with taxes taken out was working at the now-defunct Blockbuster video chain. I was fifteen or sixteen and I worked the register, shelved videos, and assisted customers. My worst job was probably the summer before my senior year of college. I worked for a small public relations firm and I had to type up press releases for a company that made chain saws. It was totally soul-sucking and horrible, and the people weren't very nice. I quit after a few weeks and got a job waiting tables at a pizza place and was much happier. I was supposed to have spent the summer getting a "resume-builder" of a job, but I learned an important lesson that summer, which is that it's never worth it to stick with a job that makes you completely miserable. Life is too short.

What book is on your nightstand now?

I just finished Ava Dellaira's *In Search Of Us*. It's a beautiful book that weaves together two stories of a mother and daughter, both when they were seventeen. I have been waiting for her second book since falling in love with her debut, *Love Letters to the Dead*. She is such a terrific writer. I read her sentences over and over again just to try and figure out how she put them together. And I can't believe it's taken me so long to get to it, but I'm also finishing up Lindy West's *Shrill*. She is hilarious and so, so smart.

What inspired you to write *Moxie*?

Well, I wanted to write a book about the '90s Riot Grrrl movement because it was a huge and important part of my life when I was younger, but I realized that if I wrote a Riot Grrrl novel, I would be writing historical fiction! I really wanted to write something contemporary, so I came up with the idea of making the mom the Riot Grrrl instead. Ultimately, I was inspired to write *Moxie* because I wanted to write a book that showed young readers that living your life as a feminist is actually a super joyful way to live your life. Because I'm a feminist, my marriage to my husband is stronger and my friendships with women more meaningful and supportive. It's made me a better mother to my son, too. Feminism is beautiful, fun, and for everyone—it's about living our lives as full human beings.

What was your favorite Riot Grrrl band?

I would have to say Bikini Kill. The songs "Rebel Girl" and "Feels Blind" are two of the most masterful pieces of grrrl punk art ever made, and I will listen to them when I'm old and in a nursing home. Sleater-Kinney was sort of on the tail end of the Riot Grrrl movement, but I loved them so much, too, and saw them live more times than I can count. A lesser-known band of that era that I loved was Team Dresch, a queercore band out of Portland. Their album *Personal Best* is legendary.

How did you celebrate publishing your first book?

I had a launch party at Blue Willow Bookshop, my favorite indie bookstore in Houston, and I had a party with friends after that. Because *The Truth About Alice* is set in Texas, I had cookies made in the shape of Texas. They were so yummy.

Where do you write your books?

I type them on my laptop at the dining room table in my house, and sometimes I work at a little coffee shop down the street from where I live.

Did you ever experience bullying growing up?

Of course I experienced a lot of mean girl drama that drove me to tears on occasion, but no, I never experienced the sort of chronic abuse that to me defines bullying. Unfortunately, I have to say I witnessed bullying. There was a girl I went to school with when I was around eleven or twelve who was horribly made fun of by many in the class the entire time she was there, for three years, and while I don't think I actively participated, I never tried to stop anything. It's one of my biggest regrets.

What advice would you give someone who is facing bullying?

I know it's advice that's heard over and over, but I would recommend that they keep telling the adults in their lives until someone listens and helps. One thing I would never tell a teenager is, "It gets better. Just hang in there. You won't even remember this when you're older." That's terrible advice. When you're sixteen, a year in your life feels like forever. And serious bullying can leave lifelong scars. Keep asking for help. And find an outlet—music, writing, art, running around the block—to release your anger or sadness.

What is your favorite word?
I love the word *mortified*. I think it's such a delicious word, and I use it as often as I can.

If you could live in any fictional world, what would it be?
I would love to visit an Edith Wharton novel, just for a week or two, to witness the world of the super privileged of her day—it would be terrific people watching! As for living somewhere permanently, I think I would love to be best friends with Anne Shirley and live next door to her in Avonlea.

Who is your favorite fictional character?
It's impossible to choose just one, but I would say Margaret Simon from Judy Blume's *Are You There God? It's Me, Margaret*; Johnny Cade from S. E. Hinton's *The Outsiders*; Ruby Oliver from E. Lockhart's Ruby Oliver books; Park Sheridan from Rainbow Rowell's *Eleanor & Park*; and Merricat and Constance from Shirley Jackson's *We Have Always Lived in the Castle*.

What was your favorite book when you were a kid? Do you have a favorite book now?
My favorite book of all time when I was growing up was *The Outsiders*, and that's why it inspired my new novel, *Bad Girls Never Say Die*. The characters were so real to me, it's like I thought I could drive to Oklahoma and meet them. I think if I met S. E. Hinton, I might cry. It was just such a beautiful story with such heartbreaking characters. To be honest,

it still ranks as one of my favorite books. I keep a list on my author website with some favorite books of all time, including books I fell in love with as an adult. I actually read a lot of nonfiction in addition to fiction. I love Chuck Klosterman, who writes about pop culture in such an intelligent way. One of the best books that I've read as an adult is called *Random Family*. The writer, Adrian Nicole LeBlanc, spent ten years following teenagers in a very poor section of the Bronx during the 1980s and wrote about their lives. It's so compelling and it's all true.

If you could travel in time, where would you go and what would you do?
Well, I'm obsessed with the 1950s and early 1960s because of the clothes and furniture. So I would go back in time and purchase all the dresses and shoes and chairs and sofas I could carry in my time machine and take it all back to the present day with me. Today's dollars would go so far back then. But I wouldn't want to live back then because even though it was glamorous in many ways, the era was far too conservative for my liking.

What's the best advice you have ever received about writing?
I once heard a saying that there are only three rules to writing but the problem is that no one knows what they are. The truth is that every writer is different. I've heard some writers say they love to write in longhand. Other writers I know plot out every single scene before they start. But that advice would never work for me. I think the best advice I have ever received is to just write and find the way that works for you.

What would you do if you ever stopped writing?
Sleep more and watch too much bad television.

Do you have any strange or funny habits? Did you when you were a kid?
I used to eat paper as a kid. I remember my sixth-grade English teacher, Mrs. Mullery, would catch me, and she would remind me of all the inks and dyes in the paper and how bad they were for me, and I would still tear little pieces off the corners of pages and eat them. Fortunately, I've retired that habit. I don't know that I have any strange or funny habits now, but if you ask my husband, I bet he could list a bunch.

What do you consider to be your greatest accomplishment?
Getting up every single day and trying to be a compassionate person.

What would your readers be most surprised to learn about you?
I was a cheerleader in high school. Sometimes that one even surprises me.

Can you tell us about your next novel, *Bad Girls Never Say Die*?
This is a book I've wanted to write for so long! Something I've always wondered about ever since reading *The Outsiders* many, many years ago is what it was like to be a greaser girl, a so-called bad girl. As much as I loved that book (and still do!), I always felt we didn't learn too much about those sorts of girls in that story, so I decided to

imagine what their lives might be like. In addition, I wanted to explore what it means to be "bad" as a young woman. Our society has found all sorts of ways to shame girls, but I've always felt that the shaming is connected to sexuality, standing up for herself and her rights, or just a girl's desire to live life on her own terms. I wanted to write young female characters who were breaking conventions at a time when the rules associated with being a girl were even more strict than they still can be today.

Everyone thinks they know the
truth about Alice, but there's only
one person who does.

Keep reading for an excerpt.

I, ELAINE O'DEA, AM GOING TO TELL YOU
two definite, absolute, indisputable truths.

1. Alice Franklin slept with two guys *in the very same
   night* in a bed IN MY HOUSE this past summer, just
   before the start of junior year. She slept with one and
   then, like five minutes later, she slept with the other
   one. Seriously. And everybody knows about it.

2. Two weeks ago—just after Homecoming—one of
   those guys, Brandon Fitzsimmons (who was crazy
   super popular and gorgeous and who yours truly
   messed around with more than once) died in a car
   accident. And it was all Alice's fault.

The other guy Alice slept with was this college guy, Tommy Cray, who used to go to Healy High. I'll get to Healy in a minute, and Brandon dying, too, but first, I should probably tell you about Alice.

It's weird, because *Alice Franklin* doesn't sound like a slutty name. It sounds like the name of a girl who takes really super good Chem notes or volunteers at the Healy Senior Center on Friday nights passing out punch and cookies or whatever it is they do at the Healy Senior Center on a Friday night. Speaking of old people, Alice sounds like a total grandma name. Like tissues-tucked-in-the-sleeves I-can't-find-my-purse what-time-is-*Jeopardy!*-on-again grandma. But that's totally not Alice Franklin. Hell no.

Because Alice Franklin is a slut.

She's not *overtly* slutty looking or whatever, but her look could go either way. She's a little taller than average but not freakishly tall, and I totally admit she has a really good figure. She never has to worry about her weight. Maybe her mom makes her count Weight Watchers points with her like mine does, but then again I don't think so, because Alice's mom doesn't seem to care that the entire town thinks her daughter is a total ho. I don't know if Alice's dad would care because Alice hasn't had a dad for as long as I've known her. Which is forever.

Alice has short hair that's cut sort of pixie-style, and she's one of those girls with naturally full lips. She always, always has raspberry-colored lipstick and lip liner on. Her face is standard pretty. She has multiple piercings in both ears, but she's not weird or punk or whatever; I guess she just likes a lot of earrings. In fact, she kind of dresses up for school. Or at least she did before all of this went down. She liked to wear pencil skirts and tight tops which showed off her boobs, and she'd always have on these open-toed sandals that showed off her raspberry toenails. Like even in February.

After it all happened, it's like she didn't care what she looked like. At first she came to school dressed all normal, but lately she's been showing up in jeans and a sweatshirt with the hood up lots of the time. She still wears the lipstick, though, which I find weird.

She hasn't ever been super crazy popular like me (I know that comes out conceited, but it's just the truth), but she's never been like that freak show Kurt Morelli who has an IQ of 540 and never talks to anyone except the teachers. If you're thinking of popularity as an apartment building, somebody like me is sitting on the roof of the penthouse, the band geeks are sleeping on the floor in the basement, and that freak show Kurt Morelli isn't living in the building at all. And I guess Alice Franklin has spent most of her life on some middle floor somewhere, but on the top of the middle.

So she was cool enough to come to my party.

You need to understand that this thing with Alice sleeping with two guys and Brandon dying in a car accident are *the* two biggest things to go down in Healy in a really super crazy long time. I don't mean just big with the kids who go to Healy High.

I mean big with like everyone. You know how there's this whole world that exists only to teenagers, and adults never know what's going on there? I think even the adults are aware of this phenomenon. Even they realize that they don't know what a certain word means or why a certain show is popular or like how they always get so excited to show you a YouTube video with a cat sneezing that you already saw twenty hundred years ago or whatever.

But Alice sleeping with two guys and then Brandon dying have become part of the whole world of Healy. Moms have talked about it with other moms at meetings of the Healy Boosters, they've asked their daughters about it, and they've looked at Alice's mom in the grocery store with a look that's always, "I feel so sorry for you, you terrible, terrible mother." (I know this because my mother has done all these things, including staring at Alice's mother in the dairy aisle while looking for some fat-free pudding she'd heard about at a Weight Watchers meeting. The pudding was only two points, so of course my mother was nuts for it.)

And this thing about Brandon dying is even crazier because he was Brandon Fitzsimmons, King of Healy, Texas. Quarterback and totally handsome and funny and everybody knew him. The dads have been talking about it at meetings of the Healy Boosters and in line at the Auto Zone, and they shake their heads and say what a damn shame it is that Brandon Fitzsimmons had to die in a car accident just a few weeks into football season. (I know this because my father has done all of these things, including wondering out loud why that Alice Franklin Slut, as he put it, had to go and mess up Healy's best chance at the 3A State Championship since he played for the Tigers back in, like, 1925.)

Football is enormous in Healy, but Healy itself is not. It's basically the kind of place that is just far enough away from the city that it can't really be considered a suburb, but it's not big enough to be considered much more than just a small town. There are two grocery stores, three drugstores, and, like, five billion churches located in strip malls. The movie theater shows one movie at a time, so you never get a new one, and the big thing to do on the weekends if you're under twenty is go get fast food and beers and park in the Healy High parking lot and talk shit about people or hope that someone's parents go out of town so you can have a party. Most people either love it here and never plan on leaving, or they hate it here and can't wait to go.

Healy isn't as bad as it sounds. I know it's totally lame that the biggest store is a Walmart and we have to drive an hour and ten minutes to go to a real mall, but still, I love it. I guess, yeah, it's all I know, but I love walking into almost any store in town and people know me and smile at me, and they ask me about my mom and dad and they ask me if I'm on the varsity dance squad this year (yes) and if I'm planning on being on the junior prom committee (yes) and if I think Healy has a chance at state (always). And the things I do seem to be the things that everyone else at Healy High wants to do. Like when my girlfriends and I were freshmen and we started using toothpicks to write letters on our nails with fingernail polish, so we could spell out ten-digit messages like I AM SO CUTE! and SCHOOL SUX! In about a week practically every other freshman girl at Healy High was copying us.

But back to Alice Franklin.

In the movies, high school parties are always these huge, crazy events with five hundred kids jammed into one house and naked people jumping from the roof into the pool, but in reality, high school parties are nothing like this. At least not in Healy. Healy parties basically consist of people sitting around the living room drinking, texting each other from across the room, watching television, and every once in a while someone goes into the kitchen to get another beer. Sometimes two people will go upstairs to one of the bedrooms and everyone makes a joke about it, and around midnight or 1 a.m. people pass out on the couch or go home.

Not so exciting sounding, I know, but I suppose what makes them exciting is the possibility that one of these nights, at one of these parties, something will happen.

And I guess that something did.

DON'T MISS THESE OTHER EMPOWERING, THOUGHT-PROVOKING BOOKS BY JENNIFER MATHIEU.

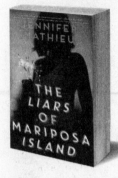

COMING SOON

*Sometimes bad girls are the best friends
a girl could ever have.*